THE BEFANA DRAMA!

THE BEFANA DRAMA!

BY GIANNA HARTWRIGHT

DEDICATION

This book is dedicated to my wonderful son, my parents, my Nan and the mothers of Woody and Archie Lee and Oliver and Harry Warburg, without whose belief in me, this book might never have been written.

Chapter One

The woman with the piercing emerald eyes had been staring intently at the rude boy, from over the top of her twisted spectacles, for precisely seven minutes and twenty-two seconds without blinking once. As the second hand of his watch reached seven minutes and twenty-three seconds, he'd become scared witless, taken the hint and let her sit in his place on the packed bus. She hadn't appreciated the way this boy with polka dot spotty skin had barged past her to grab the last seat, so had decided to spook him with her 'no blinking' trick. It had worked a treat and she'd chuckled to herself triumphantly. Spooking people was what being a witch was all about. She was proud of the stare she'd used on the ignorant boy. She'd been perfecting it over the last two centuries.

Now she was wishing she knew some other useful tricks, as she tried to negotiate her way off the bus, bent almost double and leaning heavily on her creaking, wooden walking stick. The rattling vehicle had no sympathy with her and screeched to a stop outside the medieval town walls, almost sending her flying on to the lap of a man sitting by the door.

'Mamma mia,' she muttered. 'I can brake better than that even when landing my broomstick on the roughest of roof slates.' The rude boy heard her and squirmed in his seat.

As she struggled down the steep, merciless steps, there was a sudden commotion. A black cloud of bats swooshed out of the ancient church roof and darkened the sky in a most strange and sinister manner, completely blocking out the hazy Italian sun. A rickety old man crossing the cobbles looked skyward.

'That's not good ... not good at all,' he declared. 'Bats flying by day? Trouble's brewing.' A scrawny, ginger cat arched its back and scarpered up an alley, sending a tin can clanking noisily as it went. It too could only predict something exceptionally bad looming on the horizon.

The grumpy passengers getting off the bus hardly noticed the sudden eclipse, being far too busy complaining at being held up by the slow, doddery old woman to be unnerved by it. She was equally tetchy. Her ancient legs had been cramped up in the packed bus for a good fifty minutes. Walking across the cobbles was the last thing she wanted to do, having been a sardine in a tin for nearly an hour.

'And they call that the fast service,' she grumbled as she rubbed her stout legs to try to get some

2

feeling back in them. 'Things were much better back in the fifteenth century when we travelled by horse. At least one could breathe the fresh Italian air back then.'

As she continued to vigorously slap her legs, a fellow passenger threw her a strange glance and pulled his wife closer.

'That old woman's just said things were better back in the fifteenth century,' he whispered. 'Give her a wide berth; she's obviously raving bonkers!'

That wasn't a bad conclusion to draw. Her poor clothes didn't suggest anything different. Her tatty patchwork dress had been mended on more occasions than even she could remember, as the centuries had passed by. Long threads dangled from its loose stitching and fabric squares were all hues of the rainbow, speaking volumes about how it had been patched up with a scrap of material from here and a piece of curtaining from there. Large parts of the dress were stained black with soot and a grubby white apron made her look in need of a good wash. A black scarf tied tightly around her head made her rather large, wart-ridden nose seem even more unattractive and oversized than it actually was, but to cap it all, she was shuffling along in absolutely enormous suede shoes that flapped and slapped and slapped and flapped against the cobblestones. How she managed to walk in them was a mystery to all.

While she looked truly ridiculous, those

following in her flapping footsteps saw nobody laughing; quite the opposite, in fact. Elderly, bespectacled men, who had been seated at café tables, stood to attention and raised their hats in respectful salute as she waddled along like a rather fat goose. One passenger could have sworn two young women standing in a shop doorway had curtseyed politely as she approached.

The old woman drew her hand-knitted shawl tighter around her neck and shivered.

'So much for all this talk of climate change,' she mumbled. 'The temperature was higher than this back in 1541!'

The man and woman, who had followed her since leaving the bus, elbowed each other.

'Told you,' said the man triumphantly. 'Absolutely raving mad!'

A local workman, with particularly keen hearing, also caught her words on the wind and responded. 'Come on, La Vecchia! What about May 2009? You can't deny that the temperature soared to over 32 degrees then!'

'If you say so,' the old woman replied curtly, decidedly displeased at being contradicted. To have the last word, as she had always liked to over the centuries, she quickly added, 'But on the whole, you can't deny that November has become chillier and chillier over the last 150 years.'

The man laughed loudly and carried on with his

work, as she began to cackle so much that it made her cough and splutter.

'I am right, as always!' she declared. 'Nobody can ever argue with me when I go back over 100 years!'

In a painstaking fashion, the strange hunched figure made her way to the town's main piazza, where long, silent shadows from the ancient palace were already being cast across bright white restaurant tablecloths. Many local men were occupied with discussions about the latest football results, the errors made by their politicians and the grape harvest. Even they stopped chattering as she passed.

One particularly nosy individual could not resist finding out more. 'Befana,' he called out. 'What are you doing here today?'

'Various things,' she answered, not willing to give too much away. 'Checking how many births there have been for one.' Then, in a very matter-of-fact way, she added. 'I need to get my records up-to-date. Time's running out.'

The man nodded, as if he fully understood the need to know about new babies. He picked up his newspaper and carried on reading the sports pages, allowing her to continue on her way, sensing she did not wish to be delayed further. Within minutes, he was on his phone, spreading the news that the Befana was in town.

Eventually, the old woman found herself standing in front of the glorious palace, her black shawl standing out against its beautiful pink walls, which were glowing in the autumn sunshine.

'This was all down to me,' she said proudly. 'Now when was it that I told the young Duke to build one of the most beautiful palaces in all of Italy? Was it 1434, or a little later? My mind plays such tricks on me nowadays. I do recall instructing him to put in many fireplaces, of course. After all, where there's a fireplace, there's a chimney and where there's a chimney, there's the Befana. He was such a wise and good boy to listen to me.'

While speaking to herself, she spotted something out of the corner of her eye. She took one step forward and began to run her fingers across words roughly grooved out of the beautiful palace's wall.

'Mamma mia!' she declared, for the second time in ten minutes. 'How many times did I tell that boy NOT to graffiti the walls! Controlling those fifteenth century boys was such hard work!'

She rocked from side to side, like a boat tossed on stormy waves, as she took her old creaking joints to the steps of the Church, which she climbed extremely slowly. A heavy door groaned loudly as it allowed her to enter, as if displeased to admit this particular visitor. Sitting in near darkness, a young woman spun around and smiled warmly at the old woman.

'Buongiorno, Befana,' she said. 'Come take a pew. I can't wait to share the baby news with you.' She began to shuffle papers and files, perhaps to avoid eye contact, as the old witch ran her finger through thick dust on the top of the woodwork and wrinkled up her wart-ladened nose in disgust.

'Marianna, you really must tell the priest to dust more often,' she announced bossily. 'And just look at the brass. Nobody's shined that for at least three years. Once upon a time it was cleaned every week and I even did it myself back in the 17th century, when the cleaners fell out with the priest and refused to come in and polish.'

Marianna found nothing extraordinary in this. She'd heard the tale hundreds of times and also knew to brace herself for what was coming next. Sure enough, the old woman thudded down like a lead weight, sending vibrations right down the pew and causing Marianna to drop her pen. Blowing out her cheeks she declared, 'Hit me with it then.'

'Well,' said Marianna, rescuing her pen from the floor, before tapping it by her notes. 'We've had four new babies here in town and 44 in the province since I last updated you. In total, over 500,000 babies have been born in Italy this year and so all need to be added to your present delivery schedule. Some are at houses you already visit of course, so we must make sure that we leave the correct number of presents at each house. That's the tricky bit.'

The old woman had a delighted look on her heavily wrinkled face. 'It's such a relief that fewer babies are being born,' she said. 'It's so tough visiting every child's home in just one night. It makes my stockings wrinkle terribly and I get broomstick-lag for weeks after.'

'Indeed,' said Marianna. She decided it was time to butter up the old lady. 'And how you get up and down all the filthy chimneys, keeping the broomstick under control and remembering to give good children candy and fruit and naughty youngsters a nasty big lump of coal, is beyond me!' she said. 'Santa Claus has it easy. He just ignores the naughty ones. Your life would be much easier if you didn't have to punish the mischievous children.'

The ancient lady was exceedingly pleased with this flattery. She'd always known she worked twice as hard as her beloved Santa Claus.

'It's because men cannot tackle more than one thing at once,' she explained, 'whereas we women can juggle as many balls, pieces of coal and presents for well-behaved children as we wish. It's just the way Mother Nature intended and, if memory serves me correctly, she was quite some woman. I only met her once, at an earth summit back in the 11th century, but her words have stuck with me ever since.'

Marianna's eyebrows shot up like caterpillars. This was a tale she hadn't heard before! She tried to concentrate on her notes again, though secretly keen to learn more about Mother Nature. 'We need to order your coal … well, find some actually, as the mine in Turin has closed,' she said. We may need to get it from Russia this year, which will be a real pain.'

'Whatever, whatever,' said the old woman. 'As long as I have some in time for January 3, so it's all loaded up by the 5th. I must have that lovely black stuff on board my broom, to remind the naughty children of all their bad deeds this year. It's such a pity it stains my apron so, but what can I do? Just make sure – and I sincerely mean this Marianna – that you contact all those lazy people with blocked chimneys and insist they get them swept. Do NOT take 'no' for an answer! They caused me havoc last year. That's really what I came to tell you. Make it number one on your to-do list and don't forget! Now I must get on. Lots to do and it won't do itself!'

With that, she desperately attempted to get to her swollen feet, but twice fell back on her bottom with an enormous bump. Marianna gave her a huge shove from behind and eventually the witch managed to teeter to her feet. Looking rather embarrassed by having had to have the assistance of a bottom push, she quickly darted to the door and, with a 'Grazie and arrivederci', left Marianna kissing the air, rather than her wrinkled cheek. Witches like her didn't 'do' kissing, or anything soppy of that kind!

'It's amazing how full of beans she becomes when she thinks about delivering presents,'

Marianna muttered, wishing she'd managed to give her all the other information on the list. She'd heard a few rumours around the town and had wanted to warn the old lady about them, but now it was too late. She prayed she wouldn't hear it from someone else, as she heard bats flying back into the rafters above.

Sure enough, the old witch was already making speedy progress down the street when, out of the blue, a football came firing towards her and hit her squarely in the stomach, stopping her in her tracks. She grabbed hold of the ball, with green steam coming out of her ears.

'I'm so sorry, Befana,' called the eight-year-old boy who'd committed the ball crime. 'I didn't mean to hit you. It was an accident. I've been so good all year … honestly I have.' He was almost crying as he tried to defend himself.

'Alessio, if you don't take better care, there will be a large and particularly crumbly lump of coal in your stocking this Epiphany! You can't kick balls at people as old as me,' said the Befana, now looking as red as a beetroot.

'But nobody's as old as you,' replied the boy, quaking a little. He noticed an angry twitch in the witch's slanted eyes and didn't like it one bit, so quickly added, 'That's why we love you so much!'

He bowed his head, convinced that finding dirty, messy coal in his stocking this year was now inevitable and knowing there'd be eruptions at home once his parents realised he'd fired a ball at the Befana. He looked up to plead his case again, but the old witch had just vanished. The spring in her step had quickened thanks to knowing she already had a house at which to leave some coal!

CHAPTER TWO

All was perfectly as normal in the streets of her home town, until the old woman spotted him – the man with the twitchy eye who seemed to always do his very best to annoy her. She gave a sharp intake of breath as he approached, instead turning her attention first to the children who had zipped their mouths they moment they saw her and then to the shop windows, all packed with pots, plates, vases and jugs that carried her picture. Some showed her riding a broomstick, others pictured her sweeping the floor, while her favourite was the one of her popping candy into the stocking of a child who had been beautifully behaved all year.

Full of pride, she was almost up to the speed of an old lady's sprint as she approached the twitcher, who actually happened to be the mayor. She headed towards the 'Befana House', specially built in her honour to show off to tourists. Of course, she didn't live here; perish the thought! Her own house was actually tucked away in a narrow street where she made sure no tourists could find her!

She felt exceedingly pleased with herself as she passed her own special postbox, where children could post their letters to her, describing what they wanted in their stocking. She was full of joy as she saw the posters in the windows of shops and houses that were advertising her very own stupendous January festival – the one that showed the world what a superstar she was in these parts. The festival was simply her favourite time of year. No doubt the man with the twitchy eye wanted to discuss that.

Despite all this, she was nervous. He was heading straight for her and, as she was sure he spent 90 per cent of his time breaking into a hot sweat with jealousy about her stardom, that wasn't good. He was a foolish man and foolish men did foolish things. She was sure that, without her, the town would become extremely poor. Thousands of people came here each year, wanting to see her and only her. But he, being a nincompoop and an ever-so-slightly-peeved mayor, could never seem to see that!

'Signor Marini,' she called out, in a slightly croaky voice, trying to get in first and prevent his drivel. 'You will be pleased to know plans are coming together exceedingly well for this year's present drop. We just need to collect all the candy, fruit and figs together, along with the coal. We will then be well on our way to getting everything in place long before the end of December.'

'Befana,' said the mayor seriously, so seriously in fact that his glasses were almost falling off the end of his nose. 'Could you just step inside the town hall for a moment? I called round to your house earlier, but didn't find you there. I wanted you to be told as soon as possible.'

'Quite, quite,' said the Befana, heading towards the building. 'I am very keen to know the festival schedule. How many Befana lookalikes will be flying down from the church tower this year? I'm not keen on that Guiseppe Rodini mimicking me, especially after he flashed those revolting red-spotted under-pants at the crowd last year and, I have to say, that I didn't think Eduardo Santini a suitable choice either – far too fat to be me, even if one uses imagination by the bucketload!

'And what about the biggest pair of shoes in the world?' she continued, not allowing the mayor to get a word in edgeways. 'The largest sock in the world will be fine, if it's survived the last year without a moth attack, but I did notice a few parts that needed darning last year. However, the shoes really need to be worked on, if they are to look anything like mine! My shoes don't look a bit like that awful pair you wheeled out during the last festival and I was very disappointed to see the lack of effort that had gone into the colour match.'

The mayor tried to butt in again, but the witch was in full swing now.

'The letters must reach me by December the 20th at the latest, or I won't be able to reply to all the children who have written to me. My eyes aren't what they were in 1900 and I haven't yet decided whether laser treatment is for me. Then there's the issue of the music. That little Giovanna Vallin simply cannot play in tune and has no sense of rhythm.

'Last, but not least … by no means least, is the fact that I was hit by a flying orange during last year's festival and I am not prepared to be sidelined by a citrus this coming January … talking of which, I think I've forgotten to mention the stray rocket that went off at a tangent during the firework display and almost flew up my nose as I was flying up above.'

Having got all of this off her chest, she slumped back in the chair the mayor had shoved towards her. Silence reigned for all of thirty seconds. The mayor was turning a definite shade of white and trying to steady the fingers that were gripping a pen rather tightly. His eye twitched nervously.

'The thing is, Befana … and I hate to be the bearer of bad news, but I may as well get straight to the point here.' He paused, looking extremely edgy. 'We are having to downsize the festival this year.' He paused again and then, as if he had contracted verbal diarrhoea and needed to spit out the rest of the sentence as fast as humanly possible, mumbled 'with a view to then cancelling it altogether.'

His shoulders dropped and he crossed his arms, refusing to make any eye contact with the witch known for her staring contests. He knew he'd dropped a bombshell.

'What am I hearing here?' shrieked the old woman, waving her hands wildly in the air. 'How can you possibly think of cancelling my festival? Are you mad, stupido? I am worshipped by Italian children and Italian families around the world. Millions of children have grown up with me. I attract 50,000 people a year to the festival. I am the VIPB of all VIPBs!'

'VIPB?' stuttered the mayor, looking totally bewildered.

'Yes, VIPB – Very Important Present Bringer! Without me, children would wake up on January 6 without any rewards for their good behaviour and without any reminders of their bad actions. There will simply be uproar if you cancel my festival. If it were summer, I would think that you'd taken in too much sun and become befuddled. Have you had a few too many glasses of wine perhaps? Do you think the pressure is becoming too much for you? Have you consulted a doctor?'

'B B B B Befana,' stammered the mayor. 'I must explain a few things to you. We've been carrying out some research in recent years and have noticed … how shall I put it? … a trend.'

'A trend!' shrieked the old witch. 'What are you talking about? What trend is this?'

'Well', he continued slowly, awaiting more screams and shrieks. 'As you know and so rightly say, Italian children have grown up with you as their present-bringer for many years. For children of my generation and long before that, you were the only 'VIPB' as you put it, and you had no competition. You were simply the kindest, sweetest witch in the world and all children adored you, even when you left them only coal in their stocking.'

The old woman took all of this in, furiously nodding her head in agreement.

'However,' continued the twitching mayor, 'at the end of the Second World War, Italian children discovered Santa Claus. Of course, when he first arrived here, we Italians just dismissed him as a silly old man in a red coat, breeches and boots, but the children of today … what can I say, they see things differently.'

'What, what, what?' shrieked the Befana. 'What are you telling me here?'

'Well,' said the mayor slowly, 'all of our recent opinion polls show there are now more children believing in Santa Claus than in you. Our postmaster tells me more letters are now going to Lapland, addressed to Santa Claus, than are posted in your own postbox here and the sales of vases featuring your dear self are down 22% each year, while some items celebrating Santa Claus are up by 64%. I am afraid that the writing is on the wall and we simply cannot afford to stage what will soon become an economic disaster for this small town of ours.'

The old lady's face had turned a violent shade of purple and her cheeks were blown out like a puffer fish. She rapped her fist on the mayor's desk.

'Santa Claus. Santa Claus! What's going on here? I'm engaged to the man and we had an agreement that he would operate in the north of Europe and I, and I alone, would look after the Italian children around the world. Now you're telling me that he's invading my VIPB patch! This is ridiculous! It just can't happen. He hasn't even got a foothold in Sicily, let alone here! Someone is telling porky-pies here – lies, lies, lies! I won't hear of it. Get the festival plans back up and running. This is total and utter nonsense!'

'I beg you Befana,' said the mayor. 'Open your eyes, adjust your spectacles and look around you. Let's take a walk to the town and you will see what's happening.'

They walked out into the main street and looked in the shop windows. She reached into the pocket of her apron and pulled out her spectacles, the frame of which was badly bent, having been sat on several times during the last century. Settling them on her nose, in a twisted fashion, she noticed, to her horror, that sales stickers were stuck to the windows. The words, 'Everything must go,' 'Sconto – 90%', or even worse, 'Buy one, get one free!' leapt out at her.

'Two for the price of one!' she howled. 'How disrespectful and disgraceful. Who do these shopkeepers think they are? Their fathers, grandfathers and great-great-great-great-great-great-great-great-great-great-grandfathers would never have treated me like this!'

They turned a corner and found that the Befana's tourist house had been semi-boarded up.

'We just couldn't pay to have helpers in there any more,' said the mayor apologetically. 'People are just not turning up to see you these days.'

The old lady squinted, pulling a most bizarre face.

'What in the name of heaven does that say on the board down the side?' she demanded.

'Erm,' said the mayor nervously. 'It says, 'Santa Claus here as from next year'.'

'WHAT!?' yelled the Befana, 'Are you trying to send me to my grave? How can you do this?'

She swung around, hearing a noise behind her, only to find her mailbox being sealed up. The workman was explaining to a young mother than no more letters could be posted to the Befana this year, but that the post office would be sending sacks of letters to Lapland, with replies from Santa guaranteed to arrive by Christmas Eve at the latest.

'How can this be?' shrieked the Befana. 'I have my very own rhyme, chanted by children across Italy:

La Befana vien di notte
Con le scarpe tutte rotte
Col cappuccio rosso e blu
Noci e fichi butta giù

How can you ignore this?'

'Befana,' explained the mayor all in a jitter now. 'Let's just examine this rhyme. It says, the Befana comes at night, with shoes all broken, with a hood that's red and blue and with nuts and figs to throw around – or that's the gist of it, isn't it? Well, nowadays, Italian children are very fashion conscious, just like their parents and, quite frankly, they are not likely to see shoes like yours on the catwalks of Milan. On the other hand, Santa has upped his game, wearing this year, I believe, some fabulous Gucci boots and an outfit designed by Versace, to make sure he really appeals to the average Italian child.

'Furthermore, you don't wear a red and blue hood any more – not since the famous soot incident in the Vatican some years ago, so your credibility is at an all-time low. Even Little Red Riding Hood scored higher in the last poll that we ran – at least her hood is actually red!

'Finally, nuts and figs just will not cut it for an Italian child these days. When Santa is bringing them Playstations, football shirts, Barbie dolls and Lego, you're fighting a losing battle my dear. It's the march of progress and, over the years, it's overtaken you.

'To be honest, your little fruity freebies are a real disappointment for children. Even the tooth fairy brings them money, putting a few Euros in their piggybank. You, on the other hand, just cause them to make visits to the dentist, when your candy sticks to their teeth. You also create more housework for their already overworked mothers, when the pieces of coal crumble and send coal dust flying everywhere. But above all, let's face it, Italian children can get their gifts a whole 12 days earlier if they believe in Santa and not you! You don't arrive until the night of January 5th!'

By now, the Befana's face was puce coloured and, had she been wearing her blood pressure monitor, the reading would have been skyhigh. Her brain felt as though it were popcorn, rattling around her skull, and her eyes had widened so much that she resembled a bush baby.

'Rubbish,' she shouted, 'You're talking rubbish. What is this conspiracy against me? What are these wild accusations and false figures? Is it because I left a bit of coal on your seat at the end of the festival gala dinner last year? I didn't mean anything by it – I just thought you had been particularly pompous all night and needed a reminder of your bad behaviour. How was I to know you'd sit on it and ruin your brand new, white suit?

'I've been bringing presents to children for centuries and I've seen off all ne'er-do-wells and pretenders to my throne. One word, just one word, to my fiancé Santa Claus will send him packing back to the North Pole and all this nonsense can end. In fact, I'm going to bid you farewell right now and go and make that call!' Off she stomped.

'Lies, lies and more lies,' she muttered angrily. 'Children love me. I'm worshipped and adored. I'm the kindest, sweetest witch in all the world. I was chosen by the Three Wise Men, who didn't have a clue how to find the Baby Jesus until they sought me out. I soon pointed them in the right direction and I could have been there at Jesus' birth had I not decided to stay behind and tackle more cleaning. They begged me to go … almost packed my bag for me and even had a friendly word with their camels to make my journey as bump-free as possible.

'But I had to stay and clean. The floor was a bit grimy once they'd plodded all over it with their sandy shoes. What choice did I have? A woman has to keep her house clean and tidy! By the time I'd finished, they'd disappeared into thin air and although I searched high and low, in stables across the world and under all the brightest stars in the heavens, I just couldn't find them.

'But let's not forget that I was rewarded by the Lord and allowed to look after all the children in my country, to guide and lead them. That is my mission and I've stuck to it, year after year, going up and down chimneys like a jack-in-a-box, humping coal and candy around with me, even when my back ached. The mayor and his silly little committee have been brainwashed into thinking that a Gucci boot-wearing interloper can dethrone me. I am the Befana and nobody messes with me!'

The kind, sweet nature of the Befana was by now being taken over by anger never before seen. Those passing by hardly recognised her and could swear there was actually vapour coming out of her ears. Her apron seemed to be stood on end with stiffness no amount of starch could have produced and her twisted spectacles were misted up.

'I will not listen, I will not listen,' she shouted, as she pounded across the paving stones.

Reaching her house, she shoved the door and then slammed it shut with a huge thud that made the whole doorframe shake rather alarmingly. She then snatched her broom and started to brush the floor with such force that it began to scratch the wood, making sparks fly. Pushing all the dust into a heap, she opened the door and swept it out into the street in a most frightening manner.

'Look there!' she heard a sarcastic voice say, 'That mad old witch who wears those ridiculous shoes really does have obsessive compulsive disorder like everyone says. Look at her trying to clean up: she's crazy! Go on old woman, brush, brush, brush and sweep, sweep, sweep – you're making me wet my pants just looking at you!'

'Who are you talking about?' asked an inquisitive boy, poking his head over a wall. 'Oh that one,' he laughed, 'Yes, nutty as a fruitcake. Have you heard her new rhyme, by the way. I heard it in the playground the other day. It goes like this:

The Befana comes at night
With shabby shoes – an embarrassing sight
In the 'hood' her head's all askew
Figs, you old witch? Only a PC will do!'

Tears welled up in the Befana's eyes. Her heart was beating furiously and she felt like a volcano about to erupt, spilling molten lava across the cobbles of her beloved town. As she stared at her magic calendar, she noticed the details of the 'Regatta Delle Befane', in which men dressed exactly like her, while racing along the Grand Canal in Venice. It was being automatically erased before her eyes. There it went – first the R, then the D and finally the B. All gone.

'Ungrateful wretches,' she screamed, like a possessed spirit taken over by unkindly thoughts. 'Just you wait. You will see. It will be a house full of coal for you all, never mind one piece and I won't be sweeping up my sooty footsteps before leaving as I normally do! Oh no. Oh no. I haven't felt so angry since a fireplace was blocked up in a home in Naples and I had to spend a good half hour jumping up and down before I could get down the chimney. Where's the Befanamobile? I need to call Lapland immediately and get my dear Claus to set the record straight. It's obviously a gross misunderstanding. We VIPBs have to work together in such trying times.'

She rushed back into the house, flying around the parlour like a cat with a scorched tail. Knocking into things left, right and centre, she sent objects flying off tables and shelves and crashing down to the floor. In her frenzy, she knocked over the radio that hadn't worked since 1922 and it fell heavily downwards, somehow mending the fault it had suffered for decades, but crackling madly at full volume.

She adjusted the knobs to try to cut out the distracting noise that was addling her brain and, at that very moment, heard a familiar voice – the deep, masculine tones of her beloved fiancé, Santa Claus, answering questions posed by Renata Rizzo, the most famous radio presenter in the country. She twiddled the knobs again, to get a clearer reception finally resting the set on the top of her head, where it finally seemed to stop crackling.

'So Santa Claus, or can I call you Babbo Natale, like so many Italian children now do?' enquired Renata flirtatiously. 'All these details about reindeer and elves are all very nice, but can I be so bold as to ask you about your relationship with our own VIPB here in Italy, the Befana? If my research is correct, you met her at a 'Joy and Goodwill to All Children' conference, held in Capri in 1901, where I believe you fell in love and became engaged. I believe you were separated during World War II, but she gave you introductions into top Italian circles in 1947. Is this accurate?'

Santa Claus began to cough nervously, a hoarse noise becoming audible over the radio waves.

'Ermm,' he said, in a hesitating manner. 'Ermm.'

'Well?' asked Renata, intent on not letting go. 'I can understand that it's perhaps something of which you do not wish to be reminded, but if it's not true, this is your opportunity to set the record straight and give the whole of Italy and the Italian-speaking world the truthful version of events.'

She ended the sentence triumphantly, knowing he was now in a corner and would have to say something.

The Befana's ear was now almost glued to the radio.

'Tell her Claus, tell her about our relationship and agreement to divide the world between us. Everyone knows that we are co-operating and that you have no intention of invading my VIPB patch. Tell her how in love we were. Just tell her the truth!'

Rather than hear these things, the Befana could not believe her ears.

'Who did you ask about?' asked Santa Claus. 'Let me rack my brains. Ah yes, I did once know someone called the Befana, but I could have sworn it was a few hundred years ago now and nowhere near as recent as 1901. I seem to recall she was a much older woman than myself and we only met briefly. I really can't remember where or under what circumstances, but maybe it was a conference. I fact, yes, I think it was and all the excitement of knowing that we would be thrilling children across the world made us rather, how shall we say … soppy.

'We had a mad notion of being engaged, but it was just ridiculous. We've never seen each other since and our paths don't cross. In fact, I wasn't sure she was still on the scene. I'm now very big in Italy, but haven't encountered her down a single chimney since I became the number one Very Important Present Bringing celebrity in these parts. Needless to say, this was almost immediately, ho ho, ho!

'I am, of course, very happily married to the lovely Mrs Claus now – you may have seen our wedding photos in Gello magazine, in fact. She's quite a stunner and a wonderful cook. As for the Befana woman, I don't even know whether she's still hanging on in the present-giving world, or whether she's hung up her stockings, so to speak. I would imagine children find her pretty outdated and dull these days. Hardly a fashion icon like myself and Mrs Claus, ho, ho, ho!'

In a little house in a very ancient town in Italy, an old and previously kind and well-meaning lady, with a tatty dress, shabby oversized shoes, black scarf and white apron, knocked tear drops off the end of her long nose, started to count to ten, but only got as far as five – or cinque as she called it. Suddenly, the whole of the town heard a rattling of the glass in the window frames, felt a trembling of the ground beneath their feet and were deafened by the howling of family pets petrified by a high-pitched noise only they could pick up.

As the Befana jumped up and down in fury, wildly flapping her shabby big shoes, tremors spread all around the town and many miles beyond. A real sense of foreboding could be detected on the wind.

CHAPTER THREE

Families peered out of their windows with trepidation following the weird shakes felt all around the province. To their amazement, when they twitched their curtains a little, they saw that a torrent of aniseed balls was streaming down the street, all shapes and sizes having been unleashed by the Befana's annoyance.

Next came thousands of mintballs, mixed with pink sugared almonds, red chocolate hearts, liquorice sticks and candied chestnuts. All the sweets came together to create a multi-coloured, rolling carpet of candy that children found truly exciting. But it swept up those walking the pavements and carried them along, with grown men and women being transported by a very fast-moving conveyor belt of confectionery.

'What in heaven's name is going on?' exclaimed an elderly gent clinging on to a lamppost in an attempt to avoid being swept away.

'No idea,' said another, who had shinned up a

drainpipe and on to a roof. 'At first, I thought it was hailstones, but it's all colours of the rainbow. Is it something to do with the greenhouse effect?'

As the candy balls bounced and pinged and pinged and bounced with the ferocity of ball-bearings firing around a pinball machine, the Befana stomped down the street, following hot in pursuit of her raging stream of candy. She glowered at everything and everyone, pounding down the pavements at a pace at which she hadn't travelled for at least three centuries. She shoved everything in her path out of her way with a forceful swipe of the arm and ducked and dived from the candy balls that were bouncing off objects in a never-ending vicious circle.

'Did my eyes deceive me, or was that the Befana?' asked the man on the roof.

'Surely not,' replied the other, still clinging to the lamppost. 'She doesn't move that fast!'

The witch was searching the streets wildly, heading up and down different alleyways muttering to herself.

'I've seen one somewhere. I know there's one somewhere in this town. Think, think, think!'

She banged her fist into her head whilst compelling herself to recall where the infernal place was located.

'It's an orange sign, a gaudy orange sign,' she shouted out loud. 'It's completely out of place in this town and I've thought it a million times. Why can I not remember where it is?'

She looked up to the heavens as if seeking divine inspiration and then she spotted it. There, a few doors up, on the opposite side of the street, swung a little orange sign saying 'Internet Café'. The Befana bounded across the cobbles like a wild wallaby, pushing open the door and bursting into the small room behind.

'Pronto,' said a very nervous-sounding voice coming from underneath a counter full of information leaflets on how to surf the Internet. 'Who's there?'

'I am the Befana, but who are you and why are you hiding like a child who's afraid of the dark? Is this, or is it not, an Internet Café and can I use this so-called Internet? I've heard you have to surf and all I have ever done is ride my broomstick!'

'Ah, Befana, sì, sì,' answered a young man, trembling so much beneath his white shirt that it was making creases in the cotton. 'Sorry, I thought Vesuvius had erupted and we were all going to be swept away by molten lava.'

'Don't be so melodramatic,' snapped the witch. 'Candy balls,' she declared, 'Mere, unappreciated candy balls.'

'Oh, I see,' said the youth, even though he didn't see at all and hadn't seen a thing. He had shot underneath the counter the minute the earth had begun

31

to shake. 'Come and sit here and I will get you logged on – well, I will if it's still working,' he said nervously.

He fiddled with a few plug sockets and began to tap the keyboard. 'I will get you into Google,' he said.

'I don't need any goggles,' barked the Befana, 'I need to find the offspring of the Three Wise Men. Remove this goggles thing and help me to do that!'

The youth smirked slightly, suddenly feeling he had the advantage. After all, knowledge is power.

'This is a search engine,' he explained, 'but, if you prefer, we can use Yahoo.'

'Yahoo, Yabba dabba doo, Scooby doo – I don't care one of my own figs,' bellowed the Befana. 'Just find me the descendants of the Three Wise Men, or it will be boo hoo for you!'

'I really don't think that will be possible,' replied the Internet Café attendant, wishing he'd swapped shifts with his colleague. You can't just tap something crazy like that in and expect to find it.'

To prove the point he did just that, looking triumphant when nothing came up.

'Want to bet?' asked the Befana, clicking her fingers and managing to bring up a whole new set of search results, the first one of which said, 'Where descendants of the Three Wise Men now live'.

'What use is that?' she screamed. 'Only half of it is there!'

'Click here,' said the stunned young man, not sure himself what might happen when she did.

Up popped a whole piece of text about the descendants of the Three Wise Men. The Befana adjusted her contorted spectacles and managed to rest them further up her nose.

'Does it say that they live in Dubai?' she enquired. 'I can't quite make it out. If that's what it says, where is that? I don't think it's on my normal broomstick run.'

'It's in the Middle East,' explained the youth.

'Don't be ridiculous,' said the Befana. 'I know the area just southeast of here like the back of my hand and there's nowhere called Dubai.'

'No, not middle east of Italy,' scoffed the Internet wizard. 'The Middle East of the world. I suppose you would head to Sicily and then keep flying south east.'

He himself couldn't quite believe he was giving directions to a broomstick user, but in another way it seemed almost normal. It had been a strange day so far.

'Oh good gracious,' said the Befana. 'That's the way I tried to go when I attempted to join up with the Three Wise Men all those centuries ago. I got hopelessly lost around Palermo and then drifted off course due to a strange wind swirling around the top of Mount Etna.'

'I'm sure it happens,' sniggered the youth, wishing he could record the conversation and play it back to his friends later.

'Oh well, there's nothing for it: I'm going to have to give it another go,' stated the witch. 'Does it say where they live?'

'The Jumyatt Hotel, by all accounts. OK for some, isn't it!'

'What?' snapped the Befana. 'What do you mean by that?'

'Well, they must be loaded – rich, I mean. You need to have a lot of money to live there.'

'Really,' replied the Befana. 'That's very interesting; very interesting indeed.'

'Shall I print the page out for you?' asked the youth. 'There's even a picture of the three male descendants here. Would you like that?'

'Indeed, indeed,' said the Befana. She positively snatched the paper out of the youngster's hands the moment it had printed.

'No time to delay. Got to get the broomstick fuelled up with potato peelings and horse manure and it will hopefully get me there in three hours or so. One part manure to 100 parts potato peeling usually gives me a big tuber-charge.'

The youth didn't dare argue. The sooner he got this mad woman out of the door, the better. He would then visit the doctor to see if he'd suffered a nasty bump on the head that was making him imagine all of this.

The Befana wasn't hanging around. She was heading back home snapping her fingers in a curious manner every few yards or so. Observers at first thought they could see locusts flying out of the buildings that she passed. On closer inspection, the mirage proved to be potatoes, zooting out of kitchens, restaurants and grocers' shops and heading straight for the Befana's house. As the Befana entered her home, she noted, with satisfaction, potatoes being sucked up by the handle of the broom. There, they were being processed and turned into fuel, thanks to the addition of a bit of horse manure. This had handily already arrived in a big red bucket.

'Perfect,' said the Befana. 'It won't take long now. It's just as the English would say, 'a broom with a poo', or should that be a room with a view? Who knows?'

She cackled to herself and pulled down a massive, red leather-bound manual from a shelf.

'Now I must try to remember who brought what gift,' she said, talking to herself over and over again. 'Now was it Gaspar who had the gold in his saddle-bag, or was that Balthazar? If Gaspar carried gold, who had myrrh? My memory's not what it was back then and I'm a bit confused now. Think, think, think, think, think!'

Once again, she furiously banged her fist into her head.

'Eureka,' she suddenly yelled. 'Sorry for pinching that line, Archimedes, but I don't expect you'll mind,' she chortled. 'Now the plan's coming together. Now something's hatching. Afoot with the soot! Afoot with the soot! Revenge sounds like a plan! Now where's the compass?'

She reached inside a chest of drawers and pulled out her special VIPB navigation tool, only used by the select few Very Important Present Bringing A-Listers. She tapped it violently on her wooden desk, causing the needle to spin furiously.

'Now don't you let me down,' she threatened.

'All we need now are food supplies for the journey,' she muttered.

She snatched up a loaf and shoved it into her apron pocket. Next, she opened a sack of fruit and retrieved two oranges. She reached under her dress and popped these into her knickers. She then hung a necklace of pre-strung nuts around her neck and shoved a salami up her sleeve.

'Now we're in business,' she guffawed, in a slightly insane way that reflected her foul mood. 'Now as the broom has its final charge, I think a few stretches are in order.'

She swung one leg up and rested it on the edge

of the sink, beginning to stretch her hamstring in a decidedly odd fashion. She then repeated the same routine with the other leg.

'NOW, we're all limbered up and ready to fly.'

Her cackling voice echoed down the medieval streets and was picked up several miles away by a cow that shook its head in panic. That mad witch was on the warpath!

CHAPTER FOUR

It was a chilly night and huge clouds emerged from the Befana's angry mouth whenever she breathed out. Eerie shapes appeared in the night sky and she cackled with delight as she started to shape her 'mouth clouds' into pigs and sheep, pasta shapes and candy twists.

'Now for the Tower of Pisa,' she shrieked, breathing out furiously and moving her head from side to side so much that her broomstick wobbled violently. Sure enough, an enormous, elongated shape appeared, tilted to one side. She made several short, fierce blows and the arches of the Tower's structure suddenly came into view. Down below, a man and woman were walking hand in hand.

'I must be seeing things,' declared the amazed man, rubbing his eyes and blinking hard. 'I could swear I just saw the Tower of Pisa floating in the sky.'

'That will be all that beer you've just drunk,' laughed the woman. 'It wasn't the Tower of Pisa – it was the Eiffel Tower!'

The witch was having a wicked time in the sky. Her anger had pumped up her energy levels and she was performing incredible somersaults and loops as she made her way south towards Sicily. Her broom was truly tubercharged tonight and she had seldom flown with such reckless abandon, or in such a demented fashion, in the clear skies above Italy.

Her twisted spectacles were perched precariously on the end of her nose and her dress was ballooning out as air currents swept beneath its much-patched-up fabric. Her enormous floppy shoes were making a dreadful racket as they slapped up and down uncontrollably throughout the flight.

The huge island of Sicily and a fiery glow came into view. The volcano of Etna became her guide as she steered the broomstick down towards its orange-red molten mass.

'That's going to blow before too much longer,' she speculated. 'I haven't seen it look that angry since 1971, when it destroyed the cable car. A few people will have to make a crater escape!'

She cackled weirdly, the sound echoing across a bank of cloud that she suddenly hit. The turbulence caused her broomstick to tilt almost vertically but, not at all put off by this, the Befana decided it the perfect excuse to fly upside down for a few miles.

'Come fly with me, come fly, let's fly away,' she began to sing, in a very out-of-tune fashion. She skipped a few lines. 'In llama land, there's a one man band and he'll toot his flute for you,' she continued. She did two cartwheels on her broom and then resumed flying in an upright position.

'Those Sinatra children,' she said to herself, 'always left me some lovely nibbles although, when I had to fly to Las Vegas, the sand really made me sneeze!'

Having made no headway on her journey for a while, enjoying her own antics on the broom far too much and simply going round in circles, she had almost forgotten that the last time she had tried to find the Three Wise Men, she had failed miserably – and, more or less, at this very spot in the sky. Something suddenly jolted her into action.

'I can feel you, you beast of a wind,' she bellowed. 'You might have blown me miles off course last time, but I'll get the better of you tonight.'

Her face was set with a look of grim determination that tightened up the wrinkles in her face.

'Now where is Palermo?'

She adjusted her twisted spectacles, set a hidden switch on the side to night vision – an innovation she had introduced a decade ago – and peered down through the patchy clouds. She could just make out the shape of the Teatro Massimo, one of Europe's largest opera theatres.

She shut her eyes tight. Her face looked like a bloodhound's.

'Visualise. Visualise,' she chanted, in a hypnotic

fashion, as she tried to recall the map she had seen in the Internet café. 'Which way Dubai?' she asked herself. The map came into her head.

'First over Lebanon, then I'll skirt the border of Iraq, maybe dipping into Saudi Arabia and then over the sea, being careful not to get caught out by the sea winds. Then I will tackle the last stretch to Dubai. Total distance: 4363 kilometres, or 2711 miles, flying in a south-east-easterly direction. Boy that's a long way! I hope the tubercharge is up to it.'

Despite her fears, the hours began to whiz by. Her broom had seldom seemed so forceful. As she flew over the dry deserts of Iraq and Saudi Arabia, she dropped her altitude, realising that a few camels and Bedouins were hardly likely to cause an international stir if they spotted her. She already had the power to avoid radar-tracking devices, having equipped herself with that skill a few decades back. Now, what was most bothering her was the dry air, mixed with granules of sand stirred up by desert winds. She quickly whipped off her apron and used it as a mouth cover, as she'd seen cowboys do in old Western movies. This seemed to do the trick and it was not long before a huge expanse of water became visible below and the makeshift mask could be removed.

'Not long now,' she said. 'Roll out the red carpet, folks. The Befana is coming to town!'

She performed a few more cartwheels on her

broom, leaving a vapour trail behind her. Delighted with this, she decided to do it again, creating a fabulous pattern in the sky.

'Those aircraft display teams have nothing on me,' she declared pompously. 'And as for those so-called brave wing-walkers, they should be embarrassed. Let's see them try to perform somersaults on a broom!'

By now, she could spot twinkling lights. She could see the outline of huge, impressive buildings and then grand houses built out on a spit of land stretching out into the sea. She admired glamorous boats harboured in a marina. In fact, she was so mesmerised she nearly hit the top of the fourth largest building in the world.

'Goodness me,' she stuttered nervously. 'This is worse than negotiating buildings in New York and Chicago. Thank goodness there aren't any Italian children on my present schedule here!'

Now she was stressing. 'What was the name of the place where those guys live?' she asked herself. 'What was it? What was it? Let me think. The Gum Drops Hotel? No, that wasn't it. The Jumble Hotel? No, that wasn't it either. The Yummy Hotel? No, that would just be ridiculous. She banged her fist into her head. The Eyelet Hotel? The Higher Hotel? The Dumb-Haired Hotel?'

Nothing was working, but her luck was in. Suddenly, as she swept around the city, she saw a huge, strangely shaped building, all lit up with neon bulbs and the lights shining through bedroom windows. She instantly knew this was the building she'd seen on the Internet. She circled its top, flying around a flag and aircraft warning lights. She then began her descent to the ground, noticing a strip of beach in front of the majestic hotel that seemed a perfect landing place.

'A softer spot on which to land, one couldn't hope for,' she stated, in a matter-of-fact way. 'Let's hope it's as kind on the soles of the feet as the beach is in Rimini.'

The broom's speed began to slow and each circuit of the hotel saw her flying height drop. It was almost as if she was building up the courage to land, but with so many centuries of experience, this was not the reason. She just liked to make her landings as graceful as humanly possible, having based her technique on that of butterflies.

After about ten circuits of the building, she was only two metres off the ground. She began to swoop very swiftly now, flying right down the strip of the beach. Dropping, dropping, dropping, her feet were only around a ruler's length off the sand.

'Geronimo!' she screeched, as her floppy shoes touched down. 'I've still got it!'

Sand flew up her skirt in a huge cloud, getting behind her spectacles and showering her dress with granules. She got to her feet, threw the unwelcome sand up in the air, shaking her dress furiously and tipping the itchy pile of sand underneath her feet out of her shoes.

'This is where it gets interesting,' she cackled, leaning her broom against the trunk of a palm tree that she found as she marched towards the hotel's reception.

CHAPTER FIVE

The spectacular, marbled reception area of the Jumyatt Hotel was almost deserted. The time here was three hours ahead of that in Italy and many hours had passed since the Befana had started her long and tiring journey. A few guests lounged around in deep, plush chairs. The elderly night porter was yawning; the reception staff looked bored.

The witch's very wide skirt rustled as it swept along the marble floor. She also left a trail of sand as granules continued to fall out of her massive floppy shoes. The night porter looked at her with disgust. He instantly reached for a broom housed in a cupboard behind his desk and dashed out to sweep the sand into a little pan, following in the Befana's tracks so as to sweep up every last granule of it.

The newcomer's strange clothing began to attract attention. Intrigued guests began nudging each other. The duty manager tilted his nose snootily at this ridiculously dressed woman who was clearly in the wrong place.

'Can I help you Madam?' he asked in a snobbish fashion. Helping was actually the last thing on earth he wanted to do if she was here for a job, let alone a room! He had quickly darted out from behind the counter, so that he could take her into a quiet corner. He was sure she was a tramp who'd just wandered in off the beach.

'I am looking for three men,' she explained, as he raised his eyebrows. 'I believe they live here in the hotel and I must see them straight away.'

'Madam, have you any idea what time of night it is?' sneered the duty manager. 'We simply cannot be disturbing people at this hour, even if you do claim that you know them.'

He looked her up and down and down and up. He wondered where on earth her very strange accent came from and why she looked so dishevelled. A strange whiff was coming from her clothing, which smelt like boiled potatoes. Perhaps she was a cook, or a cleaner who had just finished her job for the night. He looked her up and down again. Finally, his eyes rested on her crazy, large and tatty shoes. Nobody wore shoes quite like these!

'I didn't say that I know them,' retorted the Befana in annoyance. 'Far from it. They must just be young whippersnappers. It's their ancestors I knew. I met them just about as BC as it gets.'

The duty manager wrinkled up his arrogant nose. 'BC? Do you mean PC – politically correct?'

'No, I mean BC, ' snapped the witch. 'Before Christ, but only just. Within weeks, it was AD.'

The self-important duty manager began to tell himself that this old woman was completely insane and started to plan how to call the police and have her removed.

'If you don't know them, I very much doubt that I can assist you,' he stated, rather too officiously for her liking.

'They're probably called Gaspar, Melchior and Balthazar,' she bellowed. 'You must know them!'

A sign of recognition flashed across the face of the duty manager. 'I believe I may know these men,' he said, 'but I really cannot pass on their details to you.'

The 'you' in his sentence was spoken with such snobbery that the Befana felt her hackles rising.

'I MUST see them,' she insisted. 'It's absolutely crucial. Now please do not delay me. I have come over 4500 kilometres tonight and I am not as young as I used to be. Please just give me the details of where they live and I will crack on with my schedule.'

'Madam, I really cannot disclose such details,' replied the duty manager. 'I cannot have my guests pestered by strangers. You are very misguided if you believe you know anybody who lives in this hotel.'

'Misguided? Misguided? Shrieked the Befana. 'I'll give you misguided! Give me the number now!'

'No,' replied the duty manager firmly.

'Give it to me,' she yelled, causing guests to turn their heads and snigger.

'No,' he replied again.

'Give it to me. Give it to me. Give it to me!' screamed the witch, dancing around in a circle and poking the duty manager with one of her bony fingers.

The Befana was mad. She caught sight of the pigeonholes in which keys and letters were posted for guests. Most were empty, but one row, separated from the rest, was rammed with envelopes. Something told her that these were holes for residents, rather than holiday guests.

'Very well, young man. I bid you farewell,' she declared rather dramatically. With that, she clicked her fingers. Suddenly, the post in the pigeonholes fluttered out and started flying through the air, following the Befana as she left the building. It flew within five inches of the duty manager's startled eyes and right past the end of his nose.

'What's happening?' he shouted, trying to catch the letters, each of which eluded him and actually teased him by darting to and fro. The mail moved towards his grasp and then cleverly dodged it, following the Befana once again.

'Help me!' he yelled to his colleagues behind the counter. 'Shut the doors,' he shouted to the night porter.

'Oh no you don't,' laughed the Befana, clicking

her fingers and rooting the night porter to the spot. The transfixed employee simply could not move his arms and legs properly and although he managed to waddle like a penguin, only took a few steps before falling flat on his face.

The Befana was by now outside the hotel and the letters were hot in pursuit. Once on the steps, she opened up one of her enormous apron pockets and all of the post flew inside it.

'That's theft!' said the duty manager. 'Come back here, right now!'

He tried to chase her, but she clicked her fingers and sealed up the door. He pressed his nose up against it, shaking his fist and mouthing the words, 'I insist you come back.' However much he tried to slide the doors apart, he just couldn't manage it. It seemed as if they had been sealed up with magic glue.

The witch chortled as she sneaked around the corner and hid under a palm tree. She quickly leafed through the letters, discarding ones of no use and throwing them to the ground. By now, she was getting a bit desperate. None of the names had so far been useful and there was only a handful left.

'Don't tell me. Don't tell me,' she muttered in a frustrated manner.

She scanned the third from last letter and threw that one aside too. She read the next-to-last. Once again, she saw nothing to encourage her. Finally, one letter remained and she suddenly started to chuckle with glee. There on the envelope was the name Balthazar, with the address, Suite 7, Jumyatt Hotel.

Although she was over the moon at having discovered an address for at least one of the Wise Men's descendants, her heart sank. How could she now get back in? She could still hear the furious banging on the door and she watched the arrival of a blue-overalled workman, who seemed to be attempting to prize the doors apart. She looked up at the building. The only means of approaching the three men she needed, or at least identifying who they were, appeared to be through a window. This hotel had no chimneys, which were her preferred way of getting into any building.

'I daren't risk the broom,' she muttered. 'I can't run out of tuber-power and get stuck here and hovering simply drinks up the fuel. What am I going to do?'

Her eyes scaled the strange-shaped building once again and she sighed heavily.

'I am so, so tired,' she puffed. 'Maybe I need forty winks to think about this immense and tricky problem.'

Her eyelids began to close and she slumped back against the trunk of the palm tree. She pulled her shawl around her, though it was by no means cold. The banging on the door had stopped and she could once again hear voices from inside the hotel.

'Have your mail back,' she huffed before she drifted off. In an instant, a stream of letters was once again flying through the air, reversing the route they had taken previously. The doors opened momentarily to let the post back in and it flew past the duty manager like a flock of geese in formation. It gracefully slid back into the pigeonholes from which the Befana had taken it.

'Will this madness never end?' screeched the duty manager, shaking his head and wondering what sort of magic this could be. Outside, hidden in the undergrowth, at the base of a palm tree, a witch was snoring loudly and oblivious to the saliva dribbling down her chin.

Chapter Six

Voices in a foreign tongue that she did not recognise awoke the Befana, even though the first of the sun's powerful rays had been striking her wrinkled face for a few hours. She'd overslept and looked like a dozy hen just coming to its senses.

'Fiddlesticks! What on earth is that strange sound?' she muttered grumpily.

All she could hear was a terrible clanking and squeaking. She poked her head between two palm fronds and squinted. In the haze of the sun, she could just about make out some sort of machine. Two men were sitting in it and it was lifting them up into the air. What on earth were they doing? She squinted again and smiled broadly. They were doing one of the things she loved most, if you didn't include performing cartwheels on her broom and making mouth clouds in the sky: they were cleaning!

The contraption clanked up and down the side of the building, as the workmen washed the windows of the impressive hotel.

'What utter genius,' murmured the Befana appreciatively. 'Such a fabulous means of assisting the noble art of cleaning.'

Mesmerised, she watched the cab swing from side to side and up and down as the workmen moved from one window to the next. She counted the windows in a vertical line, moving up from the base of the hotel.

'Uno, due, tre, quattro,' she began to count, trying to focus and not blur lines of windows and count incorrectly as a result. 'Cinque, sei, sette, otto, nove and … dieci!'

She put a huge amount of emphasis on the word 'dieci' as she reached the tenth window from the bottom and noted that the outside of the building seemed slightly different at this point. Perhaps this meant that the suites were located there. She rubbed her hands with glee. This mechanical contraption was the ideal means of getting into Balthazar's suite. She began to trot towards it.

The two men in overalls who were working the device were now coming down.

'What on earth are they doing?' she asked herself, as the cab came closer and closer. She turned her back and pretended to inspect some shrubs and flowers in the garden. The men jabbered away, but she didn't understand a word. As they reached the ground, they both hopped out of the cab and began to stroll towards a door. The Befana looked inside the cab.

'Fantastic!' she said, as she realised the men had left the machine in ready-to-run mode. She jumped inside and started to erratically pull on levers. All of a sudden, she shot up a good two metres, with none of the smoothness shown by the men who'd operated the same machine. Her teeth rattled together as she desperately tried to regain control, grappling with the levers to try to slow the thing down. Rows and rows of windows zipped past her eyes.

'Uno, due, tre, quattro, cinque, sei!'

The cab jerked to a halt, but she'd lost count now! Was she on the sixth row, or was it the seventh? She tugged on the lever again and shot up a few more metres. She adjusted her spectacles and peered inside a window.

'How frustrating,' she declared. There was nothing to see. She moved along the row, getting the same result through every window. Curtains were pulled tight as some people spotted her. A little child screamed as she saw the witch's face peering through the glass. Within ten minutes, the Befana ran out of windows. She had failed.

Below her, there was a real commotion. The two workmen had returned and were waving their arms in a furious manner. She waved back merrily, knowing that she had to do something, or she would be arrested. She swung the first lever back and started to descend, quickly grabbing a cloth and pretending to clean. She spotted a man below and decided he looked as if he could communicate with the workmen.

'Do you speak English?' she asked. 'And maybe Arabic too?'

The man puffed out his chest. 'Naturally,' he said.

'Then can you please explain to these men that I am an inspector from head office and carrying out some routine checks. If they can give me half-an-hour, I will be finished.'

The man conveyed the message and the men strolled off, throwing chewing gum into the bushes as they went.

'Thank you for your assistance,' called the Befana merrily, as she shot up in the cab once again.

Now she had a real dilemma. Where on earth could Balthazar's suite be? She was getting nowhere, moving from window to window, when she suddenly caught a whiff of something very familiar up her left nostril, which began to flare like a horse's.

'Frankincense!' she declared. 'I'd know it anywhere! Now where is it coming from?'

She used her sense of smell to guide herself to a window where the scent was at its strongest. The window was open and she could see a gold coloured frankincense burner on a table. There was nobody to be seen within the empty room.

'Gaspar,' she called out in a very high voice. 'Gaspar'.

Nobody responded. She knocked on the glass, but nobody came. The workmen had now returned and were looking up at her. She knew she didn't have long. She had to do something very bold.

She tugged at the window frame and a gap appeared. She wondered if she could squeeze through it, but realised that, with her rather big belly, this was going to be a rather tight squeeze. She shuffled across the cab, swung her legs over the side and managed to sit on the edge. Stretching with all her might, she just about reached the window. She clung on tightly and started to pull herself towards it, hoping against hope that she wouldn't fall and land on something prickly in a flowerbed. She started to squeeze herself under the window frame and then toppled head first into the room.

She landed with a large thud on the floor, rubbing her head hard and scrambling around the floor, furiously feeling for the spectacles that had just fallen off her nose. She found them and put them back on the end of it, securing them with a wart. She could see steam coming out from beneath a door and realised someone was taking a very powerful shower. She began to move around the luxurious suite.

'Very nice,' she said, as she touched posh cushions. 'Expensive though, I would imagine'.

She picked up designer clothing that had been discarded in various chairs and plonked herself down on a sofa that had its back to the bathroom door. She could wait. She was absolutely sure this was Gaspar's suite.

The noise of the shower stopped. Someone was now singing. The bathroom door swung open and she could hear bare feet slapping against the marble floor. The occupant of the suite was walking towards her, but she was still well and truly hidden, sitting on the sofa. A man emerged in front of her, wearing just a towel around his waist. As he leaned down to pick something up, she spoke.

'And you must be Gaspar,' she said loudly, making the man jump out of his skin and almost lose his towel. He screeched with fright.

'Who are you?' he stammered nervously. 'How did you get in?'

'Through the window, my dear boy,' she replied. 'You really shouldn't leave it open like that; you could have all sorts of strange people climbing in! I am the Befana, by the way. No doubt you have heard of me?'

The man looked alarmed, but denied nothing. After several seconds, he uttered the words, 'The Befana? The real Befana?'

'Of course,' said the Befana in a very irritated

tone. 'How many more could there be? There's only one of me and I am it! Sit down before you drop that towel and cause us both a lot of embarrassment. Now where are the other two?'

'Do you mean Mel and Thaz?' he asked shakily.

'Don't be dumb,' said the Befana. 'Of course I mean Melchior and Balthazar, or Mel and Thaz as you seem to want to call them. Now tell me all about the three of you.'

'We're a boy band called 'The Three Kings' actually,' he replied. 'Haven't you heard of us? We've loads of fans.'

'I don't have a clue what you're talking about,' said the Befana. 'I'm always far too busy. Is it music? I think the last music I listened to with any seriousness was by that dear man Verdi. I'm glad to see you are all together though. Just as your great-great-great-great – oh I haven't time for all of that – grandfathers would have wanted.'

'Yeah, we're really good mates,' said Gaspar, rubbing his eyes in disbelief that the woman of legend, whose tale had been handed down through generations and generations of his, Melchior's and Balthazar's families, was actually sitting in front of him.

'Get them round,' demanded the Befana. 'We need to talk.'

Gaspar strolled to the phone and picked up the receiver. He dialled 21 and waited until he heard a voice. 'Mel, it's me. Come round quickly,' he urged. 'We've got a situation to deal with.'

'Situation, indeed,' muttered the Befana. 'What a way to put it!'

Gaspar was now on his second call. 'Thaz. You need to shift yourself and come round right now,' he said. 'Something's happened. You won't believe it!'

The witch wrinkled up her nose again. 'Now, I'm a something!' she snapped.

'If you don't mind me saying so, you seem a little stressed and angry,' said Gaspar. 'Is there something wrong? Can I get you a nice cup of peppermint tea, or something to calm you down?'

'Just wait, just wait,' said the Befana. 'It will keep until the other two join us and I'm not one for tea – that's one for the English, along with their bowler hats and umbrellas, but I am glad to see you've inherited your great-great-great-great – oh I can't be bothered with all that – grandfather's manners.'

There was an urgent knock at the door. Gaspar leapt up and opened it quickly. The Befana had got to her feet and was staring intently at Melchior and Balthazar as they entered the suite.

'Do come in boys,' she urged, with steel in her voice. 'We need to have a little chat. Now, let me see … you in the purple must be Balthazar and wearing that very distinctive gold 'bling', as they put it these days, you can only be Melchior. No doubt you realise exactly who I am?'

The two boys looked down at her massive, tatty shoes. They stared at her grubby dress, shawl and apron and nodded, dumbstruck and unable to communicate other than through gestures.

'Very well then; let me begin,' said the strange witch standing in front of them.

CHAPTER SEVEN

Sitting on a cream leather sofa, facing the Befana, 'The Three Kings' looked every inch a boy band. They were each handsome in their own way. Gaspar and Mel had natural, olive brown complexions and no need for awful fake tan, while Thaz's black heritage gave him superb skin and naturally beautiful white teeth. Gold dripped from Mel and Gaspar was certainly a pin-up boy. The Befana could fully appreciate how popular they might be with young ladies.

For their part, they were mesmerised by this rather odd Italian lady and looked her up and down in total awe. For generations, their families had talked of the old woman who had helped the Three Wise Men find the Baby Jesus and given them shelter, food and a nice clean dwelling in which to spend some time on the way to Bethlehem.

Gaspar recorded how he'd been told about her on his tenth birthday. He had been firmly instructed that, if she ever turned up, he was to give her whatever she asked for. Melchior remembered how his grandfather had left him a gold casket in his will. When he had opened it, he had found an ancient piece of parchment that detailed everything about his ancestor's meeting with the Befana. Balthazar, on the other hand, had been summoned into his great uncle's study one day, forced to sit in a leather chair and made to watch a presentation on the role of the Befana in his family's life.

'What can we do for you?' asked Gaspar, summoning the courage to speak to a woman he had never truly believed to exist.

'Well boys,' said the Befana firmly, 'We have what I suppose you, Gaspar, would call 'a situation' and it's one that's making my blood boil, my artichokes pickle and my garlic features gasp. Not to pour more olive oil on troubled waters than is absolutely necessary, that fat old man, Santa Claus, is up to dirty tricks and, for a woman with an obsession for cleaning, dirty tricks are just not acceptable!'

The Befana was talking in riddles. 'The Three Kings' shook their heads in sympathy, without having the slightest clue what was going on.

'Santa Claus,' said Mel eventually. 'But he's such a kind old man. How can he have upset you?'

'Kind old man? Kind old man?' shouted the Befana, so loudly that the chandelier began to shake, 'He is breaking every law ever decreed in the world of Very Important Present Bringers and has infiltrated my patch. He's turning children against me.

My Befana celebrations have been downsized, with a view to being cancelled altogether next year and he thinks he can replace my simple gifts of coal and candy with commercial gadgets and gizmos. He is also a man who has broken his promises and has not advised his own fiancée of his marriage to a Mrs Claus!'

The Befana jumped up and down in anger, stamping her feet in her oversized shoes and causing objects to fall off shelves. The boys had to act quickly.

'So where do we fit in?' asked Thaz. He had plans today, having his eye on a new yacht that was up for sale. He didn't want to miss out on buying it.

'I need various things from you and your great-great-great-great, oh I can't be bothered with all that, grandfathers promised that I would always be able to call in favours from them, or their descendants, in a time of strife. Believe me, this is that time!'

Gaspar nodded his head. Mel did the same and Thaz uttered the word, 'sure'. All three again recalled the day they had first been made aware of this woman and what they had sworn to do.

'It's good to see you are aware of this crucial fact,' said the Befana.

'So what do we need to do?' asked Mel.

'You, my dear, need to get to your vault and supply me with enough gold to stock up on fuel for my broom. I also need to buy enough coal and candy to potentially deliver a piece to every child on Santa's run, as well as my own.'

'OK, consider it done,' said Mel, sadly reflecting that his fortune would dwindle, but knowing that his family had held gold bullion in the family vaults for years and years, just in case the Befana ever needed some.

'And me?' asked Thaz.

'You, Thaz, if I must call you that, need to organise some beauty potions for me using myrrh. I need to control my warts, get rid of my acne and skin irritations, reduce those terrible mouth sores that trouble me in winter and then stimulate my blood flow, so that I have sufficient energy to get around the world on my broom without feeling exhausted. Oh, and I nearly forgot, it needs to get rid of a pimple on my bottom.'

Thaz winced. 'Too much information,' he thought to himself, without daring to say anything out loud.

'What was that?' snapped the Befana, detecting his unspoken thoughts.

'Nothing,' trembled Thaz nervously, not wishing to upset this rather volatile woman.

'And what do I have to do?' asked Gaspar kindly. The Befana smiled at him sweetly, thinking how much like the original Gaspar he was.

'My dear, dear boy,' she said, 'I need you to concoct a potion that will cast a sleeping spell, wherever and whenever it is used. It must be concentrated enough for me to carry with me on my travels and only the slightest drop in the atmosphere should be capable of sending an enemy to sleep. Now can you do that for me?'

'I have a book of chemistry that was handed down to me,' replied Gaspar. 'It's full of formulas for all manner of lotions and scents, though I've never known why it was needed.'

'That's the one,' said the Befana with glee. 'I wrote that book centuries ago with your great-great-great-great, oh I can't be bothered with all that, grandfather. We built upon his knowledge of aromatic oils and my own witchy, wondrous wisdom. I was hoping the book still existed. It took us all of twelve hours to write!'

She paused, before summing up. 'What all three of you need to do,' she declared, 'is use your popularity to appeal to your fans. You must ask them to request that the Befana this year brings them coal or candy and the simple things in life, rather than mass-produced, commercialised toys, games, computers and so on. A public appeal on TV should do the trick.'

'Whatever you say,' said 'The Three Kings', in perfect unison.

'It sounds like a plan then,' said the Befana triumphantly. 'We have a few days to get the strategy up and running, but with no further ado, I need to get back inside that window-cleaning contraption and hand it back to two men in overalls, who are probably now very angry with me. Get the wheels in motion and find me in day or two. I'm under the third palm tree on the right, if you're making your way to the beach.'

'OK, will do,' said 'The Three Kings', in unison once again.

'Favoloso. Fantastico. Stupendo!' laughed the Befana. 'Nobody tramples on my floppy shoes and gets away with it!'

With no further delay, she started hauling herself out through the window. Gaspar rushed to hold her feet as she stretched out towards the cab, inching her way in. As he finally let go, she fell in, once again having to grope around for her spectacles.

'Arrivederci a tutti!' she shouted, shooting downwards at pace, having pulled a lever rather too sharply. The boys stood at the window watching her go, a look of total astonishment written across their faces.

CHAPTER EIGHT

During the course of that sticky and humid night, the Befana hardly slept. Palm fronds stuck in her back and insect noises kept her awake. She had to think carefully how to win back the hearts of her Italian children. What she needed was a disguise, but she was so old and haggard. She was wrinkly and worn. If only she could be young again ... that would fool everyone. She tossed and turned with this one thought in her ancient, centuries-old head. After many hours of this, she came to one conclusion ... she needed to seek out Old Father Time.

She'd only ever heard whispers about this man, with his name uttered occasionally by her mother and grandmother, who themselves had listened to tales about him when they were younger. All the Befana knew was that he lived in a cave, somewhere in an ancient city carved out of rock. She had been told that a witch could only call upon Old Father Time's assistance in the most pressing of circumstances, but wasn't that now? What could be more pressing than trying to win back the hearts of her Italian children?

Under the palm trees, she tapped her broom gently. 'Broom,' she said, with urgency in her voice. 'I must find Old Father Time. I am sure he is not too far from here. Could you take me to him?'

The broom tilted its head to one side, as if thinking. It leapt up and hit the ground once. She took that to mean 'yes'.

'How many kilometres from here does he live?' she asked anxiously.

The broom lifted itself on end and drew the figures 1998 in the sandy soil.

'That is good broom … not that far at all,' she said in delight. She figured that anyone who saw her flying in the sky in this heat would put it down to a mirage, so pulled the broom out of the trees and down towards a clear patch of land.

'Come on broom, let's go,' she urged.

Up they surged and along they sped, in clear skies that only very rarely threw a tricky cloud in their path. They flew and flew, until a pink glow appeared beneath them – the pink of rock glowing in the sun. Down the broom dropped, lowering them towards the beautiful pinkness below.

Landing was tricky. Everything was rocky and sharp and looked most painful as a landing base. She expected her broom to put her down between the high rocks, but it had other ideas. It circled and went round and round until it started to hover above a rocky ledge. Instead of gliding into position, it plopped straight down, right outside a cave.

'Surely he doesn't live in this barren, hot place?' questioned the Befana, as she stared into the dark hole of a cave. The broom leapt up and tapped once. 'So he does then,' she replied in amazement. 'Rather him than me!'

A big rock partially covered the entrance. She squeezed past it, but could see nothing in the dark. Although she was a witch, her nerves jangled slightly. She thought about turning back, but it was too late.

'Who wants me?' bellowed a gruff voice. A shaft of light emerged in the darkness as a lantern swung. It lit up the face of a bearded, large-framed and extremely old man, with the whitest hair she'd ever seen.

'The Befana,' she replied, quaking in her floppy shoes.

'You don't look like a farmer,' said the man she presumed to be Old Father Time.

'Not a farmer!' she said rather tetchily, 'The Befana! Wash your earholes out!'

'What do you want?' he snapped.

'To look like a 30-year-old again,' she answered, shaking a little and wishing she hadn't been so rude.

'I could make that happen in an instant, but why do you want that so much?' he asked.

The Befana told him the whole sorry tale relating to the loss of her Italian children's affections. She explained why she needed a disguise. She touched his heart with her words, as he sat on his rock stool and listened.

'Going back in time and becoming young again is not easy. No, no, just the opposite, in fact. You will have to use your new-found youth wisely and make the right decisions.'

'I will,' she said, 'All I want to do is win back my Italian children.'

'Are you sure they will not love you as you are?' he asked. 'Being young and pretty is not everything. They may prefer you to be, shall we say 'wrinkly'?'

'They are downsizing my festival. They mock me in the street. I am not up-to-date enough for them,' she replied.

'Very well then, look into my eyes for thirty seconds,' he said. As she did so, he pulled out a huge gold clock on a chain. 'Watch this and do not take your eyes off the hands of the clock face,' he urged. 'It is essential that you do not lose eye contact with it.'

She did exactly as he asked, becoming slightly dizzy in the process.

'I am now going to count back slowly in centuries,' he said. 'Be sure not to take your eyes off the watch. Are you sure you wish to be thirty years of age?'

She nodded and kept her eyes fixed as he counted backwards, 21st, 20th, 19th, 18th and so on, right back to before Jesus' birth and beyond. As each century was announced, she felt a little different, but dared not take her eyes off the clock. Eventually, Old Father Time reached the year in which she had been thirty years old.

'Take your eyes off the clock now,' he stated firmly.

The Befana looked down at her hands. They were no longer wrinkled. Her skin was tighter and a different colour, free from age spots. She felt her face and the skin was firm, not flabby. She felt full of energy and had lost a huge amount of weight. Her dress was almost falling off her shoulders.

'Your body is thirty-years-old again,' said Old Father Time, 'but your knowledge of the centuries will be unaffected. Use the wisdom of the years wisely.'

'This is favoloso,' said the Befana. 'Nobody will recognise me now!'

'No, and you can no longer refer to yourself as The Befana,' said Old Father Time, in a most serious tone. 'This is the price you pay for rejuvenation. You must take another name, so as to not confuse time. If you ever call yourself The Befana again, you will re-age and become who you were. Of course, you may wish to do that; it's up to you, but be warned!'

The Befana scratched her head. 'I shall call myself

Bef,' she said, forcefully. 'I rather like it. It sounds trendy and very new-me!'

'Very well, my child,' said Old Father Time. 'Now leave me in peace so I can rest and await another visitor in a hundred years or so. That seems to be the passage of time between visitors.'

'Thank you,' said Bef. 'With your invaluable help, I am sure I can achieve my mission.'

'You are very passionate, my child,' replied Old Father Time. 'God speed.'

With that, he turned his back, blew out the lantern and disappeared into the darkness. In the pitch black, Bef felt her way out of the cave, stumbling a few times, but eventually returning safely to her broom. She hitched up her voluminous dress, trying to keep it on her now slim body.

'Back to Dubai, broom,' she ordered.

With no further to-do, it swiftly lifted them off the ground and took to the desert skies once again, leaving the charming and fairytale pinkness of Old Father Time's location far, far behind them.

CHAPTER NINE

It was Thaz who came to find Bef under the third palm tree on the right, a few days later. In the meantime, feeling a little grumpy that the boys hadn't completed their tasks in 24 hours, Bef had banged her head hard and tried to remember some of her old spells, finally managing to summon up a rather splendid, red designer dress. In full disguise, she had entered the hotel and logged on to the Internet, somehow discovering where she could find coalmines, candy stores and Santa's home. She was now all geared up to take revenge for her public and global humiliation in the VIPB world!

Thaz was extremely nervous at having to face the witch on his own.

'Are you there?' he whispered, trying not to alert any guests walking to the beach. He pretended to be tying up a shoelace on his rather expensive trainers, while looking around constantly, to see if anyone was watching.

'Of course I'm here!' came the reply. 'Whatever

took you so long? These palm tree fronds are playing havoc with my back at night. I'm as stiff as a board!' With that, she stepped out from the trees.

'Who on earth are you?' screeched Thaz in alarm. 'I was looking for a friend, but you're not her!'

'Yes, I am,' replied Bef, delighted that Thaz did not recognise her. She came face to face with him, eyeing up his very loudly patterned shirt with disapproval and doing up two buttons, as if she were his mother.

'Right, let's get cracking!' she said, as her stomach gave an enormous rumble, reminding her that she felt as if she had been on a hunger strike lately. She longed for her beloved polenta and pasta, wild mushroom risotto, boiled potatoes, lashings of ragu and scrumptious panna cotta. All she had managed to swipe lately were a few dates, quinces and very strange fruit, so now her stomach felt like a big empty cavern.

Food was desperately needed so that she could think straight. She had discovered that the largest coal mines in the world were in the USA, Russia, China, India and Australia. She would need to visit at least one of these. All the issues of how to buy her coal and candy were whizzing around her head and making her dizzy. How on earth was she going to manage to visit all the children that Santa Claus dropped in on?

She was jealous. He was so lucky to have all that

reindeer power to help him whiz through the night. He also had a very handy sleigh on which to load things, but she only had her trusty old broomstick. That had no carrying capacity at all, other than what she could load into a sack and carry on her back, or sling around the broom, so that the contents were beneath her as she flew. This caused terrible instability and the number of times she had to land and restock with coal and candy was just incredible. What was to be done?

'How did you manage to become so normal looking?' asked Thaz, breaking her train of thought.

'I visited Old Father Time,' she replied, in a very matter-of-fact way, as if it were an everyday occurrence.

'Oh, I see,' said Thaz, not seeing at all. He shepherded her into the hotel and into the lift. Up they rode until they arrived at Gaspar's door.. As they walked in, the other two of 'The Three Kings' were watching TV. They jumped out of their skin when they saw Bef.

'Who is this?' asked Gaspar.

'Where's you know who?' enquired Mel.

'Guys, may I introduce Bef, formerly known as The Befana,' announced Thaz.

Bef chortled loudly as their jaws almost hit the floor in amazement. Had they not recognised her cackle, neither of the boys would have believed Thaz for one minute. There was not a sign of a wart or a wrinkle. All they could see were laughter lines around her eyes. She was slim and stylish … only her hair needed a bit of attention.

'Hee, hee, hee,' laughed Bef, 'It's me and none of you recognised me! Mission accomplished! Bow down to the new-look woman, who must now be called Bef.'

'Why is that?' asked Gaspar.

'I promised Old Father Time,' answered Bef.

None of them looked any the wiser, but didn't like to probe.

'I love it when a plan comes together,' said Bef. 'Now tell me where you've got up to with your tasks,' she added, hungrily tucking into the fruit in the bowl in front of her.

The boys briefed Bef on their progress and sat back, awaiting her response. She just looked at them quizzically, her mind still whirring and worrying about her massive delivery problem.

'What happens now then?' asked Thaz, after a good few minutes had passed by.

'Now, my dear, I must start to really crack on with my mission,' answered Bef, speaking slowly, as if finally determining what had to be done. 'Firstly, we must firm up my route around the world and then, secondly … and unfortunately … and I say this with the heaviest heart and absolute fear and dread, I must make some very important enhancements to my broom.'

The left eyebrow of all three of 'The Three Kings' simultaneously lifted two centimetres. Predictably, it was Thaz who communicated what they were all thinking.

'Why the fear and dread?'

'Fear and dread and more fear and dread, because there is only one person in the world who can possibly make those enhancements,' explained Bef. She stopped abruptly. Again, the left eyebrows all went up.

'And who's that then?' asked Mel, having received a sharp jab in the ribs from Thaz, who wasn't prepared to risk annoying the witch by asking another question.

'A man around whom fearsome legends have been constructed. A man whose name strikes terror into the hearts of those who hear it. A man who can make the knees of the bravest knights in the land knock together with fear. A man who can fell trees with one swipe of his hand. A man who can ignite a forest fire with just a puff from his lungs,' explained Bef dramatically.

'Not Santa, surely?' asked Mel.

'Don't be ridiculous!' retorted Bef. 'Santa indeed! The thought is laughable. Of course it's not Santa! I'm talking about Bernhardt Bürstenfrisür – Bernhardt of the Forest, or as he is better known, the Most Fearsome Feller in Folklore … and that's feller as in tree feller, by the way, not just fella as in man!

However, we do also refer to him as the Terrible Torta!'

'Why?' asked Gaspar.

'Well, it's just a joke among Very Important Present Bringers actually. Torta is the word for cake and at one VIPB conference we had all had a little bit too much eggnog and thought it extremely funny to name him in this way, as he lives in the heart of the Black Forest, which is, of course, world famous for its gateaux!'

She chortled loudly and then stopped, as a veil of fear descended over her face. 'Of course, this is no laughing matter. Taking a broom to Bernhardt Bürstenfrisür really is a last-resort measure. Nobody in their right mind would seek him out otherwise.'

Thaz immediately thought, 'but you're not in your right mind', which Bef picked up on immediately.

'What do you mean, not in my right mind?' She clipped him around the ear and he winced. 'I have to seek out this man who, luckily, I have never had the misfortune to meet. They say he stands over three-metres tall, casts shadows as long as the fir trees in the forest and has a dwelling in which he has to sleep with his feet sticking out of the window, because he is so huge. One thump of his foot sends earth tremors all the way to the South Pole and when he sneezes, the pollen flies off all the forest flowers and causes huge clouds to descend over Germany, making hay-fever levels soar.'

The boys' faces were just wrapped in amazement.

'Wow,' murmured Thaz.

'Awesome,' added Mel.

'I cannot let you go alone,' stated Gaspar.

Bef peered over the top of her still twisted spectacles.

'Are you volunteering to come with me?' she asked.

'Definitely not,' said Thaz.

'Too right we're not,' added Mel.

'Yes, I am,' confirmed Gaspar, as his friends stared at him as if he were insane.

'Have you finally lost the plot?' asked Thaz.

'I can't let her go alone,' explained Gaspar. 'Our forefathers wouldn't have wanted that. What she has to do is dangerous and she might need me there.'

'What on earth can you do to protect her from a three-metre giant?' retorted Thaz in a mocking tone. 'You're a pop star, not a giant slayer!'

'I don't care, I'm still going,' replied Gaspar bravely.

'You dear, dear boy,' said Bef. 'Together, I'm sure we can charm Bernhardt Bürstenfrisür.' She crossed her fingers behind her back, being pretty certain this was a rather hopeful thought given the stories she had heard about the man.

'I'm guessing that people must have come away

from encounters with him alive, or you wouldn't know so much about him,' said Gaspar.

'Yes, of course! I am sure he can be completely reasonable when not rubbed up the wrong way! More importantly, he is a demon with a broom and can do marvellous things beyond the imagination of any other broom builder or 'adaptation artisan', which is what he calls himself, apparently. Only he can supply me with the means to fly right around the world delivering my coal and candy, so beggars cannot be choosers and we simply must face him and see what he can do for us. We will fly tonight!'

'Fly?' said Gaspar. 'We won't get tickets in time.'

Bef burst into laughter. Tickets! Tickets! We don't need tickets to fly through the night skies. We just hop on the broom!'

Gaspar went white. 'I hadn't thought of that,' he said. 'Can't we just book some seats to Germany for maybe tomorrow, or the day after? I could get us into first class.'

'Of course not!' boomed Bef. 'I don't have such a thing as a passport, or documentation. What would I put down as my age, for a start? We don't need anything other than the broom to get us to where we need to go and, to be honest, I don't exactly know where that is. The Black Forest is a big place, so I am going to have to perform a little magic to let my broom steer us to Herr Bernhardt Bürstenfrisür's abode.'

Gaspar had now turned whiter still, resembling the colour of his lovely Egyptian cottons sheets. 'Can I pack a few things?' he enquired innocently.

'Yes, put a little bag together, if you wish, but not too much, or you will cause an imbalance on the broom and it does not like that; it does not like that at all! You will need something warm for the shoulders, as it can get nippy in the night skies, before the sun rises. And try to find a scarf for your head. One of your Arab headdresses will be ideal. Now toodle-pip! I have to get my own wardrobe together!'

Left on their own, the boys considered how on earth they could keep Gaspar safe, deciding that his newly created sleeping potion could be his greatest asset, if things turned nasty. All three knew, however, that he had not tested it out fully and, although it had made Thaz doze off, that was hardly a sure test of its effectiveness, as he could even fall asleep to the sound of the vacuum cleaner! A gloom of immense proportion descended on a very luxurious apartment in Dubai, as a rather famous boy band contemplated how they would cope if one of their members was trampled underfoot by the Most Fearsome Feller in Folklore.

CHAPTER TEN

'The Three Kings' slouched glumly by the third palm tree on the right. They had absolutely no idea how long the trip to Bernhardt Bürstenfrisür might take, or whether they would ever see Gaspar again, after he and Bef had faced the awesome giant of the Black Forest.

'Please keep ringing us and let us know what's going on,' said Thaz, placing a hand on Gaspar's shoulder.

'I doubt there will be any signal in the middle of the Black Forest,' replied Gaspar, 'and where on earth am I going to charge my phone?'

'Good point,' said Mel.

All three looked down at their feet, realising the folly of this whole mission. A click of new stiletto shoes on the paving stones made them raise their eyes.

'Here you are,' said Bef. 'I've been up and down the so-called elevator to your apartment and just couldn't find you. At least five minutes has been wasted and dusk is falling boys … dusk is falling.'

The boys considered themselves thoroughly ticked off. She bustled around in the undergrowth, retrieving her broom. Her floppy shoes poked out from within a very large bag and her apron and shawl were under her arm. She shook the broom from side to side and then tapped it hard, three times, on the base of its handle.

'Bef to broom,' she chanted. 'Bef to broom.' Suddenly, the end of the broom began to glow.

'Broom, we have an important mission,' she explained, with a chanting type of rhythm to her voice. 'Now, as you know, we used up a bit of tuber-power going to see Old Father Time, essential though that trip was. Consequently, I now need you to set a course for the dwelling of Bernhardt Bürstenfrisür.'

The broom started to shake violently, swaying from side to side.

'What's wrong with it?' asked Mel.

'It doesn't like what I've just told it,' whispered Bef. 'Broom, dear broom. I know that you know where Herr Bürstenfrisür can be found, because I know that he made you, long before you fell into my good hands one snowy day in 1044, so I want you to concentrate hard and direct me to his home.'

The broom shook again, this time doing a little dance across the floor of the palm-fronded area in which they were standing.

'No broom. I am sure his reputation of being the 'Most Fearsome Feller in Folklore' is exaggerated. Think of him more as 'The Terrible Torta' and I am sure you can get through this. Only he can help us, broom. If we don't go to see him, our status as Very Important Present Bringers will be a joke across the world, pushed out of our own country by a Johnny-come-lately and forgotten about my millions of children and those of future generations.'

The broom bowed its head.

'Thank you, trusty broom,' said Bef, stroking it gently and wiping a tear away from her eye, brought on by the terrible possibility of which she had just spoken. If children forgot about her and that Johnny-come-lately Santa took over, she would be finished; a woman without a purpose … an old woman with nothing to do other than make minestra and polenta chips.

The sky was darkening and pesky mosquitoes were beginning to emerge, getting ready to buzz, annoy and bite. Bef wafted a few away.

'Let's head to the beach,' she declared bossily.

They walked dejectedly down towards the sea. Dubai was lit up – every building a blaze of illuminated light bulbs and neon signs. At least nobody would notice them flying through the sky.

'Broom, you know what you have to do,' stated Bef firmly.

At that moment, chefs in hotels around Dubai

stared in amazement as potatoes began to fly out of their kitchen windows. A stream of potatoes, one following another, arrived by the shore and were sucked up by the broom, which made a weird churning sound as it transformed them into broom power.

'Favoloso. We are ready for take off,' said Bef.

She straddled the broom, slipped her feet back into her huge shoes and tied her shawl around her shoulders and fixed her scarf around her head.

'Jump on board,' she said to Gaspar, patting the area where she wanted him to sit.

He nervously put one leg over the broom and sat down. Amazingly, it felt just like having a seat, even though his transport just looked like a pole!

'It's actually quite comfy,' he said, as Mel and Thaz stared at him. 'Not as bad as you might think,' he continued.

He wore his elaborate headdress and fine Arab robes, with his jeans underneath. 'Wear lots of layers,' was what his mother had always told him, when there was uncertainty about the temperature. At least he could remove some, if he got too hot.

The broom started to vibrate and rumble, causing grains of sand to be stirred up all around. Thaz and Mel took a step backwards in alarm.

'We'll be thinking about you mate,' said Thaz.

'Be careful,' urged Mel, 'and don't try to be a hero!'

'And what about my safety?' asked Bef indignantly.

'You too,' replied Mel, rather begrudgingly.

'Get ready for lift off and distribute your weight evenly,' instructed Bef, tapping Gaspar on the knee. 'There are 10 seconds to go now, so hold on tight, 9, 8, 7, 6. 5, 4, 3, 2, 1 Goooooooooooooooou … andiamoooooooooooooo!'

The broom soared upwards at an angle of around 45 degrees, just clearing the tops of the first palm trees. Gaspar could hear the distant voices of Mel and Thaz shouting their goodbyes, but all was a blur. He closed his eyes as they approached the first hotel rooftop and just managed to skim across it, seconds before hitting it!

'I really must steer better, remembering that there are two of us on board,' explained Bef. 'Sorry if I've petrified you already!'

Gaspar accepted her apology. He was clinging on for grim death, not daring to trust his balance and preferring to grab Bef's waist, as if on a motorbike. They seemed to be very high now, but he could detect jumbo jets flying above them. Surely the passengers would spot them, if they looked down.

'Can't we be seen?' he shouted in Bef's ear.

'Sometimes,' she replied. People usually think they've imagined it. Who would believe them? They just rub their eyes and, by the time they look again, we've zooted out of vision.'

'And radar?' asked Gaspar.

'I fitted a radar-fogging device when that started to be an issue,' explained Bef. 'I found an excellent Italian radar expert who helped me to do it.'

Gaspar seemed satisfied by the explanation. They had left Dubai now and all he could see was desert below and sea in the distance. He settled backwards, feeling a bit easier on this unusual form of transport now.

'Are you ready for some loops?' asked Bef.

'Are you serious? Just keep flying straight and I'll be OK.'

'Where's the fun in that?' thought Bef, but she didn't wish to unsettle him. He was, after all, her favourite.

Gaspar was getting used to the feel of the air currents on his face and was in awe of the things he could see all around him – stars, the moon, planes, birds, desert, expanses of water and Bef's huge flapping shoes. He came to realise that the shoes were actually excellent devices for keeping flocks of birds away, the loud, slapping noise that they created frightening the creatures and forcing them to adopt a different path. He actually thought he could get used to this sort of travel.

Every so often, Bef would screech, in a voice that he thought would be heard across the globe, such instructions as, 'Peep at those pyramids,' or 'Eyes down for Etna', or even 'Wonder if the Pope is at home today?' as they flew over places of interest, such as Egypt, Sicily and Rome.

Gaspar saw the beaches and Orthodox churches of Greece, the beautiful canals and buildings of Venice and the snow-clad, magnificent Alps – the latter a little too close for comfort as Bef flew frighteningly close to the mountain peaks, raising the broom at seemingly the very last minute and darting in and out of different mountains, through gaps that appeared barely wide enough to give two people and a broom a safe passage. On each of these occasions, Gaspar just closed his eyes and prayed, recognising that the worst thing to do would be to yell, disturb Bef and affect her navigational skills.

'How are we liking it?' she would enquire, over and over again, each time a new sort of terrain appeared beneath them, or new sights emerged on the horizon.

'It's cool,' replied Gaspar, uncertain himself what he actually thought of it, with a mixture of awe and fear tangling up his stomach. On the one hand, the sights were truly amazing and he was sure that, as long as he lived, he would never do anything quite like this again. On the other, the risks Bef seemed to take were terrifying. Above all, he was worried sick what might happen when she met up with Bernhardt Bürstenfrisür. It was all very well throwing caution to the wind on her broom, but it might be a terrible mistake to do so with the legendary tyrant of the

Black Forest. Gaspar felt a shiver go down his back and pulled his clothing tighter around his body.

They were now heading up central Europe, but Gaspar wasn't exactly sure where they were.

'Do you have any idea where this is?' he enquired, jabbing his finger downwards to the land below.

'Yes, of course,' answered Bef, 'it's Switzerland. Can't you hear the tinkling of cowbells on the wind?'

Gaspar strained his ears and attempted to pick up the sound, but could hear absolutely nothing. 'No, I can't' he replied.

'Goodness, you need to get your ears tested,' barked Bef. 'Listen again!'

With that, she pointed the broom downwards until they were flying almost vertically and heading straight for the pastures beneath. When it seemed as though they were going to crash straight into the ground, she straightened the broom, to allow them to hover around 90 metres above the land.

'Now can you hear them?' she bellowed.

Gaspar strained his ears again and, sure enough, could hear the cowbells chiming in a truly sweet fashion.

'Yes,' he answered. In his own head, he was thinking that Bef must have the hearing of a dog, picking up on sounds that true humans simply could not detect.

'And precisely what sort of dog do you think I

am?' she asked. 'An Alsatian perhaps, or do you see me more as a Chihuahua? Pray, do tell!'

Gaspar flushed a bright red colour and could feel his cheeks burning. 'I just thought it was amazing that you could hear that sound right up there,' he answered apologetically. 'I couldn't hear a thing except the flapping of your shoes.'

Bef didn't appear to care about his explanation, merely pointing the broom virtually horizontal and soaring back up until they were flying at their previous altitude.

'Germany will be next,' she yelled, as they continued their journey. 'You need to help me now. We must spot the River Rhine and follow its course into Lake Constance. From there, the broom can take over and guide us towards Bernhardt Bürstenfrisür's dwelling. If you see any gnomes, we've gone off course and ended up flying over Zurich!'

Gaspar looked puzzled.

'There aren't really gnomes in Zurich,' he eventually stuttered. 'It's a nickname for Swiss bankers.'

Bef started to chortle. 'So they've got you fooled as well,' she laughed. 'Of course there are gnomes! They live in caverns under tree stumps in the woods around Zurich and only venture out by night. They wear hats and have lamps attached, so by night you can see a whole line of them snaking through the fields. I often see them when I'm taking presents to Italian-Swiss children.

'The gnomes also care for the biggest watch in the world, housed in a secret location, somewhere in their territory, but nobody knows where … absolutely nobody. This allows them to keep perfect time with everything that they do. Luckily, humans rarely spot them and, if they do, are carted off to a sanitarium and told they are insane. The gnomes can switch off their lamps instantly, whenever they detect a human and are experts at camouflage. Being largely green-skinned helps, of course, but they can blend into grass, tree bark, almost anything in the world of nature.'

'Why do they go out at night?' asked Gaspar, intrigued by this tale.

'To go to the mines,' replied Bef. 'They mine for quartz to feed the biggest watch in the world, which requires quartz in order to run. If they didn't go mining, the watch would stop and their whole world would fall apart.'

'Wow,' said Gaspar. 'I never knew.'

Bef didn't seem to be listening, staring downwards, trying to detect the winding River Rhine. After a few minutes, she succeeded.

'There it is,' she cried, 'now let's track the river to the lake.'

Tracking the Rhine wasn't as much fun as it sounded. Rather than just flying in a straight line, it involved turning and twisting, as the river wound along its course. Gaspar began to feel a little sick.

There was a sudden turn left at one point and, lacking concentration, he almost fell off the broom. He corrected his seating position, hoping Bef hadn't noticed, though it was almost inevitable that she had. She didn't miss much.

Gaspar shut his eyes, wondering if this jerky movement was really necessary. These were thoughts he didn't voice, even though he actually wondered whether the broom could take over right now and save them from having to carry on in this awful fashion.

Bef was still gleefully pointing things out.

'Liechtenstein to the right,' she bellowed, like a pilot telling passengers what they could see underneath them.

Gaspar could hardly be bothered. His stomach was churning at the thought of having to meet Bernhardt Bürstenfrisür and he was beginning to wish he hadn't been quite to quick to offer to accompany Bef. Thaz and Mel were probably either sleeping soundly, or having fun in the sunshine. Suddenly, his train of thought was broken.

'Grazie a Dio,' yelled Bef.

'What?' replied Gaspar.

'Thanks be to God. There's Lake Constance.' She pointed to a mass of water just ahead of them. 'We will just follow the river a bit further and then my darling, clever, brave and all-knowing broom will take over.' She ended the sentence as if expecting a response, but nothing happened. 'Won't you broom?' she said, rather emphatically.

The broom shook a little, in response to this firmer tone.

'Yes, he will,' explained Bef, as if now interpreting broom language for Gaspar. 'This broom and I go back centuries; he won't let me down.'

Secretly, Gaspar felt it would be no bad thing if the broom refused to find Bernhardt Bürstenfrisür. If it couldn't locate the giant, it might be a stroke of luck for all concerned, particularly himself! He almost prayed they wouldn't find the river's course at the other end of the lake, but his prayers were not answered. Although they did lose it at first, Bef circled around three times, until she spotted it once again and triumphantly pointed it out to Gaspar when it reappeared. His heart sank.

As they carried on, something strange started to happen. Bef closed her eyes, humming to herself and uttering some sort of spell. A shuddering and rattling emerged and he could feel the broom vibrating. A horrible burning smell entered the nostrils and then a roaring sound followed. They shot forward with a huge spurt, both he and Bef being catapulted forwards towards the front of the broom. The broom's bristles, positioned behind Gaspar, stood on end and a whirring noise sent his ears crazy.

They zigzagged, moving here and there, darting upwards and downwards and moving in circles again and again. Gaspar began to question whether they were actually making any progress at all. It was clear the broom was now steering their course, Bef still chanting some weird words Gaspar didn't understand. They shot forward again and Gaspar could see a huge forest.

There was no light from below, just a mass of dark, gloomy pine trees and foreboding shrouds of mist. To his despair, the broom began to descend, at first gradually, tilting itself just a few degrees downwards, as if searching for something, but not willing to take too much risk. That all changed without warning. All of a sudden, the tilt became a plunge and the pit of Gaspar's stomach ended up in his mouth, as if he were on a rollercoaster at the funfair. They dropped rapidly, the forest drawing ever nearer and shapes of actual trees emerging in the murky atmosphere. They darted and threaded in and out of trees, with Gaspar just closing his eyes at times, sure that they were about to collide with a tree trunk, or hit a branch.

The ground was 30 metres below them now and he felt truly sick. Without any warning whatsoever, the broom decided to land. Gaspar gasped in horror. The broom's speed hadn't altered at all and they were heading straight for a massive tree, with a circumference of well over 27 metres. It was simply a giant of the forest and he couldn't predict anything right now other than a mangled mass of broom, Bef and one of 'The Three Kings'! He felt a thud and then a massive skid along the forest floor, though his eyes were still shut tight. They were motoring through the pine needles at a huge rate of knots and fragments of twig and leaves were filling his shoes, as they scraped along the ground.

He opened his eyes bravely, but panicked. They were zooming towards a fallen tree, its trunk strewn directly in their path.

'Watch out,' he shouted loudly.

The broom twitched beneath him, as if annoyed by his interference. They were now just a couple of seconds away from hitting the tree and all seemed lost. Gaspar started to pray and suddenly the broom jerked and lifted itself at the very last minute, hurdling the obstacle, reducing its speed at the same time and landing the other side quite neatly, finally coming to a grinding halt in a leafy glade.

'I think we've arrived in The Black Forest,' declared the now non-spell-chanting, youngish witch. Gaspar sank back on the broom realising that he just wanted to burst into tears.

CHAPTER ELEVEN

The intense scent of pine filled Gaspar's nostrils, as he reached for the bottle of sleeping potion, to check it was still intact and not smashed to smithereens. Luckily, he had wrapped it well and it was still in one piece.

Bef had snapped out of her trance. She shuffled across the forest floor, her enormous shoes causing a loud rustling noise.

'Ssh,' urged Gaspar. 'We don't want him to know we're here!'

'My dear boy,' replied Bef patronisingly, 'do you not think he might have already been alerted to our arrival, considering the noise we've made?'

'That depends,' said Gaspar. 'Ask broom if Bernhardt lives close to here, or whether he's put us down some distance away.'

Bef seemed a little annoyed by this suggestion, but crouched down and whispered something to the broom. It leapt up about a metre and put itself down again.

'Apparently, we're about 800 metres from Bernhardt's house, though the broom can't remember exactly which tree trunk that is. I can only imagine it's an enormous one and one where his feet would have an opening to poke through when he is asleep.'

'Remember the one we nearly crashed into?' said Gaspar. 'That one was massive. Do you think that could be it?'

Bef scratched her chin in deep thought. She clearly didn't have a clue.

'We must let the broom take us,' she finally declared. 'It must follow its homing instinct. All brooms know how to find their way home, even if they don't want to.'

The broom leapt up another metre or so and landed with an indignant thump.

'Come on,' instructed Bef. 'You carry that end and I'll take the bristles.' She picked up one end of the broom and nodded her head towards the other. Gaspar adjusted his Arab headdress and did as he was told. They carried the broom like a log of wood, walking through the trees and traipsing back, just as Gaspar had thought, towards the gigantic tree they had first seen.

'I told you,' he whispered. 'We're heading back the way we came in.'

'Be quiet,' growled Bef. 'Broom tells me it's the middle of the night here and Bernhardt Bürstenfrisür is likely to be asleep. That would give us time to think of a strategy, once we know where he is.'

Gaspar shuddered. The thought of having to negotiate with a mad, three-metre tall giant was not one that sat easily with him. He cast his eyes down, wishing he were anywhere but here.

Bef forged on, placing her feet purposefully so as not to rustle. Every so often, she stopped and looked all around her in a very exaggerated fashion, checking whether the enemy might be watching. In Gaspar's head, it was as if every tree in the forest had a pair of eyes fixed upon them and as if every creature were sending messages back to 'The Most Fearsome Feller in Folklore.'

The broom was motionless, now resigned to the fate of meeting its original master. Totally subdued, it showed not a flicker of response to anything that happened, other than when Gaspar nearly dropped his end, having tripped over a trailing plant. At that point, the broom shook in his hand, as if telling him to be more careful.

'I think this is it,' whispered Bef, after a trek of about twenty minutes, though trek was hardly the right word, given the snail's pace at which they had approached to keep the rustle of Bef's shoes down to a minimum. They both put the broom down and crouched behind a tree, staring at the gigantic trunk that was clearly the same one they had almost hit.

'I can't see any feet dangling out,' said Gaspar. 'Maybe he's not asleep after all.'

'Maybe he's asleep standing up,' answered Bef, trying to reassure herself that he might be in the land of nod. 'The tree certainly looks big enough for him. It must be his home or broom wouldn't have brought us here.'

'What do we do now?' whispered Gaspar. 'Do we wait for him to wake up, or do we go and knock on the trunk? I'm not too au fait with protocol when it comes to Very Important Present Bringers.'

'He's no Very Important Present Bringer,' hissed Bef. 'We true VIPBs voted to kick out his application. What place in history does he have as a present bringer? It was just a joke and the committee wouldn't hear of it. Just as we thought we were going to have to concede and let him in, and just as all the lesser VIPBs were wavering, a final vote swung it. This casting vote allowed us all to breathe easier again. Good job his visa to the conference was refused though, or he could have caused uproar there. We're told the thumping of his feet jumping up and down in anger caused tremors right the way to the South Pole!'

At that moment, something over to the right caught Gaspar's eye. He stared in amazement. A pair of pyjama-bearing legs was waving around in a kicking motion, but they were extraordinarily tiny legs, no more than a third of a metre long, or maybe 45 centimetres at the most.

Gaspar dug Bef in the ribs and pointed. She fixed her eyes on the sight of the stripy red and white pyjama bottoms writhing in the tree.

Out of the blue, a tiny man suddenly jumped down and came striding angrily towards them, shaking his fist.

'Very een-teresting. Very een-teresting indeed,' he shouted, with a heavy German accent. 'So who was it who blocked the application, pray tell. Who was it who had ze casting vote and prevented Bernhardt Bürstenfrisür from becoming a Very Important Present Bringer?'

Gaspar could not believe his eyes. This man was talking as though he might be Bernhardt Bürstenfrisür, acting as though he was Bernhardt Bürstenfrisür, with a lot of anger and animosity, but how could he possibly be 'The Most Fearsome Feller in Folklore'? This was no three-metre tall giant, but a tiny little man of no more than a metre in height, but with hair that stuck straight up another 45 centimetres, streaked ginger, black and forest brown. It almost resembled a dirty brown candyfloss on a stick and Gaspar couldn't take his eyes off it, no matter how rude he knew it was to stare. He had never, ever seen hair like this.

'What are you staring at?' barked the little man.

Bef brushed Gaspar aside and took a step forward.

'We are looking for Bernhardt Bürstenfrisür,' she declared. 'Please take us to him, as you are clearly in his service.'

'Een his service. Een his service,' shrieked the little man in a very shrill voice. 'It iz I! He iz me! I am ze von and only Bernhardt Bürstenfrisür, he of legend and myth, or myth and legend, if you prefer. But who, Madam, may I ask, are you, coming here, waking me up and acting as through you are a Very Important Present Bringer?'

Bef's hackles rose, as though she had forgotten that she had had a complete change of appearance. She took one floppy shoe pace towards the little man.

'You are not Bernhardt Bürstenfrisür,' she stated rather boldly, 'whereas I, on the other hand, am Bef, the VIPB formerly known as the Befana!'

The little man took in a lung-full of breath, paused and then rolled backwards with laughter. His surreal chortles echoed around the forest, causing birds to stir in the branches and squirrels to dive back to their dreys.

'Very güt. Very güt! How funny you are Madam,' he shrieked. 'The Befana iz an ugly old witch, not a glamorous girl like yourself! I like your humour. I like your humour very much … very much indeed! Come with me. Let it not be said that Bernhardt Bürstenfrisür did not give his guests a cup of acorn tea. Then, whilst you are drinking tea, you can tell me who you really are and who blocked my application.'

He turned around and started to march back to the tree from which he had just jumped down.

'You can't be Bernhardt Bürstenfrisür,' insisted Bef. 'He is three-metres tall, a giant of the forest and capable of sending earth tremors all the way to the South Pole.'

'Ha, you fell for ze old propaganda,' laughed Bernhardt Bürstenfrisür weirdly. 'It iz so easy to make people believe anything and very advantageous when you are actually only 0.9 metres tall plus hair. You then live in a gigantic tree and let people think you are too tall even for zis house when, in fact, your feet dangle from a bed only 40 centimetres long!'

He chuckled to himself in a crazy manner and Gaspar began to feel very uneasy. This tiny man was obviously insane, wound up by rejection and out for revenge. When he discovered who had cast the final decisive vote that had blocked his application, hell would have no fury like a tiny, half-crazed forest monster with hair like a toilet brush!

They tried to follow Bernhardt Bürstenfrisür through a door in the massive tree trunk, but could not get through, even he struggling and having to bend at 90-degrees to get his hair through first.

'Ach mein Gott,' he shouted. 'We vill have to go

to ze entertainment suite.' He stomped to the back of the giant tree and swung a door open there. 'Come zis way,' he shouted. 'Be quick because ze wood-burning stove is only set to low and I don't want ze heat to escape.'

Gaspar suddenly remembered the broom and tracked back a bit to pick it up. The broom slapped in his hand, in annoyance at being remembered. It seemed it had no desire to meet its maker.

Bef had entered the tree and Bernhardt Bürstenfrisür stood beside the opening, propping the heavy wooden door open. A thought flashed through Gaspar's mind that Bernhardt could simply usher them inside and lock them in. He felt for the sleeping potion phials inside the little bag attached to his waist. All was still in place. He walked gingerly towards Bernhardt Bürstenfrisür, whose top half was almost blending into the background, whilst his red and white pyjama bottoms stuck out like a sore thumb.

'Normally, I would remove my pyjamas and change into something more appropriate,' he explained, seeing Gaspar eyeing him up and down. 'But zen, you are hardly a picture of elegance your-self, are you?' he continued, pointing to Gaspar's Arab headdress. Gaspar forced a smile and stepped towards him. At that moment, the broom tucked under his arm came into full view.

'Vot iz zis? Vot iz zis?' exclaimed Bernhardt

Bürstenfrisür. He tilted his head backwards and began to inhale, filling his nostrils with some smell he was detecting on the breeze. He jerked his head downwards and started to sniff, like a hound following an aniseed trail across the hills. He lifted his nose up and down and up and down, until it was two centimetres away from the broom, which he suddenly grabbed and wrestled away from Gaspar.

'Von of my beauties. Von of my beauties indeed,' he confirmed to himself.

Any thought of locking them inside the tree evaporated as he ran inside and slapped the broom on a huge pine table. Bernhardt ran his nose right along the broom, trying to detect something. Bef watched him disdainfully, obviously less than impressed by this strange, tiny man, who in no way matched up to her expectations of Bernhardt Bürstenfrisür.

The broom genie himself did not seem to notice, now in raptures and oblivious to anything else going on. He ran to a wooden dresser, curved perfectly to suit the shape of the tree trunk, and whipped out a pair of wooden-framed spectacles. He perched these on his nose, making his appearance even more bizarre. He inspected the broom closely with his fingers and then reverted to sniffing it again. It seemed some sort of ritual that he wanted his audience to observe in detail. Ten minutes passed by, until he suddenly leapt up on to a wooden stool.

'Around 993 AD,' he shouted at the top of his voice, having triumphantly aged the broom.

'You could be right,' conceded Bef. 'It reached me in the snows of 1044, when I think it was seeking some sort of refuge from the heavy falls in the mountains.'

Bernhardt Bürstenfrisür adjusted the angle of his spectacles and then threw them on the table.

'1044? 1044? Who are you?' he shouted. 'You are not old enough to have lived in 1044 and I do not like people trying to make a fool out of Bernhardt Bürstenfrisür. Indeed I do not!' He slapped down his foot and a few chairs shook – hardly the earth tremors of myth and legend.

'I have already told you, my good man, that I am Bef, formerly known as the Befana,' declared the witch. 'I may look very good for my age, but I have recently had some 'work' done, as they say in celebrity circles. I am here to see the giant Bernhardt Bürstenfrisür, which I now see might be you, although you are a mere shadow of the man I was expecting.'

The little man shook in anger. 'Sizeist now are we?' he shouted. 'Size iz not everything and little men really do have a chip on their shoulder, particularly when they fell a lot of trees in ze forest! Do not push me Madam, as I vill not like it. I vill not like it von little bit!'

He banged his fist on the table and the broom shot up a metre.

'Now, why are you here? Why do you come to my forest, disturbing Herr Bernhardt Bürstenfrisür, waking him from his slumber and bringing back his broom.'

'Possession is nine-tenths of the law, making that my broom,' snapped Bef. 'It's been with me for centuries and only recognises me as its owner. However, I have a very important vendetta to wage and my broom needs to be adapted. It needs to become the most powerful, fastest, most ingenious broom in the world, so I recognise that only the genius, or should I say reported genius, of Bernhardt Bürstenfrisür, given that nothing else said about you seems to be correct, can give me the broom I need to have.'

Bernhardt Bürstenfrisür nodded, flattered by the reference to genius.

'A vendetta you say. A vendetta. How von loves a vendetta! Nothing better in fact; nothing better at all!'

He began to dance a little jig around the room, slapping his pyjama bottoms as if they were lederhosen. He waltzed around the table, all the way to the door, making a circle around Gaspar, who was still standing up. He then jigged all the way towards Bef. Suddenly, his face shot right up in front of her, so his nose was just a centimetre away from hers.

'So tell me Madam. Bef Madam. Frau Befana,

or whatever else you might want to be called, why should Bernhardt Bürstenfrisür do anything to help you? Why should Bernhardt Bürstenfrisür assist an enemy who has helped prevent him becoming a Very Important Present Bringer?'

Bef looked shocked and backed away slightly. Gaspar touched the phial of sleeping potion again. Things could be turning very nasty.

'Because,' answered Bef, or 'Perché' as we say in Italy …'

Gaspar felt sick. She was obviously buying herself time, to try to get out of the hole she had dug herself into thanks to her comments in the forest.

'Because,' she continued … 'because Santa Claus once rejected your brooms, slated them in fact, ridiculed them across the globe and rejected them in favour of reindeer power!'

Bernhardt Bürstenfrisür began to shake, at first as one might describe as 'like a leaf', but then uncontrollably. A very strange sobbing sound emerged and tears rolled down his little pale-green face, completely changing him from tyrant to toddler in just ten seconds.

'Zis iz true. Zis iz so true,' he cried. 'The shame of it. The looks I received. Ze Gnomes of Zurich, who used to be my friends, cast me aside. I was forced to live here, alone and with nothing except my dream of becoming a Very Important Present Bringer to keep me motivated. I created all zat propaganda about being a giant to make myself feel better, but deep down nothing worked. I was heartbroken, destroyed and so, so angry. SO SO ANGRY!'

He banged his fist on the table once more, jumped up and down and quivered. All tears disappeared, to just leave the very angry face of a man who had been scorned by the world.

'And so, vot difference does this terrible insult make?' he shouted. 'Zis iz still no reason to work on your broom. Santa Claus slighted me, but you voted against me.'

He pointed his finger accusingly and jabbed it into Bef's ribs.

'You sat there and mocked me by laughing when zay called me 'The Terrible Torta! Ha, you thought I knew nothing of zat, but you are wrong Signora, very, very wrong. I know it all. I have my spies. Walls have ears and nothing – well almost nothing – escapes Bernhardt Bürstenfrisür. So why, why, should I help you, you old witch?'

A thoughtful look descended on Bef's face. She rose to her feet and towered above Bernhardt Bürstenfrisür, the tip of his hair not even reaching as far as her chin. He took two steps back.

'Because,' she said, 'it is against him that I am waging my vendetta.'

Bernhardt Bürstenfrisür ran his hands up his tall candyfloss hair, smoothing down the sides. He jigged a step towards her, as she stepped back, a sort of dance emerging between them as they moved towards each other when making a point and backwards when listening to the enemy's point of view.

'Rubbish,' shouted Bernhardt. 'You are his fiancée.'

Bef's face clouded over. 'I was once. I waited for years for him to hang up his boots and come to live with me in Italy. He told me to keep delivering presents to children in Italy and the Italian-speaking world, whilst he handled his patch. Then I hear that he has stolen the hearts of my children. My celebrations are downsized and seemingly no longer loved by my kiddies. To add insult to injury, I then hear, on one of those new-fangled radio shows, that he has been married for years and there is a Mrs Claus!'

For a moment, she looked downcast and dejected, then she lifted her head and shrieked, 'And now it's payback time!'

Bernhardt eyed her up and down. 'I like zis approach. I like zis attitude. In fact, I like it very much … very much indeed. Ha ha, there iz little better than revenge – a dish served cold, as they say. And how I want revenge. Revenge iz what keeps the blood coursing through my veins and von day I will know … know exactly who had ze casting vote that prevented me becoming a Very Important Present Bringer. When zat day comes, ze forest vill shake and ze squirrels will scamper like never before!'

Bef looked pleased with herself. The little man

circled around the room, his hair perfectly bolt upright and his feet tapping on the wooden floor of his entertainment suite. He spiralled around and around, making Gaspar dizzy as the stripes of his pyjamas became blurred and fuzzy. He danced his way towards Bef and suddenly leapt towards her, his feet just stopping short of landing on her toes.

'But, but, but my dear Signora, despite the fact zat you are nowhere near as ugly and wart-ridden as legend would have us believe, and fabulous as revenge iz, I want more from you. I want, want, want ze name of ze person who had ze casting vote and zen and only zen vill I work on your … no, vot am I saying … MY broom.'

Bef pushed him away.

'It's my broom. Have you never heard the say-ing, 'finders keepers, losers weepers'? I am giving you nothing until you have adapted my broom and then, and only then, will I tell you what you want to know. Do we have a deal?'

She raised her eyebrows and held out her hand. Bernhardt Bürstenfrisür considered the proposition for ten seconds and then spat on his hand, rubbing his spit into Bef's palm as he shook on it.

'Now, I don't have time to mess about, so please attend to the matter urgently,' insisted Bef. 'The sooner you complete the task, the sooner you will get the information. Please get on with it!'

CHAPTER TWELVE

As instructed, Bernhardt Bürstenfrisür leapt into action, having another long sniff up the broom's handle and a close inspection of its bristles. He began to tap his long, tapered fingers up and down the handle, listening intently to every sound he made, as if he were a musician playing an instrument. Gaspar stared, as he gave judgement after every tap.

'Ze broom has been bruised very badly here,' pointed Bernhardt Bürstenfrisür, indicating a spot two-thirds of the way up the handle.

'That was during World War II when we were hit by shrapnel,' responded Bef. 'It was enemy fire that caught us completely by surprise.'

'And here,' said Bernhardt accusingly, 'ze broom has had quite a soaking. Water has seeped into its internal organs and weakened its flying mechanisms.'

To prove this fact, he reached inside a drawer in the dresser, withdrawing a stethoscope. He placed this on the broomstick and listened silently for a few minutes.

'And do we have an explanation for zis?' he asked.

Bef blushed with shame.

'I splashed down in the Adriatic in the 1700s when a violent storm broke out,' she explained. 'We were in the water for just a few seconds, but the broom found it hard to recover. It was a good year before we reached our previous speed again.'

'I am not surprised. Not surprised at all, am I,' tutted Bernhardt. 'Zis type of wood is very rare and precious and needs to be handled with kid gloves, not flapping shoes!' He glared at Bef, who glared back.

'Nevertheless, I can remedy ze results of such mishandling when making ze adaptations. How fast do you want to fly?'

'Like the wind. I need to get around Santa's patch, as well as my own a few days later.'

'Hee, hee, hee,' responded Bernhardt. 'Zen I vill make it happen!'

For a while, the little man was lost in a reverie. He squeezed the broom tightly, massaged it along its entire length from end to bristles and rammed the stethoscope into his tiny ears as far as it would go, to listen to the heartbeat of the broom.

'Güt, güt,' he pronounced after a while. 'Zis

broom is one of my best. It has ze capacity to carry more, just as you wish.'

Bef breathed a sigh of relief. Gaspar was too dumbstruck to say anything. He was mesmerised by the way in which the little 'adaptation artisan' operated, jumping around in his stripy pyjama bottoms with all the jerky movement of a Mexican jumping bean.

'I can give you your wish very easily,' said the broom builder extraordinaire. 'It iz very güt zat there are three of us. My potion requires zat there are three present, to give it ze full force.'

Gaspar nodded, pretending that he understood the plot. Bef was otherwise engaged. She had found a cloth made from fern leaves and was scurrying around with it in her hand.

'What are you doing?' asked Gaspar, as he watched her act like a madwoman, using her fern leaves to dust everything she encountered – dresser, rocking chair, wooden stumpy table and shelves. On and on she dusted, until she arrived in front of Bernhardt Bürstenfrisür and started dusting his nose.

'Mein Gott in heaven, what are you doing woman?' he asked, pushing her away as he tried to stroke the broom.

'It's dusty and dirty in here,' said Bef, still dusting away.

'I think it's her compulsive cleaning disorder

kicking in,' explained Gaspar, trying to elicit sympathy from the broom maker.

'Well keep her away from me,' shouted Bernhardt in a very intimidating manner for one so small. 'I must concentrate.'

He ran to a wooden stool, pulled it across the floor, causing a terrible screech, and then positioned it in front of the dresser. He jumped on to it and stretched with all his might, almost toppling off. Eventually, he managed to pull down a piece of apparatus – clear tubing, as whirly as a snail's shell. Next came a little device that looked like a Bunsen burner. Both were plonked on the tree stump table, around which Gaspar and Bef were now sitting. Bernhardt Bürstenfrisür studied the faces of both.

'Make me angry,' he declared with great authority.

'Why?' asked Gaspar.

'Perché?' asked Bef.

'What for?' continued Gaspar.

'Why are you wasting our time with this?' added Bef.

'Wasting your time! Wasting your time!' shouted Bernhardt, trembling with rage. 'I think, Madam, zat it is you who are wasting my time!'

He was certainly mad now, running around the tree stump in his stripy pyjama bottoms at a real rate of knots. Before he made himself too giddy, he took the only other available chair, sitting between Gaspar and Bef, and flung both of his arms out.

'Hold my hands,' he demanded.

Neither of his guests moved.

'Now!' he shouted loudly.

Reluctantly, Gaspar stretched out his hand. Bef flung her hand into Bernhardt's, rolling her eyes in frustration. Their little host opened his mouth as wide as an alligator's. An enormous ball of fire came flying out, instantly lighting the Bunsen burner with a spindly flame. Bernhardt reached forward and poured some yellow liquid into the tubing.

'Quickly now,' demanded Bernhardt, 'spit into the tube.'

He jumped on the table and spat wildly into the top of the snail-shaped device. Gaspar got to his feet and followed suit. Bef crossed her arms.

'A Very Important Present Bringer does not spit,' she declared haughtily.

'Well, gob in it then,' suggested Gaspar, recognising that the deed needed to be done.

'Gob in it? Gob in it? What is that?' demanded Bef.

'The same as spitting, but it might make you feel better if you call it gobbing,' replied Gaspar.

Reluctantly, Bef got to her feet and spat a huge amount of saliva into the tube. This started whirring around, heated by the flame below.

'Perfect. Absolutely perfect,' enthused Bernhardt.

'Now we can begin. Now we have ze ingredients to allow your broom to fly at a super-tonic speed.'

Suddenly, a green coloured liquid started pouring out of the end of the tube. Bernhardt produced a little dish from his pyjama pocket and began to collect it. Gaspar and Bef slumped back in their seats, exhausted by the energy shown by this little fellow. He ran to his broom and started spreading the green mixture down the whole of its length.

As he rubbed the mixture in, various bulges in the broom popped out.

'Here we have your storage facilities,' he shouted with glee. He dived under the broom and spread more mixture on the underbelly. A whole second tier emerged. 'And here we have your extra super-tonic speed function, complete with more carrying capacity,' he declared, with obvious delight at his own genius. 'Zay don't call Bernhardt Bürstenfrisür ze 'adaptation artisan' for nothing,' he screeched in sheer pleasure.

He jumped up in the air and landed on the wooden table, causing Bef and Gaspar to shoot out of their seats. The broom shuddered slightly, shot bolt upright and then slumped back to its original position.

'All adaptations are complete,' yelled Bernhardt triumphantly as he lifted both arms upwards and stared at the ceiling. Within seconds, he had collapsed on the table and was on all fours, staring into Bef's eyes.

'So now, my dear Signora, it is for you to tell me who it was who cast ze deciding vote to prevent me becoming a Very Important Present Bringer.'

Bef went pale with fright.

'I can't recall,' she declared.

'Can't recall! Can't recall! Who do you think I am? Some sort of simpleton? Of course you remember. I know you do! Now who was it?'

He pulled a tiny fork out of another pyjama pocket and pointed it at her.

'I am sworn to silence,' said Bef defiantly, pushing the fork away.

'Zen, I vill readapt your broom,' replied the angry little man.

'No you won't,' shouted Bef, equally loudly.

'Yes, I vill,' replied the adaptation artisan. A full found of 'no you won't' and 'yes, I vill' then took place, sending Gaspar quite dizzy sitting in the middle of it all. Suddenly, putting an end to all of this, Bernhardt uttered the words, 'Schloss zum sperren.' Immediately, wooden shafts fell from the ceiling and surrounded the two visitors. Next, wooden planks shot out of the walls of the tree, barricading the door.

'Now we shall see who vill tell and who vill not,' chortled the broom maker. Gaspar was horrified. Bef just stared at the little man.

'You must work it out,' she said, after a good

thirty seconds in which the broom maker had stared her out across the table.

'Vot do you mean' shouted the little tyrant.

'I mean,' said Bef, 'that I cannot possibly tell you who it was outright, so you will have to work it out.'

'Tell me now, or ze broom vill be regressed to how it was when it arrived. We had a deal and now you want to change ze rules. Vot is going on around here?' He bounced up and down in anger, like a little jack-in-a-box. 'You vill stay here until you tell me,' he yelled, reaching into a wooden chest and producing a long length of rope. He uncoiled this, as his visitors watched in horror. He then deftly wielded it around his head, as if ready to lasso the pair of them.

'We're going to have to get out of here,' whispered Gaspar. He started to move his hand, to try to reach the phial of sleeping potion. 'I think I may have to act,' he continued, winking at Bef so that she got his meaning. 'The moment I make a move, block your nostrils with your hand.'

Bef looked him in the eye. Suddenly, Gaspar could read her mind and the words, 'get the potion ready the moment the bars on the door are released,' entered his brain. He nodded in acknowledgement that the message had been received.

'A clever man like you, who aspires to be a Very Important Present Bringer, should have no trouble working out the identity of the person who blocked their entry into our esteemed circle,' said Bef, with an air of authority. 'We expect all VIPBs to be able to work out clues and solve riddles. It's part of life as a VIPB.'

Bernhardt Bürstenfrisür was a little taken aback by this.

'I see,' he said thoughtfully. 'Very well, give me ze clue.'

Unbolt the doors first,' said Bef.

'No, I vill not. Tell me first,' replied the little broom artisan. 'You are here on my terms and you vill leave on my terms. Vot is ze clue?' He became redder and redder in the face, until he resembled a tomato. 'Tell me, or I vill sneeze and send pollen clouds all over Germany!'

By now, the little man had a very violent demeanour. He whirled around in a rage and shook his fist at Bef in the angriest manner Gaspar had ever seen. He picked up the rope again.

Bef said nothing. The rope began to rise of its own accord and weaved its way around herself and Gaspar.

'Very well,' she shouted, extremely annoyed to be trapped in this way. 'The clue is 'Enable Validate'.'

'Enable Validate? Enable Validate? Vot does this mean? This is nonsense, ridiculous rhubarb, something even my intelligence cannot fathom. Vot use iz ziz clue to me? I want a name and I want it now, or I shall keep you as a prisoner here forever more and nobody shall ever find you! Now vot is that phrase you people like so much … spill the beans!'

'Undo the doors now!' demanded Bef.

Bernhardt sneered in her face and shouted 'Nein' so loudly that he deafened her. At this moment, a huge gap in the floor opened up around the table and the area on which Bef and Gaspar were seated began to descend into the void below.

'You vill be prisoners in my cellar,' laughed Bernhardt erratically. Gaspar shot forward.

'Oh no we won't,' he yelled, opening up his hand to reveal a small phial of his potion, out of which he shook the tiniest drop, whilst holding his nose tight shut with the other hand. Bef had already covered her nostrils.

Instantly, Bernhardt Bürstenfrisür slumped to the floor. Bef and Gaspar were still dropping into the cellar, but Gaspar jumped back to floor level.

'Give me your hand, Bef. We haven't got that long.'

Bef reached out to him and he hauled her up, struggling at first to get her massive shoes up to Gaspar's level.

'How on earth can we get out of here?' Gaspar asked her.

Bef wrinkled her nose.

'Schloss Revertio!' she shouted. Nothing happened. 'Schloss Re-openio!' she declared. Still nothing moved. 'At a schloss now,' she admitted, shrugging her shoulders.

A strange hum, which Bef had never heard before, filled the room, followed by a thumping and banging. She looked around to see her broom standing upright and bouncing on the wooden floor.

'What's it doing?' asked Gaspar.

'I have absolutely no idea,' she replied.

Both stared as the broom continued to bounce and gyrate around the room, heading towards the door. Its humming went up a notch. As it reached the wood barring the door, the bars began to slide back, one by one, until the forest outside could clearly be seen.

'I see,' said Bef. 'These bars must have been cut from the same tree as my broom. It's talking to them. It's keeping them held back until we get out. Andiamo! Avanti!'

She grabbed Gaspar and dragged him to the door. Sure enough, the murmuring of the broom was holding back the bars, which were hovering in the air. The two of them ran outside, as the broom shot out with them with such force that it knocked them flat on their faces and left them laying amidst pine cones and leaves on the forest floor. An angry squirrel scampered up a tree and chattered to them in great annoyance from above.

'We've got to get out of here,' urged Gaspar. 'I have no idea how long that potion will last.'

Almost before he finished the sentence, the broom came back to life again, sweeping them up so both were straddled across its back. It hovered a metre above the ground and then took off at 45 degrees, just clearing the nearest trees as it soared upwards into the sky. They looked down to see an agitated broom artisan screaming at them from below, waving his legs in his red-striped pyjamas, as if they were sticks of candy.

Gaspar wiped the sweat from his brow, while Bef knocked a dewdrop off her chin. She reached under her dress to produce her old, mangled spectacles, which she shoved on to her wart-free nose.

'Off to buy ourselves some coal in Russia now,' she announced, as if nothing had happened. 'Broom, take us to Kuzananetzkova!'

With that, the broom swung around wildly, completely changing its course and flying back the way they had come. Down below, two little legs were still kicking everything in their path, in sheer frustration and anger.

CHAPTER THIRTEEN

The broom flew magnificently, as it swept across Germany, then the vast territory of the Ukraine and on towards Russia. It became decidedly chilly on board and Gaspar shivered, the cold chilling him to the core.

'Cold?' asked Bef, as she felt him quiver.

'Too right,' answered Gaspar, pulling his clothing tighter around him.

Bef muttered something that sounded like, 'Caldezza, Mezza, Pezza, Caldezza'. Jets of hot air shot out of the broom, bringing sudden, welcome warmth to the daring duo.

'That's cool,' yelled Gaspar, so his pilot could hear.

'What?' answered Bef, 'It's meant to be hot!'

'Yeah, it is,' stressed Gaspar.

'But you said it was cold,' yelled Bef, her words almost lost on the wind.

'Oh, never mind,' responded Gaspar.

Within an hour or so – faster than even Bef had

thought possible – they were reaching the border between the Ukraine and Russia.

'Aha, can you hear that?' screeched Bef. 'That's the sound of the Cossacks.'

'I can't hear anything,' replied Gaspar. 'What is it?'

'The sound of the Kalinka being danced in hundreds of homes and bars,' explained Bef. 'I passed this way in 1862 and I well recall the tone of those Russian singers. The song was top of the charts, as you say these days, and I was captivated by it. I even parked my broom to ask what the song was about. Actually, it's about the snowball tree. Just fancy that! But the words are about little strawberries and raspberries – fragole and lamponi.'

Out of the blue, the broom began to weave, moving in a snake-like manner and then circling around and around.

'Why is it doing this?' asked Gaspar, getting a bump from below as the broom objected to being called 'it'.

'La mia scopa,' said Bef referring to her broom in Italian, 'has been trying to find the way by tracing the route of the Volga. We are now looking out for the coal mine. Keep your eyes peeled!'

'What will we see?' asked Gaspar.

'A massive column of smoke coming out of a large chimney … though not the sort I would want to nip down!' Bef chuckled at her own humour.

As it was, they detected the coal mine in a completely different way. Both of them began to choke uncontrollably, as smoke entered their lungs and made their eyes smart so much that tears began to appear. Gaspar pulled his scarf tightly over his face, while Bef shoved her shawl inside her mouth.

'Take us down,' urged Gaspar, 'We need to get below the smoke.'

The broom took this as an instruction, shooting down and pointing at such an angle that both Bef and Gaspar had to cling on tight, while leaning backwards to try to stay on board. Down and down they fell and, sure enough, they stopped choking the minute they were lower than the smoke. They spotted a vast area covered in deep, white snow. The broom began to level out, when about four metres from the ground and then dropped vertically, depositing both passengers in a snowdrift.

'Yikes that's cold,' yelled Gaspar, as snow got down the back of his trousers and up his back. 'I think I've got icicles growing on my bottom already! Does it ever do a nice, smooth landing?'

Bef was sprawled across the snow, with her big floppy shoes pointing straight upwards in a truly comical fashion. Gaspar got to his feet and helped her up.

'We need to get to the mine office,' she said.

'But I can't walk in this snow,' explained Gaspar.

Bef didn't appear to be having much trouble, her

massive shoes acting almost like snowshoes. Gaspar looked at his own feet. He was still wearing sandals!

'I swear that I'm getting frostbite,' he shouted.

'I won't have any swearing or blaspheming,' stated Bef. 'It simply isn't necessary.'

'I'm not swearing,' replied Gaspar, in a rather exasperated fashion. 'I just need something more suitable on my feet.'

Bef looked at his sandals quizzically, tapped her nose three times and uttered the word 'racchette.' Suddenly, a pair of snowshoes appeared on their feet although, not surprisingly, Bef's were ten times the size of Gaspar's, seemingly being exactly the same size as her big floppy shoes.

'Where have our other shoes gone?' asked Gaspar, worrying that he'd paid 300 dollars for his designer sandals.'

'Look above you, dear boy,' answered his companion.

Sure enough, as Gaspar looked up, he saw a massive pair of floppy shoes hovering in the air, suspended in the atmosphere by goodness knows what.

'What do we do now?' he enquired.

'Follow me!' ordered his leader, as she took them trekking across the snow, leaving a trail of footprints behind them, one set much larger than the other. They tramped, with great difficulty, through the drifting snow, heading towards the silhouette of a building – a dark, menacing building lit up by the moonlight. A few twinkling lamps could be seen through the darkness and suddenly these multiplied a hundred times, with more and more twinkles emerging the closer they got.

'What are all those lights?' asked Gaspar.

Bef stroked her chin five times, shut her eyes and stared through the darkness. 'I do believe they are the lamps on the miners' helmets. I think they must be coming out of the mine, having finished their shift.'

The lights were like little glow-worms, making what seemed to be a river of light, with still more lights being added to the flow of that river as they approached the mine. As they drew closer, they saw that these men, with their blackened faces and clothing, were not only wearing helmets fitted with lamps, but also carrying lanterns in their hands. This doubled the twinkles and added to the swaying movement of the stream of light.

'Get down,' urged Bef. 'Lay flat in the snow! They may think we are spies – especially you!'

'Why me?' asked Gaspar, a little offended.

'You just look very odd,' answered Bef. 'I think it's your tan and your strange clothes.'

'Says a woman with enormous shoes!' thought Gaspar.

'That's enough of that thought,' snapped Bef, reading his mind.

They lay in the freezing snow, with Gaspar colder

than ever, as the stream of men marched by silently, hardly uttering a word to each other. As they loitered, they became aware of another source of noise, this time from behind them. Other miners were marching into the mine, to take over from their colleagues, the only difference being that these men did not yet have grimy faces. They lay still in the snow until all of the men had disappeared from view.

'Andiamo. Let's go!' urged Bef, getting to her feet and shaking the snow off her clothes. Gaspar struggled up.

'Where are we going?' he asked.

'To find the manager,' answered his companion, as if it were obvious.

They reached the edge of the building and looked around for some sort of office. Eventually, they spotted a little sign sticking out of a wall and made their way towards it. A light was casting some illumination out on to the snow outside. They approached a window and peered inside. A man with a big black moustache was smoking a pipe and lolling in his chair, with his feet on a table strewn with papers, files and books.

'This must be the manager,' asserted Bef and, before Gaspar could say anything, she was tapping on the window. At first, the man did not hear her and Gaspar realised that a radio was playing. Suddenly, the tune came to his ear.

'Cool,' he said. 'He's listening to one of our hits!'

'You're always cold,' muttered Bef, ignoring his proud moment completely and banging even louder on the window. This time, the man heard her and shot back in his chair, startled by the noise and the sight of a strange woman pressing her nose against the windowpane. He walked towards them and lifted the glass, poking his head outside to talk. He uttered something in Russian, which neither of them understood. They looked back at him blankly.

'Do you speak English?" asked Gaspar hopefully.

'Why not Italian?' hissed Bef.

'Much less likely,' replied Gaspar.

'A leetle,' he said gruffly, in a thick Russian accent. 'What do you vant?' He eyed them suspiciously.

'Carbone,' answered Bef. 'Carbone.'

'Coal,' translated Gaspar.

'Vell, you have come to the right place,' said the man, still not sure whether to trust these two strangers.

'I want,' said Bef. She stopped dead in her tracks. 'Just one moment,' she continued. She reached under her skirt and pulled out a calculator, which she tapped madly. 'I want two million kilograms of coal,' she declared, having done the maths.

The man looked staggered.

'Laydee, you must have a very beeg fire,' he exclaimed.

'Broomsticks and figs,' she replied dismissively. 'It is for my children.'

The Russian looked completely lost, obviously wondering how many children this very odd lady could have. He signalled for them both to enter the building via the window. Bef tried to get in, but got stuck half way, thanks to difficulties with her skirt and snowshoes. Gaspar managed it much more easily and was grateful for the warmth of the man's office. The manager signalled them to follow him, leading them down dark corridors that winded around and around.

'We're heading into the mine,' said Gaspar, as light gradually began to disappear and the sound of rumbling carts of coal was accompanied by that of hundreds of men chipping away at the coalface.

'You want two million kilograms of diss?' asked the manager, pointing at coal stacked in a truck below.

'Yes,' answered Bef. 'Exactly.'

The man beckoned them to follow him and they walked deeper into the mine, to discover hundreds of trucks fully loaded with coal. The man counted about forty trucks.

'Diss much?' he asked, clearly indicating that he thought her calculations askew.

'Yes,' Bef confirmed, after hammering figures into the calculator once more.

The man pulled a small notepad out of his pocket, removed a pen from behind his ear and wrote down a figure.

'He wants the money,' said Gaspar, as if Bef was too slow to realise that.

'I'm not stupid, you know,' she replied, in a very annoyed tone. 'Oro, oro, oro, oro,' she chanted, while stamping one foot. 'Oro, oro, oro, oro.'

A whizzing noise accompanied the flight of golden nuggets, zooming through the mine in a long arrow shape. The arrow of gold flew around the cavern, headed close to the manager and began to change shape as first one, and then another and another and another, gold coin plopped to the ground beside him. A huge pile of gold emerged, much to Gaspar's amazement.

'Where did all that come from?' he asked, totally baffled by what he had seen.

Bef looked exceptionally pleased with herself as she explained, 'Mel collected the gold and I've just had it transferred by BACS.'

'What on earth is that?' asked Gaspar.

'Broom and Chant Spell,' explained Bef. The gold was transferred to my broom and then sent on to me.'

Gaspar shook his head in wonder, as the manager sank to his knees, kissing the gold with his lips. He ushered them towards carts of coal, all linked together with chains. Men were summoned to hook up more trucks, while another employee brought a motorised cab and linked it up at the front. The pair were invited to get in and drive, Bef struggling with her massive snowshoes once again, while Gaspar slid in beside her.

'Where are we taking all this coal?' asked a dumbfounded Gaspar.

'Outside to the broom, of course,' replied Bef. 'Now, how do you get this thing started?'

She fumbled around the cab, but the obliging manager stopped kissing pieces of gold long enough to lean in and switch on the engine. The trucks rolled forward about half a metre and were just about to gain momentum and go trundling on, when a big black something suddenly shot down a chute and landed right in front of them.

A ball of black unravelled itself and brushed itself off, before rising to its full height – a good 2.5 metres – and shouting, 'Not zo fast!!'

A very slender, wiry woman with long black hair, which stretched right down her back and past her bottom, smoothed down her skirt and came towards the front of the cab, leaning over until she was eye-ball to eyeball with Bef.

'Vot do you zink you are playing at?' she shrieked.

Gaspar was terrified by this huge, Amazonian woman with a voice that could shatter the eardrums of dogs thanks to its shrill tone and annoying accompanying buzz. Her words echoed around the cavern in a most spooky and frightening manner, causing both passengers to cover their ears.

The menacing woman then took a step backwards, eyeing Bef from top to toe for the first time. She began to simper.

'So sorry. So sorry. I was looking for another woman, with a wizened face, warts and a bad case of acne for nine months of the year.'

'I haven't had bad acne since 1511,' shouted Bef in response. 'And that was long before you came along!'

The shrill woman stepped closer again, inspecting every aspect of this person who appeared to be a stranger, but who seemed to have more about her than met the eye.

'Eet can't be,' she said, totally mystified.

'Well it is,' said Bef, extremely pleased that her appearance was so much improved. 'Now what is it that you want Natalia?'

Having now established the identity of the imposter, the angry tone came back into the aggressor's voice, causing Gaspar to quake in his snowshoes.

'Natalia Lebedev has a big bone to pick with you lady!'

'That's Signora actually,' replied Bef, as the woman became angrier and angrier, until she shook like a totem pole in an earthquake. 'What is the nature of this bone and why are you talking about yourself in the third person? That's a right reserved for only the top Very Important Present Bringers!'

'This bone! This bone,' shouted the woman, 'is due to treachery of the highest order; betrayal of the worst kind! In fact, it shows an unspeakable lack of solidarity among Very Important Present Bringers!'

She was getting louder and louder at the end of every sentence. The mine manager was hiding under a truck of coal and urging all his men to take cover too.

'What on earth are you screaming about?' asked Bef with great annoyance in her voice.

'What I am talking about,' replied Natalia, in a way that made 'what' sound like 'vot', 'is what you have done to me. You have betrayed me to a man who can make pollen clouds cover the whole of Germany when he is in a temper. The 'Terrible Torta' now knows that I cast the decisive vote that prevented him from becoming a VIPB and the news has already spread on the Flush Telegraph. He is on the warpath and travelling as fast as his little red stripy pyjamas will stretch!'

'Flush Telegraph?' asked Gaspar innocently, speaking for the first time and suddenly wishing his curiosity hadn't got the better of him. The woman fixed him with a stony stare suggesting she was not amused by his question.

'The Flush Telegraph,' she said, clearing her throat so that she could speak even louder, 'is the way messages are communicated throughout the VIPB world, whenever a high security alert is raised.

The first I knew of the treachery was when my toilet started flushing itself and could not be stopped. Eventually, a little plastic capsule containing a message popped out and my friend Penelope Popov informed me that earth tremors, starting from within the Black Forest, were already being experienced across Europe. She then learned, from a passing raven, that Bernhardt Bürstenfrisür was charging up his broom to come and find me here in Russia!

'My other friend, Vladimir Vostok, then informed me of a rumour on the rumour mill, spread by squirrels fleeing the Black Forest. They said that Bürstenfrisür had learned about my casting vote from a woman with big floppy shoes!'

Bef seemed lost for words for once.

Eventually, she said, 'But I didn't give him your name. I just gave him a riddle, thinking that the half-wit wouldn't work it out. It was an anagram and, as far as I was aware, adaptation artisans are pretty useless at those.'

'Vell, not this one!' shouted Natalia.

Gaspar decided to ride to Bef's rescue. 'She had no choice,' he declared gallantly. 'He was holding us prisoner and threatening us in a most menacing way.'

'Yes, this is true,' confirmed Bef. 'We were about to endure torture from the Torta.'

'Not good enough,' shouted the aggrieved VIPB. 'What about our code of conduct?"

'Well actually,' said Bef, unable to stop herself from getting one up on Natalia, 'that only applies to VIPBs inducted before 1779. Johnny-come-lately VIPBs aren't protected, so stop your witching and get out of the way.'

With that, she put her foot on the pedal of the truck and jolted forward, forcing Natalia to jump sideways to avoid a collision. But then, one of Bef's snowshoes jammed the accelerator and she couldn't slow down, sending the truck plummeting into the depths of the mine, rolling up and down the metal track like a ride at the fairground. The forty coal wagons behind them jolted up and down, sending coal flying at all angles, with lumps bouncing off the walls, as if they had a life of their own.

Gaspar looked back and, to his horror, saw that Natalia was clinging on to the very last truck and was now crawling on all fours across the top of the coal, getting closer and closer to them, as their high-speed journey through the mine continued.

'She's coming for us,' yelled Gaspar. 'What are we going to do? I've never seen an angrier looking woman in all my life!'

'I'm coming to get you,' shouted Natalia, confirming his worst fears, as her shrill voice caused pieces of the cavern walls to break off.

'Where are we heading?' asked a petrified Gaspar.

'No idea,' replied Bef. 'I've not been this lost since

1660 when I suddenly found myself in the midst of the celebrations for the restoration of Charles II as King of England.'

Gaspar shut his eyes, praying for a miracle, but his eyelids suddenly detected some light ahead. He opened his eyes and pointed excitedly as he said, 'There's the exit. We'll be outside in just a minute.'

He wasn't wrong, but the trucks just trundled and bundled their way along the track, with Bef's snowshoes still jammed on the accelerator.

'I think you will have to hit the brakes,' he shouted, unable to push the pedal himself, because the shoes were in the way.

'I can't move my feet,' replied Bef in a panic. She looked over her shoulder and saw her foe just two trucks behind now, still crawling along like a toddler, but with an angrier look than ever, as pieces of flying coal jumped up and hit her in the face.

When they were just seconds from the exit and still travelling at a tremendous speed, Gaspar saw something dangling above the hole.

'What on earth?' he said, staring in amazement. There hanging down from the metal structure forming the exit was an unmistakable pair of legs, which were sporting red stripy pyjamas. Both he and Bef ducked to avoid them and, just seconds later, Bernhardt Bürstenfrisür dropped down into the very same wagon of coal in which Natalia was crouched, coming face to face with the woman who had stopped him becoming a VIPB.

He had hardly had time to shake his fist at her, when the cab came to the end of the track, stopped dead and flung both Bef and Gaspar out into the snow, catapulting Bernhardt and Natalia another 90 metres beyond them. Bernhardt got to his feet, with one intention in mind – that of settling his score with his enemy.

'Quick, get up,' shouted Bef. 'We must run to the broom and get away fast!'

Her snowshoes had been left stuck inside the cab, so she ran bare-footed across the snow with all the actions of someone walking on hot coals, with an 'ouch' and an 'oo' uttered when the cold got too much to bear.

'Scarpe, subito!' she shouted and, to Gaspar's amazement, this produced the sight of his sandals and her floppy shoes descending from the sky. 'Follow the shoes,' she ordered, as the footwear headed towards the broom and she and Gaspar pursued them, so as to find where the broom could possibly be located in the darkness of the area around the mine.

Behind them, there was an almighty yell and a piercing scream, as Bernhardt and Natalia battled it out in the snow. Ahead, a buzz and a hum told them the broom was starting itself up.

'What about the coal?' asked Gaspar.

'Carbone avanti,' shouted Bef.

Gaspar turned to see a wall of coal flying out of the trucks, as if chasing them away from the mine.

'Duck, quickly,' he shouted, pushing Bef down into the snow, just in the nick of time. The coal flew right over their heads and formed itself into a very long, straight line, just before the broom sucked it up into its underbelly.

'How is it all going to fit in there?' questioned Gaspar.

'It will be zipped,' responded Bef, 'which I think means compressed until needed. It will then expand back to its full volume.'

'Cool,' said Gaspar.

'Patience, my boy,' shouted Bef. 'I'll heat you up when we are back on board.'

Gaspar and Bef reached the broom hand in hand and jumped on as it hovered just above the snow. The witch's shoes shot back on her feet and Gaspar's sandals arrived back on his. The broom was in no mood to hang around and took off fast, soaring into the sky.

'Faster, faster,' urged Bef. 'Bernhardt's broom is down there and, if he hops aboard, he'll be chasing us around the globe.'

Down below, however, the two enemies were still shouting at each other, with Bernhardt kicking up clouds of snow and Natalia causing snowballs to form and roll towards him, merely thanks to the shrillness in her voice.

'Just look at her,' said Bef, as they continued to soar upwards. 'She never was a VIPB with any class. She only controls a very small present-bringing patch around the top end of the Volga, which she claims she inherited from her uncle. Goodness knows how anyone voted her in as a VIPB. I think it must have been the year that most of the committee suffered the Bumps and couldn't fly their brooms to the Annual Gift-bringing Meet, or AGM as we know it. There's simply no other explanation.'

'Where are we heading now?' Gaspar asked in trepidation, it all getting just a little too much for him.

'In search of candy, my dear boy, in search of candy,' answered the now coal-rich witch.

CHAPTER FOURTEEN

Even Gaspar, broom novice though he was, appreciated the new supertonic speed of the broom. They were truly whizzing through the night skies, despite the fact that Bef's floppy shoes were hardly aerodynamic. They were crossing Russia at a fantastic pace and he was beginning to enjoy the ride, particularly when the witch threw in a few broom-wheelies, which tipped them up almost on end and then plonked them back in a horizontal direction again. He couldn't help but love the way she chortled every time she did this, murmuring away to herself in Italian and sometimes appearing to have forgotten she had a fellow passenger.

'Where exactly are we heading?' he shouted with all his might, to try to make her hear. Previous attempts to elicit a reply to this question had simply produced answers of 'candy town', 'bonbon boulevard' and 'la città delle caramelle', which she had told him meant exactly the same as candy town.

When he had asked which country, she tried

to shut him up quickly, which made him specu-
late that she maybe didn't know herself. When he
pushed her on this, it became clear that this was
the case. She had answered haughtily, 'Canada or
America … I can't remember which, which is bad
for a witch.' When he had tried to help her out,
she had snapped, 'The Windy City … now are you
any the wiser?' In actual fact, though he didn't like
to tell her so, he was. 'The Three Kings' had been
on tour to Chicago a couple of years before and
they'd had great fun playing to sell-out audiences.
Somehow, he didn't think she'd like to hear about
others rivalling her own fame.

He'd assumed they would head straight for
Chicago and was totally unprepared for what happened next. Bef stroked the side of the broom – now
with quite a girth since the adaptations – and talked
to it in a whisper. The broom suddenly did a triple
loop in the sky, before weaving from side to side
and then winding its way downwards in wide ribbon shapes in the sky. It seemed to have come to
life and appeared almost gleeful, if it is possible
for a broom to present such emotions. Gaspar had
certainly never seen it so animated, as it zigzagged
and spun towards the ground.

'What's happening?' he yelled from the rear.

'We are making an important pit stop,' replied
Bef. 'Well, at least that's what the good boys at the
Ferrari factory tell me it's called.'

'Do you mean for fuel?' enquired Gaspar naïvely.

'No, I don't!' said Bef, slightly irritated in case pit stop wasn't the right word to have used. 'We are going to pick up some lovely warm clothing. I am tired of the wind blowing up my knicker leg and distressed that you keep telling me how cool you are. We'll never make it across the Arctic unless we get kitted out in something suitable.'

She was talking almost as if she was going to call in at a shopping mall. Gaspar looked below him and saw nothing in the way of highways, street-lights and neon signs.

'So where on earth are we?' he asked.

'Well, you are quite right,' replied his pilot. 'We are definitely on earth and not on Mars or Venus just yet!'

'Yes, but where?' demanded Gaspar, getting just a little exasperated by the old-yet-not-so-old look-ing witch.

'Siberia,' she answered, in quite a curtly fashion.

Suddenly, a zoosh and a zoom could be heard, as the broom shot down almost vertically. A grind-ing noise emerged from the back, followed by a squealing and screeching.

'O Dio,' shouted the pilot, 'I haven't got the hang of braking under supertonic conditions at all!'

Truer words were never spoken. The broom careered right and left as they approached the

143

ground and then shot straight forward, towards a strange glow that had appeared ahead of them. This got brighter as they drew nearer and Gaspar realised it was shining out from a small building, the door of which was wide open. With no further to-do, the broom travelled straight on through the open door. It came to a grinding halt, just as it seemed as though it would go through the back wall and out into the snow once again.

As both passengers breathed a huge sigh of relief, as little voice spoke up.

'Cup of tea, anyone?' it said.

The broom had stopped right in front of a kitchen table, in what appeared to be an aluminium box. Grey metal walls could clearly be seen, though every single wall was draped in rich tapestries, knitted chain loops, bits of brocade and white crocheted items and even full costumes, dangling on what appeared to be hangers made of tree branches.

A massive cabinet was stacked from top to bottom with balls of wool, while another contained roll after roll of material in all sorts of patterns and hues, from gingham check to sober grey serge cloth. In the middle of the kitchen table sat a sewing machine, while from the ceiling hung all manner of things – tape measures, a massive pair of scissors, pieces of tailor's chalk of enormous dimensions, knitting needles in more sizes than Gaspar could ever have imagined and strand after strand of brightly coloured satin ribbon.

Gaspar gazed around him in amazement at the spectrum of colours and the Aladdin's Cave of materials. In a way, it seemed cluttered and claustrophobic, but in another, exactly as if everything was perfectly in place and exactly where it should be.

The charming little voice struck up again.

'My dear lady, pray let me help you to your feet.'

For the first time, Gaspar saw the body belonging to the voice, just as it jumped right beside him and shook his hand warmly.

'Jeremiah Needlebaum at your service, Sir,' he said.

Jeremiah Needlebaum was quite unlike anyone Gaspar had ever seen before. He was a fairly tall and wiry man, his height being accentuated by the fact that he was wearing blue and yellow-banded legwarmers over red tights. Bright red shoes appeared to have been hand-stitched together and were of the finest leather. His dazzling tunic was purple at the bottom and bright tangerine at the top, while the puffed sleeves were the same bright red as his meticulously polished shoes.

His ears stuck out from his head at right angles and, sitting on top of those, a pointed hat, appeared to have been made out of chicken wire. This held, according to Gaspar's estimations, around fifty reels of different coloured cotton, in four rows running around the hat, while his bright red belt seemed to have pouches for needles, elastic, trimmings and buttons. His kind face was notable for its twinkling, hazel-coloured eyes and for a very short, stubbly beard, which he stroked as he pondered what his guests might wish to eat.

Gaspar came to his senses and realised that he had been very rude and had not introduced himself – something he put right immediately.

'Very pleased to make your acquaintance indeed,' replied Jeremiah in response. 'And how is my dear friend, the Befana?'

The witch looked at him quizzically. 'How on earth did you know that I am the Befana?' she asked bluntly.

'Because nobody on the planet flies a broom quite as recklessly as you,' answered Jeremiah honestly. 'I watched you looping around in the sky while stargazing – something that I do very regularly since I was exiled to Siberia for making the King of Prussia's pantaloons a little too tight across the buttocks one day.'

Gaspar almost burst out laughing, but then saw that this was no joke, as a hint of sadness came over Jeremiah's face and a tear welled up in his eye. Gaspar looked at the grey metal walls of the room and suddenly realised that this was actually a prison cell, albeit a finely decorated one now, with all of its rolls of colourful material, wools and tapestries.

Jeremiah must have read his thoughts. 'Until 1850, the doors of the cell automatically locked at 9pm and did not reopen until 7am. That year, I had a reprieve and the doors no longer locked. Technically, I am free to go, but now people just come to visit me when they need an outfit. I've actually grown very accustomed to this room after so many centuries. Why move?'

Gaspar reached out and patted him on the shoulder in a gesture of solidarity. Bef hugged him.

'You dear man. My dear friend. I have left it far too long since I last saw you.'

'You have fine new clothes,' said Jeremiah, once he had escaped her grasp. He felt the cloth of her dress and admired the way it was cut and tailored. 'Maybe a dart here and a tuck there would have been pleasing to the eye,' he asserted, 'but all in all, it wasn't a bad job. Have you abandoned the dress and apron that I made for you all those years ago?'

'Oh no,' said Bef, throwing her arms up in horror. 'These clothes are to suit a purpose, but I need something different for now,' she said. 'My companion here also needs a much warmer outfit. We are due to cross the Arctic Sea and Alaska and we simply won't make it unless we have warm suits of some kind. The heating feature on my broom is good, but can't quite work miracles.'

Jeremiah's eyes lit up.

'No outfits come along for three decades and then two come along at once,' he cried in sheer glee at the task ahead of him. 'I have so many designs and ideas for Arctic Sea-crossing wardrobes, but first let's have some tea and, while we are sipping that and making small talk, my brain can be whirring between biscuits.'

Gaspar became aware of a small stove burning in a corner and watched as Jeremiah skipped over to it and brought out a tray of freshly basked biscuity-looking things, which smelled amazing.

'Seedies,' replied Jeremiah. 'I collect the seeds in spring and summer and dry them out for my baking in winter.' He offered one to Gaspar, who immediately devoured it.

'That's absolutely delicious,' he said.

'Yes, it's amazing what the addition of a little poo from an Arctic ground squirrel can do to add to the flavour,' replied Jeremiah.

Just as Gaspar was about to spit his seedy out, Jeremiah began to roll around with laughter.

'I'm just joshing,' he chortled. 'It's so long since I had anyone to laugh with.'

Tea was poured into delicate little china cups that Jeremiah brought out from his cupboard and a multi-coloured knitted tea cosy was positioned on the teapot, to keep the tea warm. It was clear Jeremiah had created this himself, along with the knitted doilies on the table. In fact, everywhere you looked in the room, there seemed to be some sign of his creativity.

'So why do you need the dress you are wearing and why have you rejuvenated yourself and changed your appearance?' asked Jeremiah, stroking his short beard.

Bef's face turned red with anger.

'Because, Jeremiah, because …' She paused, seemingly unable to speak the truth. She composed herself and continued, 'Because that man, that Santa Claus, to whom I thought I was engaged, has married another woman and made them Mrs Claus, while I have been sitting in my little home, cleaning and looking after the needs of my many children, in the belief that he would join me one day.'

Jeremiah looked doleful. 'What a terrible discovery to have made,' he said.

'Yes,' replied Bef. 'But he also wants to take over my patch and bring presents to all my lovely children in Italy,' she explained.

'That is an insult too far,' said Jeremiah. 'So, I am guessing you have changed your appearance to show him what he is missing?'

'Mainly to surprise him when I arrive at his home,' confessed Bef. 'I have a plan to upset his apple cart and his reindeer sleigh at the same time!'

Jeremiah nodded, as if he fully understood. He left his seat at the table and began to inspect his rolls of material, using a small footstool to reach the very top row of his storage system.

'For you, dear lady, I think a fetching white outfit, to blend in with the snow, while for the young gentleman, I think we shall plump for a manly black, with grey flecks and touches.'

With that, he hauled out a white fake fur material and a heavy black material on a similar sized roll. A smaller roll of grey fake fur was then unfurled with a great flourish.

'I will trim both of your outfits in this and make Cossack hats for both of you out of the same material,' he declared.

Jeremiah pulled on a handle. A sewing table shot forth and he laid first one roll of material out and then another. He became a human dynamo, rushing over to his 'customers' with tape measure in hand, to take their measurements down and then writing these in chalk on a piece of slate, before dashing back to the cloth and cutting all sorts of shapes out of the material.

'If I could just ask you to move to the comfy chairs,' he said, snapping his fingers and producing two bean bag seats, 'I can proceed with the sewing.'

He seated himself at the sewing machine and ran up line after line of stitching, reaching into his chicken wire hat to instantly produce bobbins of cotton, in exactly the right shade, without having to think for a second where they were positioned. As the machine whirred and hammered in stitches, Jeremiah sewed faster than Gaspar thought humanly possible, although he wasn't quite sure whether Jeremiah was human or not!

Within thirty minutes, Jeremiah had sewn both costumes and was holding them up with sheer pride, cavorting around the room with both of them in his hands.

'Now for the fashion parade,' he said. He pushed a handle and pulled out a sheet of metal that folded in the middle. 'Please step into my changing room, one at a time,' he instructed.

Bef went in first and emerged wearing a full-length fake fur, white dress with matching trousers underneath and a grey fake fur overcoat and Cossack hat. Gaspar entered next and came out sporting a black fake fur all-in-one suit, with grey cuffs and trim around the bottom of the trousers.

'And now,' proclaimed Jeremiah, 'the feet!' He whipped out two pairs of grey furry boots, beautifully stitched and with real leather soles, moulded with grips to prevent slipping on ice.

'But what about my own shoes?' asked Bef, fretting as she looked at her big, floppy monstrosities.

'You will roll them and store them in this backpack,' said Jeremiah, conjuring up a grey rucksack fashioned to match her outfit. 'Here is a plan of how to fold them to fit,' he continued, producing a piece of paper filled with diagrams and instructions.

'You think of absolutely everything, Jeremiah,' said Bef. 'You truly are the best tailor that the Very Important Present Bringing world has ever had.'

Jeremiah blushed and looked very bashful. 'If only, my dear lady, I had managed to win your heart in the way that Santa Claus did. When must you fly?' asked the kind-hearted man.

'I think we could stay for the night here, if that is agreeable to you,' replied Bef, taking his hand in hers.

'Magnificent!' cried Jeremiah. 'I have some pre-made sleeping bags and rugs, which will keep you perfectly warm and cosy down here on the floor. It will be my extreme pleasure to have you here as my guests and serve you lichen porridge in the morning. With a bit of warmed up, long-life goat's milk, shipped in from Turkey, it's a veritable delight and the very best way in which to prepare you for your long, cold flight.'

He paused and acquired a hopeful look in his eye. 'For now though,' he continued, 'would you mind awfully if we played a game of cards? It's been so long since I played gin rummy that I'm almost forgetting how to do that. We could follow that up with dominoes – I knitted some about 123 years ago, at a rough guess, and get very little chance to get them out.'

Bef shrieked, 'Favoloso! I love both of those pastimes.'

Gaspar pondered and then said, 'Well, I'm good at playing the guitar, so I guess that whatever this dominoes thing is, it can't be that hard!'

Both Jeremiah and Bef chuckled loudly, while Gaspar admired himself in Jeremiah's full-length mirror and thought that he quite fancied keeping the outfit that had just been tailored for him, should 'The Three Kings' ever stage a concert in a country with a sub-zero temperature.'

Chapter Fifteen

Jeremiah was absolutely true to his word and dished up a wonderful, tasty lichen porridge, which at first had Gaspar wrinkling up his nose at the sheer sight of it, but which was decidedly delicious when you actually grabbed a spoon and tucked in. Either that, or Gaspar was just very hungry! The feast was made even more delightful by the addition of warm cakes from Jeremiah's oven, which he had risen at 3am to bake. His guests had only stirred at 6am, having found their rugs and sleeping area just as cosy as Jeremiah had predicted.

Having tucked into her porridge with great gusto, Bef thanked Jeremiah profusely for the spread he had laid on.

'You, my dear friend, have done the name of Needlebaum proud,' she declared, making her host blush ever so slightly, sending a red flush up his pale little cheeks.

She then pushed her bowl to one side and

started to roll the palm of her hand around the table in semi-circular movements. Gaspar watched in amazement as, before his very eyes, a map suddenly appeared. She rolled her hand around at the top right corner of it and the map showed only Siberia, the Arctic Ocean and Canada. Another adjustment also brought Chicago into view.

'How the devil did you manage that?' asked Gaspar, in complete amazement.

'Very simply indeed,' replied Bef. 'By using my sky bone.'

'Sky bone? What on earth is that?' asked her young pal.

'Well, in my case, it's the bone between my elbow and my wrist,' explained Bef. 'How did you think I navigate through the skies so cleverly. When it works, it's marvellous, as it's essential to check one's route before one takes to the broom, as trade winds, weather fronts, meteor showers and all sorts of other phenomena can try to send my trusty broom off course. The trouble is, it doesn't often work!'

After admitting this, she gazed at the map, totting up figures in her head. Eventually, she spoke. 'I calculate that, if we leave shortly, we should arrive in the Windy City by mid-afternoon, which would be perfect timing to get our candy supplies sorted.'

Gaspar didn't like to argue. Jeremiah nodded his head and stroked his beard.

'You must allow for those strange currents over the Arctic and please make sure that you don't touch down. Those polar bears can be very vicious, you know. One scent of a witch and they'll be on the hunt, as you witches have a very unique smell.'

Gaspar had almost turned as white as a polar bear on hearing this warning and prayed Bef would not perform any of her aerial stunts while flying over polar bear land, just in case one of them went slightly askew and they crashed rather spectacularly in precisely the wrong place.

'Of course I won't crash,' tutted Bef, reading his mind again. 'I've never had an accident!'

Gaspar remembered the explanation of water damage to the broom, which she had given to Bernhardt, but didn't like to contradict her!

The two sky travellers gathered their possessions together. The floppy shoes were neatly stowed away in the rucksack and the fine new clothing buttoned up and belted. Jeremiah looked at his handiwork. A tear came to his eye, as the time came to say farewell.

'Goodbye, my dear lady,' he said, bowing and kissing her hand in a most gentlemanly fashion.

'Arrivederci, my trusty friend,' she replied, giving him a gentle kiss on the cheek that made him blush once again.

'Ciao, Mr Needlebaum,' said Gaspar politely. Bef looked at him oddly. 'What?' he asked.

'I didn't know you spoke Italian,' she answered.

'Didn't know I was!' replied Gaspar.

Bef looked at him as if he was stark raving bonkers and shook her head. He was a strange boy at times.

They carried the broom out into the snow and prepared to board. The broom shook a little, started its supertonic charger up and began to throb. The two passengers pulled their hats down tight around their face and lifted up the collars of their coats. This was going to be one very cold flight.

Jeremiah stood in the snow, which reached above his lovely red shoes and halfway up his leggings. He seemed a forlorn little figure standing there, waiting to say goodbye to the only visitors he'd received in years.

'Don't leave it so long next time,' he urged, as the broom began to lift off the ground and more tears rolled down his cheeks.

'Bon voyage,' replied Jeremiah, watching them lift into the skies until they passed beyond the first cloud and were visible no more. 'Back to my sewing,' he sighed, realising that he needed to keep busy, to prevent getting too emotional at no longer having the pleasure of human company.

It became increasingly cold as the pair of intrepid candy gatherers clung to the broom. They were thankful that Jeremiah had kitted them out with such warm and comfortable clothing to survive this very icy mission. Although the broom puffed out a wave of heat now and again, the frost crystals soon began to reappear, no matter how many times Bef uttered her 'Caldo Cantation' spell to provide added warmth.

Below them, they could see only frozen seawaters, stretching for mile after mile, with icebergs and big sheets of ice drifting away from the polar ice cap. Beyond that, lay desolate and frozen expanses of earth that seemed to hold no sign of human life. All they could feel was the extreme cold reaching right into their bones and freezing their core, despite the best efforts of Jeremiah.

Gaspar tried to speak, but could hardly open his mouth. 'I'm not sure how much more I can take,' he jabbered, when he finally managed to unlock his jaw.

'Pazienza. Pazienza,' replied Bef. 'Not too much longer.' She began to chant something, which seemed to speed the broom up, as it raced ahead. As if he had willed it to happen, Gaspar suddenly saw some twinkling lights – lights that could only mean a town or a city, or maybe even a highway, was on the horizon. The lights became more numerous and brighter and the broom seemed to then drop them lower, so that they could ride on the thermal currents that it could now detect, using its finely-tuned sense of what to do to keep its passengers happy.

They began to pass a number of towns, headed past Milwaukee and reached a large spread of brilliant lights.

'The Windy City,' shrieked Bef with glee. 'It's an age since I was last here, bringing coal to that very naughty child who grew up to be Al Capone!'

Gaspar managed to flick icicles off his eyelashes, as he blinked in amazement at this statement.

'Look there!' shrieked his pilot, 'The Willis Tower – one of the tallest buildings in the world – and over there you can see the St Lawrence Seaway. Now all we need to do is find the candy factory!'

'How do we do that?' asked Gaspar, thinking it would be like trying to find a needle in a haystack.

'Breathe in now,' instructed Bef, 'Candium, nasalium, locatum,' she shrieked.

At that moment, Gaspar felt a tingling in his nasal passages and detected the unmistakable aroma of red cherry gummy bears on the wind. This was followed by the intoxicating smell of chocolate and then the scent of roasting peanuts, which made him incredibly hungry and desperate to tuck in.

'Where is it coming from?' he asked eagerly, as the wonderful medley of smells got ever stronger.

'My trusty broom will guide us now,' replied Bef confidently.

Sure enough, the aroma became stronger and stronger and they began to circle a large, gold coloured building, from which light spilled out into the surrounding area. Gaspar spotted a parking lot and hundreds of cars parked up. As they descended further, he saw parents taking their children by the hand and leading them into the factory. Laughter filled the air and a great sense of joy rose on the breeze.

'Here we have our candy factory,' shouted Bef. 'Look how big and bold it is. It must have enough candy to feed the whole of America, at least for the one night that I need it.' She was almost dancing for joy on the broom, rocking it from side to side and making Gaspar feel decidedly queasy.

'Take us down!' she hollered. The broom did exactly as instructed and descended towards the parked cars.

'Don't let it damage anyone's vehicle, or they'll be looking for compensation,' warned Gaspar, as the broom came far too close for comfort to some of the magnificent cars in view. But he needn't have worried. The broom seemed completely in control, dropped to 1.2 metres above the ground and then slid itself into an available car park space and stopped dead. Bef hopped off and Gaspar followed suit, trying to catch her up as she made her way through a throng of people heading to the entrance.

'Don't you think we might be a little too warm

when we get inside?' asked Gaspar. Bef stopped and looked thoughtful.

'Perhaps you are right.' She stripped off her outer coat and hat. Gaspar did the same, before Bef clicked her fingers and made the clothing mysteriously disappear.

'Where did it go?' asked Gaspar in amazement.

'Into the invisible broom cupboard,' she explained, moving the palm of her hand in front of her face, just enough for Gaspar to detect the outline of a cupboard hovering above the broom. Their clothes now appeared to be hanging inside.

'What about your rucksack?' he asked. 'Should we leave that too?'

Bef gave him a withering look. 'If you think I am leaving my shoes, you are very much mistaken, young man,' she said severely.

Gaspar felt rather like a child entering a candy store with his mother. Despite her rejuvenation and new appearance as a 30-year-old, Bef was still thousands of years older than that in terms of her behaviour. She positively marched into the candy factory and Gaspar prayed she wouldn't try to take his hand, as if he were a child needing his mother's assistance. She resisted the temptation, but almost shoved him into the queue of people waiting to enter the haven of all things sweet and chewy.

'Ouch,' he said, as she poked him in the ribs.

'Why are we queuing?' she demanded. 'Italian

people like me don't queue, unless we absolutely have to!'

'I think it's some kind of tour,' he replied, as other people started to jostle him and push him forward towards a candy factory employee, standing at the front of the group and wearing a bright yellow outfit.

'What's a tour?' asked Bef, in total ignorance.

'We're going to be shown how they make the candy,' he explained.

'O Dio,' exclaimed Bef, 'I want to buy it, not learn how to make it … I haven't time for that!'

Sure enough, the employee in the yellow outfit moved down the queue, counting up to fifty people and then instructing all those that she had counted to enter a room ahead. This included Bef and Gaspar, so they moved forward with the group of stressed out parents and over-active children. Bef looked at each naughty child in a certain way that she had acquired over the centuries, which denoted that they would be dead certs for coal and not candy in their stockings, if they didn't improve their behaviour.

The families moved into the factory, watching employees making some of their favourite sweet creations. They tasted some of the delicious samples on offer and even helped weigh out some of the nuts used in the chocolate-nutty creations. They experienced every flavour, from peach to pineapple, and marvelled at the way in which some of the candies were shaped and moulded. Everyone was mesmerised by the processes – well, everyone except Bef.

'Why are we wasting so much time on this?' she muttered, as they watched yet another gummy bear being created. 'We have to start our negotiations to get our supplies as soon as possible, but I can't possibly start bartering with all these people watching. In any case, who is the 'capo' of this factory? Could it be that man with the appalling check shirt, who showed us in, or that woman with the very lank hair? How on earth am I going to be able to get my candy when we are moving from place to place no faster than a penguin in sand!'

'Have you seen any penguins in sand?' asked Gaspar.

Bef scowled. She became a little mad inside and started to scour the factory, in search of the manager's office. She could see nothing.

The group moved on to a larger area of the factory and everyone began to squeal with delight, like little pigs in a sty. There, in front of them, stood a magnificent chocolate fountain, set like a waterfall inside a rainforest. This part of the factory was warm and humid and she and Gaspar began to wish they had left the rest of their furry outfits behind.

The children had by now already got their

hands stuck into the stream of chocolate, while adults pretended to be annoyed and then did the same. They were so absorbed by this chocolate heaven that nobody noticed a rather strange woman with an Italian accent slip away from the group and head out of the door, pulling her companion along with her as she went.

'Where are we going?' asked Gaspar, rather peeved not to have been able to get his own cup of chocolate from the fountain.

'To the top,' replied Bef forcefully, pointing to an escalator they had passed before entering the zone containing the chocolate fountain. She pulled Gaspar on to it and both began to ride up, looking down on hundreds of candy workers, who were all too occupied to notice two strangers heading upwards above their heads.

They arrived on a steel walkway, perched high above the factory. They moved along it, noting a few office doors along their route. They eventually found one that said, 'Head Honcho'. This they took to mean 'the boss'. Bef knocked on the door quite gently. She heard no voice, so knocked again. For the second time, no response was gained. On the third occasion, she rapped so hard on the door that the noise could have been heard in Kazakhstan.

Bef was still leaning on the door, when it was opened with a jerky movement from the inside, causing her to fall into the room and flat on her face. She struggled back on to her feet, clinging to the edge of a desk to haul herself up. As she did so, she came eye to eye with the 'Head Honcho', Rocky Candymeister. She instantly realised who he was, as he had his name spelt out in children's alphabet cubes, stretching right across his desk. He, on the other hand, had no idea who this woman sprawled across the floor could be.

'Can I help you, ma'am? Have you got lost while on the tour?'

As he peered down at her, Gaspar realised that his bright red, yellow and orange giant spectacles were actually made of candy, as was a big medallion on a chain around his neck and his tie. He got up from his seat and grabbed a striped candy walking stick, which he gave to Bef, thinking she might need it to get to her feet. With an extremely offended look, she pushed it away, as the overpowering smell of candy filled her nostrils.

'It is quite safe to lean on,' explained Rocky Candymeister. 'It is made of our extra-tough candy-for-all-emergencies range.'

Bef greeted this with a withering look, pulling herself up to her full height and looking Rocky in the eye.

'I have come here to buy candy,' she declared haughtily, 'not to lean on it.'

She clicked her fingers and suddenly a pile of gold started to pour out of the ceiling's light fittings, cascading to the floor all around Rocky Candymeister's feet, until he was surrounded by it right up to his knees.

'How much candy does this buy me?' she asked, secretly delighted at how much gold Mel had managed to raise.

'Well ma'am, let me just check,' said a bewildered Rocky Candymeister. He took hold of one of the coins and bit it. 'Ouch,' he shouted, 'it's real!'

'Of course it's real,' tutted Bef. 'Do you think a witch like me goes around with a pile of fake gold at the click of her fingertips?'

'Did you say witch?' asked Rocky, with a look of terror now filling his eyes. 'Say it ain't so!'

'Va bene, it ain't so,' replied Bef obligingly. 'I'm actually una strega.'

'Oh, I can cope with strangers,' said a relieved Rocky, mishearing what she had said in his sheer panic and not realising she had simply given him the Italian word for witch. He stared at the gold all around him and began to count on his fingers.

'Do you want candy sticks, gummy shapes, bonbons, chocolate peanuts, or something else?' he enquired.

'I want whatever will fit into my broom most easily,' replied Bef.

Gaspar witnessed the frightened look in Rocky's eyes once again.

'In her room,' he emphasised heavily. 'She

wants to be able to fit them into her room and eat them, as she wishes, once she gets back home.'

Rocky again breathed a sigh of relief. 'Maybe gummy shapes then,' he suggested, again counting on his fingers. 'I reckon all this gold will buy you around 2.3 million kilograms of gummy shapes, which will near enough clean out our stock, but I'm always pleased to be able to help a good customer.'

'It's a deal,' declared Bef. 'Now where is the stock?'

Rocky looked amazed. 'Do you want it right now?' he asked.

'Well, of course I do. I need to get it loaded up,' replied the witch.

'Do you have a fleet of pick-up trucks then?' asked Rocky, a little perplexed by the whole situation.

'No, of course not,' sighed Bef. 'I just have my broom.'

'Room,' shouted Gaspar. 'She just has the one room, but is sure it will be big enough.'

Rocky picked up the telephone and instructed several employees to come and remove the gold. They arrived with wheelbarrows, which they loaded up and then struggled to push out of the door thanks to the sheer weight of the cargo.

'Take the lady down to the basement,' instructed Rocky, as a sixth employee appeared.

'She needs to be taken to the gummy shapes area, to review her purchase.'

Gaspar could detect something strange about his demeanour, but couldn't quite put his finger on it. He was being pleasant enough to Bef, but something was definitely afoot.

The dutiful employee, smoothing down his bright yellow outfit to look smart, ushered Bef out of the door and along the corridor. Gaspar, however, hung back, which the employee seemed to fail to notice. They seemed to want to get Bef down to the basement as fast as possible. Something told him that things weren't as they seemed.

Gaspar stood by Rocky Candymeister's door, which was slightly ajar. He heard Rocky pick up the phone.

'Get me the FBI!' he demanded, as he spoke to the operator. 'We have a possible threat to national security in my factory and they need to get over here fast, in fact, like yesterday!'

The operator clearly began to ask questions, as Gaspar did not hear Rocky put down the phone. After a few seconds of silence, Rocky began to speak again.

'Well, as far as I can tell, the women is a witch, or maybe even some sort of alien, who has come here with enough gold to fill Fort Knox. Actually, let me correct that … the gold has just cascaded out of my light fittings. She's demanding candy and I have to question why anyone needs quite as much as she's asking for – a full 2.3 million kilograms of gummy shapes! I can only think that it is for, shall we say, sinister purposes. I have had her taken down to the basement and I have instructed that she be locked in a storage cupboard down there, until your agents arrive. Just be quick!'

He seemed to have finished his conversation, but then struck up again.

'Oh, by the way,' he said, 'she's accompanied by some sort of stooge – a rather gormless looking lad, who does look rather familiar, I have to say. I think she may have hypnotised him, as he hardly speaks, other than to correct her.'

Gaspar felt his legs turn to jelly, until he himself could have been described as a gummy shape. He was also rather miffed at being described as gormless, though rather pleased that Rocky had probably seen him performing with 'The Three Kings'. He looked down and saw the yellow-outfitted employee leading Bef down a spiral walkway. He ran as fast as he could to catch them up, but the faster he ran, the faster the pair seemed to move, forcing him to run at a speed at which he could no longer control his body's momentum.

He caught up just as the employee was opening the door to the basement. He piled straight into him, just avoiding knocking Bef out, but sending the poor candy worker flying through the air.

Both Gaspar and Bef watched in stunned silence as the employee performed a triple somersault and then landed flat on his back on the most enormous pile of gummy shapes imaginable. He sat up for a brief second and then fall back on the rather large gummy bed, groaning loudly.

'Come on, we've got to get out of here,' urged Gaspar. 'Rocky has called the FBI and is planning to imprison you down here.'

'The FBI,' tutted Bef, 'I can run rings around them and have been doing so since Hoover's time.'

'This isn't a time to be harping on about vacuums and cleaning,' stressed Gaspar. 'We really do have to get out.'

The semi-conscious, yellow-uniformed employee groaned again.

'Oh fiddlesticks,' exclaimed the witch. She closed her eyes and started to chant something that Gaspar could not understand. Suddenly, the whole pile of gummy shapes started to dance around the room, first lifting the employee up, as if being tossed around on a wave of stickiness. It then dropped him flat on the ground, before whirling the gummy shapes into a tornado-shaped monster candy that shot out of an air vent on the wall and out into the world outside, where it was promptly sucked into the broom.

Gaspar grasped Bef's hand. 'Come on, let's get out. Time is of the essence.'

As they ran out of the door through which they had entered the room, they ran slap bang into a rather triumphant looking Rocky Candymeister, flanked by three other employees.

'Not so fast, lady,' he stated in a very pompous tone, standing there in his candy tie, holding a candy walking stick and splaying his legs wide apart in an authoritative fashion. He tapped the candy stick on the ground, as if dancing with it and lifted up his enormous candy glasses using only the muscles in his forehead.

Bef danced to one side of him and then another and then suddenly shouted, 'Pietrifisico!' Rocky and his men were turned into standing statues as she grabbed Gaspar by the hand and darted like a scuttling mouse straight through Rocky's legs.

'For how long will they be cast in stone like that?' yelled Gaspar.

'Well, if it's as successful as my last attempt at that spell, which I think was in the year 1060, about 20 seconds,' replied Bef.

Gaspar turned around in alarm, as Rocky and his men came back to life and started to give chase. Their bodies clumsily jerked around uncontrollably, as the spell wore off, causing them to barge into one another.

'Run hard,' shouted Gaspar, 'and head for the chocolate fountain. I am sure I saw an exit door near there.'

By now, the rest of their tour party were just emerging, with chocolate around their mouths and bag after bag of candy in their hands. Gaspar and Bef darted around the group, trying to dodge bodies and find their way out. The vast chocolate fountain lay ahead of them, its liquid chocolate pouring out from every possibly source. Gaspar saw Rocky and his men just a few paces behind them.

'Duck,' he ordered.

Bef and he fell flat to the floor, as Rocky and his three allies flew over the top of them and straight into the chocolate fountain. They began to cough and splutter, getting to their feet with faces dripping with chocolate and rather angry eyes.

'Hardly the Trevi,' chortled Bef, as Gaspar pulled her to the left.

Gaspar had spotted an exit door, just as he had hoped and was now heading straight for it. He pushed the security bar and swung it open, revealing the parking area where they had left the broom. Rocky and his men were still trying to wade their way out of the fountain, with chocolate pouring down their trouser legs and weighing them down. Rocky's candy glasses were smeared with brown, chocolatey marks and only half-perched on his nose. Gaspar looked back and realised that a wig, that Rocky must have been wearing, was no long on his head, but floating around the pool of chocolate at the fountain's base like a rather fluffy yellow duck.

'Get the broom started up,' demanded Gaspar.

Bef chanted all the way across a car park, in which a queue of traffic was waiting to park. Engines were revving up and car horns beeping every few seconds in sheer annoyance at the wait. In the distance, Gaspar could see flashing lights and then the sound of sirens added to the noise. Ten police cars were trying to overtake the queue, to get to the candy factory doors.

They ran even faster and reached the broom, which had gone past its quivering stage and was hovering a metre above the ground. It seemed really anxious and kept emitting a beep.

'Oh goodness, it's having a panic attack,' explained Bef.

'So will I, if we don't get away now,' shouted Gaspar, as he watched the FBI pile into the car park.

They jumped on board, with no time to worry about clothing or map checking. Off shot the broom into the sky, circling the car park twice, right over the heads of amazed FBI officers. They all held up their badges, to demand that the broom cease flying, but all to no avail. The trio of Bef, Gaspar and broom were already en route for their next destination and had no intention of bailing out.

They soared higher and higher into the sky, as the broom headed for what it felt to be a safe altitude and one that would not be detected. Suddenly, it gave what sounded like a bottom burp and a dreadful smell filled the air. Gaspar could only laugh, thinking that the broom had broken wind in a place called the Windy City, which was truly apt!

'That was far too close for comfort,' he shouted, once the smell of the bottom burp had drifted off into the ether. 'Where are we headed now?'

'You, my dear boy, are headed for the airport,' stated Bef. 'I believe it's called O'Hare International and you will be able to get a flight there to Dubai. You will then rejoin the others and make your TV appeal, asking the children of the world, and all of your fans, to take Bef to their hearts and leave out stockings for her and not Santa Claus, or Father Christmas, as the English will insist on calling him. Once you have made the appeal, you can all await my instructions.'

Gaspar felt a little crestfallen. For all the terror that travelling with Bef brought with it, it was rather exciting and, at times, gave him more of a buzz than appearing on stage. While getting back to the sunshine and his bandmates would be nice, he was going to miss the unexpected, the downright dangerous and the whacky.

'So you want us to get all the Kingdergartners on side then?' he asked, in a very downbeat manner.

174

'The what? The what?' asked his pilot.

'The Kingdergartners,' continued Gaspar, 'That's what the press call our young fans. We've got a massive, worldwide fan base of nearly five million kids under the age of 10.

Bef's eyes lit up.

'Five million! Five million! Fantastico! Favoloso!' she shrieked, making the broom do a triple loop when Gaspar least expected it. 'This is great news; even better than I had imagined! Together, we shall convince the children of the world that there is only one Very Important Present Bringer and that is I! Viva Bef!'

Gaspar could swear that he could hear thousands of cats miaowing in hundreds of homes and alleys, streets and rubbish heaps below him, as they flew over the Windy City and Bef's shrieking filled the air. How he was going to miss that!

Chapter Sixteen

Dusk fell as they circled O'Hare airport. Hundreds of aeroplanes sat below them, while some came very close to the broom in airspace! Gaspar had already asked the question at least ten times, but felt it necessary to repeat it once again, as a jet whisked past at what seemed to be only half a metre from his nose.

'Just remind me how it is that you are not detected on the radar and yet jets never hit us,' he asked.

'It's the Broom Barrier,' answered Bef, slightly irritated by this line of questioning again! 'My trusty broom has an invisibility shield, which means that it cannot be seen by radar devices when flying over someone's airspace. However, it also has the skill to stay 1.8 metres away from any jet, at any time. This is the distance at which it can control the shake the jet causes as it passes.'

'That's incredible,' said Gaspar, pretty sure, however, that some jets had been closer to them than 1.8

metres! 'Does Santa's sleigh have the same technology then?'

Bef sighed heavily. 'Unfortunately so. It is a pre-requirement for the transport used by all VIPBs. However, my broom has an added skill that no other VIPB can boast.'

'What's that then?' asked Gaspar, all ears.

'My broom can detect whether a plane is carrying children with very good hearts, who have heard of me and love me with every essence of their being. If my broom knows this is the case, it lifts the invisibility shield, to allow these children only to see us flying past their window. He tips me off by shimmying three times and I give them a wave as we pass in the air. They all love that!'

'Wow, that's cool,' said Gaspar.

Bef shook her head. Even the warmest clothes from Jeremiah Needlebaum could not keep this boy snug.

They looped around in the sky, dropping ever closer to the airport terminal. Gaspar felt in his pocket for his passport. It was lucky he'd packed it. He felt inside his other pocket and reached another phial of his special potion. He had experimented greatly with this one, attempting to make it much stronger than the one he had tested on Thaz. The first had proved equally as short-lived in effectiveness, when used on Bernhardt. Hopefully, the second phial, with its greatly increased strength of Frankincense and other secret ingredients, made to the old family formula, would prove of more use to Bef, if she needed it during her next mission. What a pity he'd left it inside his overcoat before entering the candy factory!

The broom began to make its final descent, circling around the terminal building, to bring itself down to land in front of one of the terminal entrances, slap bang in the middle of the taxi rank. Gaspar expected to hear a torrent of abuse and alarmed cries from the taxi drivers, but heard nothing at all. It appeared as though the invisibility shield was still in operation.

'Can anyone see us?' he whispered in Bef's ear.

'Not at present,' she explained. 'The moment you take five paces to the left, you will become visible to your fellow humans, but they will simply think they are going, how do you put it … barmy, when you appear out of nowhere.'

Gaspar looked around. One taxi driver was reading a newspaper: another was listening to his radio and fiddling with the knobs to re-tune it. Others were too far back to see him. He reached inside his pocket and drew out the phial of special strength potion.

'Here, take this,' he urged. 'It should be much stronger, though I have no idea how long its effectiveness will last. I put in double the quantity of everything and then fiddled around a bit with the formula. I couldn't make out some of the letters on the parchment, as they'd become worn over the centuries, so I guessed a bit.'

Bef pushed it back towards him. 'The potion will only work if its creator is present,' she explained. 'Didn't you know that?'

Gaspar looked disappointed. He really didn't wish to leave his rather strange travelling companion behind. He had grown rather fond of her. Bef seemed to sense this and turned away, before she received anything as embarrassing as a kiss on the cheek.

'Off you toddle,' she said. 'Don't forget what you three boys need to do next and do NOT let anyone know where I am. It is possible that Bernhardt Bürstenfrisür may have alerted disreputable folk within his network and they may seek to track you down. Stay strong, whatever the interrogation.'

Gaspar turned white – a clever trick considering how tanned he was. Bef dug him in the ribs saying, 'I'm only joking. Bernhardt doesn't have the intelligence to track you down, whoever his allies might be!'

Gaspar breathed a huge sigh of relief and stepped off the broom. He took five steps to the left and a veil of what seemed like raindrops running down a shower screen lifted from in front of him. His ears popped and he heard noise and hustle and bustle all around him. As he walked towards the terminal door, a security guard rubbed his eyes in amazement, wondering where this man in fake fur had suddenly come from. Gaspar looked back over his shoulder, but had no idea whether Bef and the broom were still there.

When his flight to Dubai was eventually called, he was saddened. He boarded the plane and took his seat, next to a window. He stared out into the clouds, as his heart told him that a witch from Italy had taken hold of his emotions and now they could have parted company for the last time.

As his eyes welled up, the clouds parted slightly and there, right by his side, he could see Bef waving to him. He had become one of those children, or adults with the child within – the ones the broom could sense truly loved its mistress. Gaspar began to wave back, causing the man sitting next to him to stare, suspecting his fellow passenger of being a madman. As he focused on Bef, Gaspar realised that she was actually tucking into a burger. He laughed out loud, causing the man beside him to move seat, to a place where normality reigned.

The flight passed quickly, with Gaspar taking the opportunity to enjoy a much-needed nap. Thaz and Mel were awaiting his arrival at the airport, just as agreed, but were somewhat surprised to see their band member dressed from top to toe in fake fur. Gaspar sweated madly, as they walked to the car, before desperately throwing his clothing off and attempting to acclimatise to the Dubai sun.

'Did you get up to anything exciting?' asked Thaz.

Gaspar thought carefully about this, wondering how best to sum up his adventures. Eventually, he spoke. 'Well, I had to flee a mad adaptation artisan and spit into a tube to create a special potion, so that was a bit crazy. I also met an exiled tailor, living in a Siberian prison, who made me lichen porridge. I managed to escape from a very enraged VIPB in a coalmine and also had to hotfoot it away from the FBI, having left the men who were chasing me dripping in chocolate. Apart from that, no … I guess not.'

Thaz and Mel looked aghast and Gaspar could tell that they were asking themselves whether their bandmate was spinning them a very fancy yarn that would have made even Jeremiah Needlebaum proud. Neither of them dared challenge his tale for an instant, so Gaspar decided to put them both out of their misery.

'And that's all perfectly true,' he added.

Gaspar was made to tell the whole story, chapter and verse, right into the night. Thaz and Mel were absolutely dumbfounded, which is what Gaspar wanted, as he knew they had to fully understand the importance of making a video appeal to their fans. They had to somehow make their fans take Bef to their hearts and that might not be easy.

The three of them sat up for hours planning what to say, how to say it, where to film it, which lines each of them should take and whether or not to set the whole thing to music. They went around and around in circles and still couldn't agree on the right words to use. No matter how many times they tried, it never seemed suitable. Frustration and frayed tempers followed, until Gaspar explained that he was exhausted and so they should sleep on it. All agreed that was a very good idea.

Gathered together the next day, with the coffee and orange juice poured and the sun streaming through the windows, they resolved to get back to work on the script, but something broke their train of thought. A knock at the door started gently and then became louder and louder, showing a real insistence on the part of the visitor to get in and speak to them.

Gaspar looked as though he was about to be sick. 'Goodness me,' he exclaimed, 'maybe she wasn't joking. Maybe Bernhardt Bürstenfrisür has tracked me down, or maybe, even worse, it's the FBI!'

'We can't just ignore it,' said Mel, as the knocking became even louder. 'If it was the FBI, they'd have barged the door down by now. If it's Bernie what's-his-name, then we'll just have to face the music. It's not as if you were in control of anything.'

'I did make sure my sleeping potion went up his nostril,' stated Gaspar, not so sure he would be seen as an innocent party.

'Well, I can't stand this infernal knocking any more,' declared Thaz.

With that, he got to his feet and went to open the door, wondering if a little man in red and white striped pyjamas was going to come flying through in a rage. Peeping through the secure spy-hole would be no help, as Bernhardt wouldn't be seen through it, given his tiny size!

Thaz swung around, having taken a peek.

'It's a guy in a grey suit. He looks quite official, but not FBI material.'

With that, Thaz opened the door and all three of 'The Three Kings' saw the man described … a man with olive skin and jet black, wavy hair: a man carrying a briefcase and some papers under his arm … a man who greeted them not with 'Good day,' 'Good morning' or 'How do you do?' but with the one simple word, 'Buongiorno.'

All three replied in total synchronisation, 'Buongiorno.'

'Have I found the group known as 'The Three Kings?' asked the man, in a heavy Italian accent.

'You sure have,' replied Mel. 'How can we help you?'

'I am looking – in fact, searching hard,' babbled the man, somewhat nervously, 'for someone who, back in Italy, we know as the Befana. Please can you tell me whether she has passed this way recently?'

At this, the guard of all three singers went up. All

looked at each other with a glance that signified that none of them wanted to betray their witchy friend. None of them knew what to say. In the end, Gaspar took the plunge.

'And who might you be?' he asked.

'My name is Luigi Passarella,' explained the man. 'I am a citizen from the town from which the Befana comes. I simply have to find her and give her our news. I simply must know where she is. In simple terms, that's it.'

Gaspar's suspicions rose.

'Why on earth do you need to find her so desperately?' he asked, in a very guarded fashion.

'Because, my dear boy,' answered the man, with a rush of emotion and true sincerity in his voice, 'because everything in our village is a disaster since she left us. Everything has gone wrong and only she can help us get back to normal.'

With that, the man sank to his knees, almost begging 'The Three Kings' for assistance.

'I think you had better start at the beginning,' said Thaz, 'and I think we had better do this over a another cup of coffee.'

CHAPTER SEVENTEEN

Luigi Passarella sipped his coffee slowly, as he tried to find the right words with which to address 'The Three Kings'. He kept wringing his hands nervously, then decided to smooth down his hair in an equally agitated fashion. For some unknown reason, he opened his briefcase, withdrew a pair of gold-rimmed spectacles, which he positioned on the end of his nose and then finally began to speak. It was as if the spectacles gave him the serious aspect required for an explanation of the predicament in which his village found itself.

He opened his mouth. All three boys leaned forward, perching on the edge of the sofa and looking at their visitor seated in the chair opposite. All were on tenterhooks.

'It's such a sorry state of affairs,' said Signor Passarella. 'Such a sorry state of affairs.'

All three band members nodded in a agreement, without having a clue what was so sorry about things.

'The Befana,' continued Signor Passarella, 'was an icon for us – a true, kind and thoroughly fair old lady, who did her best to encourage children to behave, to tick off adults, if we let discipline slip, and to keep us on our toes all year round. She was the fabric that held our village life together and it is regretful that anyone thought they could replace her with a red-suited man, with a white beard and a string of reindeer at his disposal.'

'Quite,' said Gaspar, being as protective towards Bef as usual.

'Things have gone very awry since she disappeared,' continued the Italian gent. 'The potato crop has failed, all the candy balls in the sweet shop have turned soggy and impossible to chew and the children are totally out of control, saying that there's just no point in being good any more, if the Befana will not be there to reward them in January.'

All 'Three Kings' nodded, while their eyes urged the man to continue with his tale.

'Worst of all,' said Signor Passarella, 'there is the issue of cleanliness. Since the Befana last walked our streets, a strange dust has gathered, peppering our windows, laying on our pavements, blowing up our noses whenever we leave our houses and then having the audacity to filter under our doors and into our homes when we least expect it.

This terrible brown dust nestles in your glass, if you decide to head to a bar. It sprinkles itself upon our cappuccinos in the street cafés. It lays heavy on the books in our library and gets inside our shoes as we walk along the streets.

'There's just no escape from this horrible dust that gets down our throats and makes our children wheeze heavily on the way to school. It manages to get inside our pillowcases. It blows on to our food, just as we are giving thanks for the meal on our table. It swirls around in the wind at night, so we simply cannot sleep and it whispers one name as it twizzles around and around and that name is 'Befana.' On and on it whispers, 'Befana, Befana, Befana,' leaving us all with a heavy heart for the way we treated her. It is as if the dust, which she so religiously swept away every day, thanks to her mania for cleaning, is punishing us. The dust is laughing at a village that drove her out of her home, closed her postbox, downsized her festival and treated her with no respect whatsoever. Even now, I can hear the dust whispering that name, 'Befana'.

'This does sound pretty serious,' said Thaz, stroking his chin. 'Have you called the environmental health inspectors?'

'We cannot sleep, we cannot eat and we certainly cannot call in inspectors,' said the man, rather annoyed that Thaz thought he could present a simple solution like that and expect it to solve the issues. 'Nobody wants to come to our village any more, as news of the dust has spread. The businesses shut up at 11am, after just one hour of opening, as there is no trade to be had. Added to this, we have the other strange occurrences.'

'What are those then?' asked all 'Three Kings' in unison.

'The terrible wailing of all the cats in the village the moment the hand on the clock shows midnight. They come from every alleyway and strays are arriving from other villages. A gang of cats sits under the church tower every night and they mew and call and make the most terrible din imaginable. We have to cover our ears, but we cannot stop the horrific noise from invading our eardrums.'

The bandmates thought this was the end of the story, but there was more.

'Then there is the dreadful shuffling sound,' continued Luigi.

'Shuffling?' asked Gaspar. 'What's that about then?'

'It is the sound of her massive, floppy shoes, dragging along the streets, haunting us and taunting us for having been so shallow as to laugh at her old, tatty clothes and peculiar ways and wish to replace that with a man in designer boots and an on-trend outfit. We hear the shoes every night at a quarter past midnight, when the wailing of the cats stops and the shoe shuffle takes over. Some even say they have looked out of their window to see a massive pair of floppy shoes dancing down the street, shuffling their soles, but still not disturbing the dust enough to send it packing on the next passing wind.'

The 'Three Kings' thought this had to be the end of the tale of woe, but still Signor Passarella went on.

'And then there is the singing,' he said. He paused and looked at the boys. 'Of course, it's nothing like yours,' he said hastily, in case his hosts felt he had something against singing. 'It's a very creepy voice that emerges when someone crosses the square by the church, as if someone is in the bell tower and singing down to us. It's always the same song … the song of the Befana, but it is as if some lost soul is reminding us of what we did, by repeating the verse over and over again:

La Befana vien di notte
Con le scarpe tutte rotte
Col cappuccio rosso e blu
Noci e fichi butta giù

'We all do all we can to avoid crossing the square, but it is as if a strange magnetic force pulls us in to the piazza, just so we have to listen to that voice and that verse.'

Signor Passarella looked truly exhausted now, as if revealing the extent of the village's misery had drained him. He opened his briefcase again and out piled a load of dust, which was deposited on the rather nice marble floor of the apartment.

'Ecco! Now you see what I mean,' explained the guest. 'There is no escape from the dust and what's more annoying is that we have nothing with which to sweep it away. Just after the Befana was last seen, every broom from every house in the village stood upright, bolted for any means of exist, whether that was a door slightly ajar or a window partly opened, and flew out of the house and up into the ether, never to be seen again. Some particularly nasty brooms actually grappled with their owners, before poking them in the back-side and triumphantly marching out of the house, having won the battle.'

He paused for ten seconds before continuing.

'We have no brooms and we have piles of dust. We no longer have the cackle of the Befana, but eerie noises in the night. We have no icon – just a pin-up poster of Santa Claus that nobody wishes to see. The Mayor has had to resign and nobody has a clue how to lead the village out of this mess. Consequently, I suggested that we simply had to find her and urge her to come home to the village that does truly love her. The trouble is, that we can't find her.'

'The 'Three Kings' slumped back on the sofa, reflecting on all they had heard from this genuine-sounding man. Each had different thoughts running through their brain. Mel was wondering just how much dust there might be, if you weighed it all. Thaz was contemplating a role for a cat catcher. Gaspar was thinking more protectively.

'What on earth led you here and to us?' he asked, in a detective-sounding way. How in the name of the Befana did you find us?'

'We traced her last movements and discovered she had been to the Internet café and surfed sites that would lead her to you,' answered Signor Passarella.. 'All we had to do was pay the lad on the desk a little extra cash and he told us exactly which websites she had visited. All of these brought us to you.'

'Wow, well done you,' said Mel, before receiving a kick from Thaz and a look from Gaspar that told him to shut up.

'Good though that was and, if I may say so, very clever of you too,' said Gaspar, 'I'm afraid that she's not here. In fact, we don't know exactly where she is right now.'

He looked at his two bandmates in a way that signalled that they were not to breathe a word of anything Bef was up to.

Signor Passarella looked as though he was going to burst into tears. Thaz quickly produced a hanky – a yellow and white spotted one that looked quite ridiculous when Signor Passarella used it to blow his nose.

'Then all my efforts have been in vain,' the little Italian man said sadly. 'What is to become of us? She may never know how much we love her and how much we want her to come home.'

That was the straw that broke the camel's back …

within seconds, he had burst into tears, drops dripping off the end of his gold-rimmed spectacles. He reached into his pocket and pulled out an envelope, as another pile of dust tumbled to the floor.

'We wrote her this letter,' he explained. 'Every child and adult in the village has signed it. It seems that all I can do is leave it here with you, in the hope that she will visit you and read it.'

With that, he plonked the letter on the coffee table in front of him and sighed heavily, with all the characteristics of a man who had lost the last hope he had of finding something precious. With this same sorry air, he got to his feet, smoothed down his trousers, causing more dust to pile out and said, 'I must bid you arrivederci.'

The boys leapt to their feet to reach the door before he did, but he was already halfway through it, as if he couldn't wait to get back home and report his total failure in his mission. A trail of dust marked the route he had taken from sofa to door.

'Wow,' said Mel, after their visitor had exited. 'What a tale.'

'Do you believe he's genuine?' asked Thaz.

'Should we open the letter and check it out?' asked Gaspar.

All three boy band members slumped back on the sofa while the letter lay on the table.

'We can't open it,' said Gaspar, after several minutes.

'It's not ours to open,' agreed Mel, after another few minutes had passed.

'It's not for us to try to save her from doing something she has no need to, I suppose,' added Thaz.

At that, all three of them leapt forward to grab the letter.

'That's precisely what we've got to do,' they all cried in unison.

Within seconds, they had rushed to the kitchen, switched on the kettle and used the steam to lift the seal open without tearing it. All three started to read the letter, Gaspar holding it, Thaz hovering by his side and Mel using a footstool to stand behind them, reading the letter from above.

'Gee whiz,' they all declared. 'Now what do we do?'

CHAPTER EIGHTEEN

It had been cold as cold could be as Bef had flown north from Chicago. She had quickly eaten her burger and felt relatively warm as she had flown close to Gaspar's plane, but the moment she had found herself back in the night sky alone, icicles had started to form on the end of her nose. Though it pained her to admit it, she missed the boy who was always 'cool' and those funny ways of his that made her laugh inside. It could be lonely flying solo on your broomstick, with nobody to ride as your co-pilot. This thought had never occurred to her before, in all her years as a Very Important Present Bringer. She had surprised even herself by the extent of the affection she felt for the boy.

She quickly tried to banish these thoughts from her head. Of course she wasn't alone: she had her trusty broom, with its extra power and carrying capacity and its usual immense loyalty to its mistress. Wherever she went, it went and a person could never be alone when they had such a dedicated broom acting as the force beneath their wings. With these thoughts, she rediscovered her fight to carry out her mission, the fire in her belly increasing as she first flew over Hudson Bay and then Baffin Bay, followed by the frightfully cold Greenland, where the polar bears' growls could be heard on the wind.

She would make sure that all the wrongs that had been done against her by Santa Claus were righted once and for all. She would teach him that snubbing her and rejecting her so cruelly had been a very big mistake. She would check out Mrs Claus and discover what sort of woman had captured the heart of her own former fiancé. But before any of that, she would track down Lars Llangfjord.

Bef had not seen Lars Llangfjord for years and, in fact, his name had almost fled from her mind, until she had stopped to consider, in the midst of a triple loop in the sky over the waters of Hudson Bay, how many other people Santa Claus might have upset. At that moment, the tale of Lars Llangfjord came rushing back to her.

She had first met Lars Llangfjord when engaged to Santa Claus. Santa had hardly mentioned the chap, but she suddenly came across him one day, while at a VIPB conference and taking a quick break from the debates about how to keep sky pollution down.

He had been standing next to Santa's reindeer and, at first, she had thought he was trying to steal them, so had approached very softly in the snow, hoping its crunchiness wouldn't give her away, to spy on him from behind a large fir tree. As she had adjusted her ears, she had realised he was actually talking to the reindeer, but in a strange language that meant nothing to her. She noted, however, that the reindeer seemed to respond immediately to whatever it was that he was telling them. All at once, they would all start to hoof the ground, or lift themselves half a metre up in the air, or toss their heads and antlers on the breeze. Whatever his funny, secret language was, they seemed to speak it too.

Mesmerised by this encounter, she had rushed back to the sturdy log cabin, in which Santa was drying his socks, to ask him to reveal the identity of the strange man. She described his white beard, which reached to the ground, and the purple cape that he swooshed around in front of the reindeer, as if fancying himself to be some sort of magician. Santa had explained that this was Lars Llangfjord, his trusty right-hand man for centuries, known to everyone simply as 'The Reindeer Whisperer'.

Santa had then dismissed the man's role as being, 'not that important in the greater scheme of things'. While Santa admitted that he was 'quite good' with the reindeer, he said Lars had an inflated view of his role in the present bringing world and was also daft enough to assume that he could one day become a VIPB.

Santa had announced this in a scoffing sort of

tone, but had forgotten that walls have ears. A wise old snowy owl, which lived in a tree two paces to the right and three steps back from the log cabin, had blinked far too often in astonishment at Santa's words, alerting a migrant snow goose, who in turn told a Lapland Longspur, who made the mistake of telling an Arctic Warbler. The Warbler, being a Warbler, could not keep the story to himself and soon the reindeer themselves got wind of it. Lars then sensed that there was something upsetting his reindeer, so asked them, in the language that only they and he spoke, what on earth the problem was.

The lead reindeer, Rudolfus, a great-great and probably many more times great uncle of Rudolf, then felt it only right to tell Lars that he was unlikely to ever become a VIPB, if Santa's reaction was anything to go by.

When Lars heard the whole tale and realised just how little regard Santa had for his work, he marched in to see the bearded gent, demanding to know why he had been so belittled in earshot of a snowy owl. A furious row broke out, with the logs of the log cabin shaking as Santa bellowed and Lars shrieked. It ended with Santa sacking Lars – the worst thing that any Very Important Present Bringer could do to an employee, as it meant instant banishment to another land.

Though Lars tried to fight his case at a VIPB Skybunal, it was pointless. The judges all backed

Santa. Lars had to pack his velvet bags and purple cape and accept a wholly dreadful situation – banishment to the snowy wastelands of Iceland. His reindeer whispering days were seemingly at an end.

Bef had felt much sympathy for Lars, having seen how wonderful he was with the reindeer. She also knew that, if she had not raised the question of who he was, he would still be whispering in their ears. She had tried to speak up for him, but Santa would have none of it. Lars, however, heard of her pleas and once sent a friend to tell her how kind she had been. It was said, however, that his anger and resentment of Santa knew no bounds and that he had sworn on the ancient Rock of Erik the Enraged that he would one day seek the revenge he was plotting in his heart.

Bef knew very little about Lars' whereabouts. The friend had simply said that Lars was now living in Iceland and improving his skills in whispering, using a new technique which he called NLP – New Lars Parlance. By employing this skill, he was sure he could not only communicate with other creatures, but also persuade them to do whatever he asked – a whole new power way above that of simply reindeer whispering.

Iceland wasn't a massive country, but it was big enough to hide a very angry man with a long white beard and purple cape. Trying to find him would be very much like trying to find a needle in a haystack … though that was a skill at which Jeremiah Needlebaum had always excelled! If only Jeremiah were here now!

Thinking deeply about this, Bef realised there was only one thing for it. She would have to use a skill she was only allowed to use once every five years … that of Extraordinary Scopa Power, or ESP for short. Now, for those of you who do not know, 'scopa' is the Italian word for broom and the broom plays an enormous part in Extraordinary Scopa Power. Bef began to prove this point as she headed towards Iceland, with the chilliest of winds forming snowflake patterns on her cheeks. She began to chant something that nobody in the world except her broom could understand. She then entered into a trance and began to issue orders to the broom, tapping its top.

Every time she did so, a piece of an image appeared, but only a piece. It was almost like bits of a puzzle, emerging one at a time and then floating in the air until joined by another piece. Al the time, Bef kept chanting and then tapping and, every time she tapped the broom, it generated another piece of the picture.

When eight different pieces were floating in the air, Bef pointed her finger at each piece and moved it to a new position, locking it into place with a neighbouring piece. Eventually, she had a picture in front of her of a man with a white beard, standing in front of a huge geyser and selling tickets to tourists as the geyser bubbled away. As Bef rubbed her eyes and concentrated more, she saw the name of a place emerging within the suspended sky puzzle. She suddenly ordered, 'Broom, trusty broom, take me to Haukadelirium!'

With this, the broom surged forward, circling the coast of Iceland for many minutes, like a whirling dervish. Suddenly, it nose-dived down and down at a vast pace. Bef clung on tight, gradually seeing clouds of steam rising from a very active geyser that looked as though it might explode at any moment. As they drew nearer and nearer, she could hear a commanding voice. 'That will be 50 Krona for the tour,' it said, over and over again. From the tone of this voice, she knew she had successfully tracked down Lars Llangfjord.

'Down broom, down,' she urged, as the requests for 50 Krona seemed to speed up.

Clouds of awful-smelling gas were making her choke and she needed her broom to land as fast as possible. Added to this, the geyser seemed destined to blow and the last thing she wanted was for an eruption to catapult her sky high into the atmosphere and off to some godforsaken land whose name she didn't even know. She needed to whisper in the ear of the talented and hugely dedicated reindeer handler right this minute.

The broom responded to her requests, itself less

than happy with the odours they were encountering. It circled above the heads of a queue of people gazing at the geyser and, as it did so, Bef spotted Lars, wearing his flamboyant purple cape and sporting what seemed an even longer beard than she had remembered. He seemed to be handing out tickets to people carrying cameras, with little of the joy in his face that she had seen when watching him talk to the reindeer. He appeared downbeat and depressed, his job seemingly bringing him little satisfaction. Her heart went out to one she felt could have been a big asset in the Very Important Present Bringing world.

The broom deposited her behind the cabin that seemed to go with Lars' job. She brushed herself off, tried to hold her breath, so as not to breathe in more awful gases, and joined the back of the queue of people waiting to see the geyser. Gradually, she moved up the queue and the person in front of her disappeared. She was now face to face with Lars.

'Lars the Reindeer Whisperer,' she said, in a quiet tone. 'It has been a long time since I last saw you, but I am very glad that I tracked you down.'

Lars' body jolted as she said his name and announced his former job title. He stared at this woman, who he simply did not recognise. He looked her up and down and shook his head.

'It won't seem to come to me, so pray tell who you are and how you think you know me,' he demanded, in a curt tone.

'I am Bef, formerly known as the Befana,' she said in a hushed voice. 'I first saw you at a VIPB Conference, when you were talking to the reindeer. I then tried to fight your cause with my former fiancé, but he would have none of it and insisted on sacking you.'

'Former fiancé? Former fiancé? Shouted Lars, bouncing up and down a little. 'So did he also sack you, madam, or did you see sense and get rid of him?'

He looked her straight in the eye, standing just four centimetres from her nose. Bef didn't flinch. Invasions of personal space were quite common in the VIPB world.

'I was not aware that I had been 'sacked' until quite recently,' she said, in a bit of a huff as she had not, until this point, thought of her rejection in terms of being 'sacked'. 'I only found out, by listening to the radio, that he has married a Mrs Santa Claus, who is tucking him up at night,' she said bitterly. 'This is the reason I am here.'

Lars looked her up and down again.

'What happened to you?' he asked nosily. 'I remember a rather ugly woman with warts and tatty clothes … a woman who always wore enormous, and one must say ridiculous floppy shoes, and not a woman like you at all!'

Bef didn't know whether to bristle with anger at being described as ugly, or glow with pride. She felt her shoes kick her from within the rucksack on her back, so decided to take a little offence on their behalf.

'I am she,' she declared, 'but my shoes were, and indeed are, far from ridiculous.'

With that now out there, she continued, 'I have had what they nowadays call a 'makeover', so that I can arrive at Santa's home under cover and carry out my cunning plan.'

'Which is?' asked Lars very directly.

'To take over the whole of Santa's VIPB area and deliver to all of his children myself, while he sits and regrets the day he ever tried to march into Italy and take over my patch. As they say, hell hath no fury like a female VIPB scorned!'

'I like your thinking. I like your thinking,' guffawed Lars, in a slightly sinister way. 'It's about time that man was taken down a peg or two. Being slightly further down that ladder that he uses to get on to some people's roofs will do him no harm whatsoever!'

He started to perform a jig, in high amusement at this prospect.

'I really do like your thinking,' he repeated.

He suddenly stopped jigging and invaded her personal space again.

'So why are you here?' he demanded.

She stared him out, determined only to tell him

once he had moved back a few centimetres. He took the hint and did just that.

'Because you are the Reindeer Whisperer,' she said calmly, 'And whispering to reindeer is precisely what I need to assist my plan.' She looked him in the eye and saw a twinkle. She decided to push it further.

'There is simply no other reindeer whisperer like you anywhere on earth. You were irreplaceable Lars, which is why Santa never replaced you. You have a talent like no other. You are crucial to my mission and I will not leave here until you have agreed to join me on my broom and fly to Lapland with me.'

Bef knew this would be the ultimate temptation for Lars. Having never been a Very Important Present Bringer, he had never known the thrill of taking to the night skies. He had been very much ground crew. She could see him licking his lips at the very thought of that amazing experience. She just needed to seal the deal.

'And of course,' she said, 'you too have unfinished scores to settle in Lapland.'

At that, a broad beaming smile broke out over his face. He started to shout to the tourists who had gone to view the geyser, telling them to return quickly, or they would be locked in for the night. He impatiently swung a padlock around his long, bony finger as the last stragglers made their way back to the gate, struggling to squeeze themselves and their rucksacks through the narrow gap that he had now left for them.

'Come, come,' he urged, hurrying them along, as if his life depended upon shutting the gate in the next ten minutes. Eventually, he rounded them all up and fixed the padlock around the bars. He swooshed his purple cape around dramatically, like a matador in front of a bull.

'Now I will take you home and serve up my excellent Geyser Goulash,' he declared flamboyantly. 'I am peckish for paprika and it has always assisted with my whispering. You can tell me more about your plans while I perfect my reindeer repertoire once again and then we shall fly off together, to wreak havoc and manipulate mayhem! I have waited years for this day!'

With that, he linked arms with Bef and hopped along gleefully, forcing her to either hop at the same time, or risk falling over in the snow. The pair looked a strange old sight as they jumped awkwardly across the snowy waste between the geyser and Lars' log cabin, whispering to each other as they went along, starting to make their plans. Being peckish for paprika was highly addictive, as Bef would soon realise.

CHAPTER NINETEEN

Geyser Goulash was something Bef couldn't get enough of. She had been hungry on arrival in Iceland, but there was something simply fabulous about this dish, which forced her to demand portion after portion, until she suddenly belched loudly and realised that it was time to stop eating and start planning.

Lars had already lifted up some floorboards of the log cabin and found some rolled up maps, thick with dust, which had not seen the light of day for donkey's years. The maps covered the whole of Santa's home, a place defined by the darkness of winter, or kaamos as Lars said it was called in Lapland, by the sparkling spring snows and the very light summer nights.

Lars had a monocle strung around his neck and used this to peer at the map with his left eye only. He suddenly pointed to an area, stabbing his long fingernail into the centre of the zone he was highlighting.

'Here, madam, we have the reindeer park,' he

said. 'There will be around forty reindeer in the park right now, though none of them will remember me. What exactly is your plan?'

Bef was sitting on a high stool and she began to swing her legs around wildly, in an attempt to think clearly what the plan might be. A look of deep concentration fell over her face. She thought deeply about the question again and then opened her mouth to speak.

'The plan is,' she said, 'to make the reindeer refuse to fly. What we need is what we call in Italy 'uno sciopero,' or a strike to you and me. We, or rather you, need to convince the reindeer that they must withdraw their support of Santa and stay rooted to the spot, so he has no reindeer power for his sleigh. If Santa cannot fly, he cannot deliver presents: it's as simple as that.'

Lars looked at her in admiration. 'A truly great and well thought-out plan,' he declared, rubbing his hands together with glee. 'Now we are clear, I can work out the best way of achieving it.'

He began to stroke his long white beard as he continued to study the map. He hummed and hawed for a while, twisting part of his beard around a bony finger, as he tried to think of the best strategy. Having got his finger so stuck in his beard that he had to ask Bef to help unwind the twist he had made, he finally came to a conclusion. He jabbed a finger in the map once again but much higher up than the reindeer park.

'You must fly me to this point here,' he said, with great authority. 'There is a secret passage that starts high up in the mountains. I can enter the passage just here.' He moved his finger around a centimetre to show where he meant. 'I can then travel down the passage and emerge here, on the boundary of the reindeer park.' He jabbed his finger around nine centimetres away. 'Then I can hop over the fence and get right into the reindeer compound. From there, I will simply use my whispering skills.'

Bef was about to open her mouth to utter a response, when Lars suddenly continued.

'However,' he said. He paused for a good twenty seconds. 'I need to get myself a disguise … a new costume that will not arouse suspicion. I must also trim my beard somewhat, or I shall be instantly spotted.'

He looked down sadly at his long, white beard, which had been his pride and joy for centuries. Without any more delay, he reached into a drawer and found an enormous pair of scissors, which he struggled to lift.

'Grab hold of these,' he urged Bef, 'and chop!'

Bef looked a little unsure, but she did as she was told and hacked into his beard, at a point around a metre below his chin. Ruler lengths of white beard hair fell to the floor. Lars ran to a mirror. 'Now I too have had what you call a makeover,' he stated.

He returned to the map and quickly turned it over. 'Here,' he said, pointing once again at a point on the map, 'is where my disguise awaits.'

Lars' finger was hovering over a place with a name Bef simply couldn't have read out, even if she had tried. It appeared to be on the Arctic Circle and seemed to be in the middle of nowhere.

'What is there?' she asked, a little confused.

'It is the chief Kammi,' replied Lars. 'Here we have a traditional Lapp village, complete with reindeer hides on the seats and the best cloudberry wine you will ever taste. The recipe has been handed down for generations, as has my reputation with the Lapps. My friend the Arctic Warbler has often brought me news of the village, where the Lapps say the reindeer have never been the same since my departure.

'There has been disobedience in the ranks and the Lapps are desperate to sort their reindeer out, or so I am told. If I help them with this task, I am sure they will return the favour and let me have a traditional Sami robe to wear. Dressed in this, I will not stand out at Santa's reindeer park. People will just assume I am one of the helpers and I will slip over the fence and around the compound with no trouble at all.'

He paused and moved to within two centimetres

of Bef's nose again. 'But pray tell,' he said, staring her in the eyes, 'how are you going to get into the village and keep close tabs on what Santa is up to? How will you avoid suspicion?'

Bef had this figured out already and so declared, perhaps rather too triumphantly, 'I am going to get a job as an elf in Santa's Post Office.'

Lars looked at her as if she had gone mad.

'An elf?' he asked. 'An elf?' He looked her up and down. 'Santa already has elves and they don't look like you. What makes you think there will be a job available?'

'I don't,' said Bef, 'but you can used your skills to convince the Head Elf that he needs another helper. As soon as he puts a notice on the Elf Telegraph, I will appear and offer my services. You will be on hand, to do a spot of whispering. This will convince the Head Elf that I am the worker he needs. Once I am on board, I can start to carry out my side of the plan.'

Lars stared at her in amazement. 'What makes you think I can whisper in Elf?' he demanded.

'Because,' replied Bef, 'I believe you can now communicate with lynx and wolverine. Elf, as a language is very similar to the language of Lynx, or so my 'Old Almanac of Native Tongues in the Very Important Present Bringing and Natural Worlds' stated on page 227. This is one with the slight stain on it from when too much potato juice had been fed into my broom and it had to spit a little out. That globule of spit travelled all around my drawing room for a good thirty seconds before landing on page 227, just below the guidance on Elf speak. That's why I have never forgotten the close linguistic links between Elf and Lynx.'

Lars was now more than impressed. His blood was flowing through his veins faster than he could ever have imagined. Meeting this determined woman almost showed him why he could never have been in the same league as Very Important Present Bringers. He felt humble. And yet … she needed him to help her with her cunning plan. He felt a spot of bartering was now required.

'What is my reward, other than revenge?' he suddenly asked.

'A recommendation that you become a Very Important Present Bringer when the next round of VIPB expansion comes around,' answered Bef very cleverly.

At this, Lars' face lit up brighter than the Northern Lights. 'That,' he declared, 'is more important to me than anything else.'

Bef nodded knowingly. She knew her powers of persuasion had worked.

Lars began to jig around the room excitedly, almost tripping over the broom, which was propped up against one wall. It shook with annoyance and Lars patted it gently. 'Pardon me,' he said, in a quirky manner, 'I can't wait to fly off on you. He turned to Bef with eyes as excited as those of a child in a sweet-shop. 'When shall we fly?' he chirped.

Bef studied the clock and then the map. 'I should say that will be in precisely five hours, 23 minutes and 13 seconds,' she said. 'The winds should be favourable at that moment and we shall speed off to the Lapp village. What do you say broom?'

The broom hopped up and tapped its top against the wall three times.

'That means I am spot on,' said Bef smugly.

Lars went to a window of his cabin and opened it, having to give it quite a shove as the frame stuck and then snow prevented him pushing it open in one swift movement. He knelt on a stool, sticking his head through the window and made the strangest sound – a sort of cooing noise, followed by chirrups and tweets and much more that Bef could not under-stand. He tilted his head this way and that, as he switched between one sort of noise and another and then began to roll his head, producing yet another call as he did so.

Bef watched in amazement as this continued for several minutes. Lars then reached out to a small table and picked up what looked like an animal horn. He put it to his pursed lips and began to shove another strange sound down the horn and out into the dark night sky. Once again, this continued for several minutes.

Just as Bef was getting bored with all this hooting and cooing, a small bird landed on Lars' hand, tilted its head in the same direction as Lars' and began to chirp back to him, using the same sounds she had been hearing. This little greenish-grey coloured bird with a white underbelly was clearly communicating with Lars and Lars with it, but Bef could not understand a word. The bird began to trill loudly, before suddenly hopping on to Lars' head and using it as a launch pad as it then flew off into the darkness. Lars waved it off and then struggled to close the window once again.

'What was all that about?' asked Bef.

'That was my friend the Arctic Warbler. I have sent it off to the Lapp village, to investigate matters there, so that it can report back to us on our arrival. Once we know how the land lies, we will enter the village and I shall remind the reindeer how to behave in a manner more befitting of such a noble breed. I shall then send the Arctic Warbler on to Santa's village and again ask her to report back to me on the situation there. Once we have that knowledge in our hands, we shall proceed with our plans. Knowledge is power, madam. Knowledge is power.'

Lars attempted to stroke his long beard, forgetting that most of it had been cut off. Instead, he stroked thin air, causing Bef to grin broadly and have to quickly straighten her face, as the reindeer whisperer looked up at her.

'What a fabulous strategia!" she declared, to get herself out of trouble. 'Your attention to detail is superb Lars. I shall have no hesitation in putting you forward to be a Very Important Present Bringer.'

Lars glowed as brightly as the fire in his hearth at this news and pulled a rather large sack-like object down from a hook fixed to the ceiling.

'I shall sleep on the floor tonight in this sleeping bag,' he explained, 'while you rest in comfort in my bedchamber. Now, before we turn in, I shall fix us a nightcap of delicious reindeer milk that I have kept in storage for some considerable time – maybe fifty years or more – but it is long-life milk and it shall be a pleasure to share it with you, with a sprinkling of fern powder on the top. That shall be just the ticket for a sound night's sleep before we fly.'

Bef beamed, wondering deep down what on earth this would taste like. She realised, however, that refusing this treat would be a very rude thing to do, so decided to brave it, no matter what. As Lars poured it out, she realised it didn't look too bad after all and graciously sipped from her mug. Within minutes, she began to feel drowsy and excused herself, asking to be shown to the bedchamber. She lay down on the bed, falling asleep in seconds. Lars tiptoes up and quietly shut the door, before snuffing out the three candles that flickered in huge brass holders on the table, setting a rather large alarm clock, which sat on a shelf close to the front door and hopping into his sleeping bag.

'Oh what great fun we shall have broom,' he said quietly. 'How long I have waited for a moment and an opportunity like this! The reputation of Lars Llangfjord will be restored once again as the best reindeer whisperer the world has ever seen.'

With that, his head hit the floorboards and he too fell fast asleep.

CHAPTER TWENTY

Bef almost fell out of bed. The ring of Lars' alarm clock was so loud it seemed to shake the whole log cabin. More rattling followed. Lars was rustling up pre-flight food treats and was determined to get them off on their flight on schedule, if not before.

Once they had eaten and done a final security check of his cabin – something Lars insisted upon, because he didn't trust the Arctic foxes – they carried the broom out into the snow, sharing the load between them. Lars was now bounding around like a firecracker, beside himself with excitement about the big plans, not to mention his forthcoming reunion with reindeer.

So it was that an old, but young-looking, witch from Italy and a reindeer whisperer, now resident in Iceland, took flight on the winds and directed themselves towards the Lapp village that would offer Lars some assistance, if the words of the Arctic Warbler were to be believed. The bird should, by now, have arrived at the village and be gathering information useful to Lars. The planning was perfect and Lars' heart was full of hope, causing him to bounce rather annoyingly on the broom, creating all sorts of navigational issues.

'For goodness sake stop doing that!' demanded Bef. 'You are making me feel very broom sick.'

Lars took the reprimand very well and sat as still as a statue for at least the next thirty miles, before bouncing once again. Bef just sighed and asked the broom to ignore its rather over-excited passenger.

After a few hours of flying and circling snowy lands, a frozen river came into view and, above it on a hillside, there soon appeared a collection of Lapp huts. As they dropped down towards the ground, it became apparent that one of these was much grander than the others and even had a grass roof. Dropping further, Bef could see only mist and no sign of the huts at all. She became disturbed by an even greater amount of bouncing from the back of the broom, which almost catapulted her over the top.

'I can hear the reindeer on the breeze,' yelled Lars.

Bef slung a look over her left shoulder and glared at him. He shrivelled a little upon seeing her look so angry.

'So sorry. Pardon me,' he said. 'It's just that I haven't heard such a wonderful symphony of reindeer voices for so very long.'

The kindness in Bef's heart could not stay

hidden. She patted Lars' hand. 'Don't worry, my friend,' she said. 'You will soon be among them once again, whispering your magic words and hearing them tell you how much they adore their one and only reindeer whisperer. After all, once you find someone special, you never lose the love for them in your heart and their ancestors will have handed down stories about Lars Llangfjord, the most famous reindeer whisperer in all the world.'

Lars began to shed a tear at these unexpected words of kindness.

'Mamma Mia, stop snivelling!' urged Bef in embarrassment.

She rifled inside her clothing and produced a pristine white handkerchief, one of hundreds that she bleached each year at home. When she knew that a child was a borderline case between coal and candy, she would leave a handkerchief alongside the lumps of coal. She felt it helped soften the blow, when they cried a little with regret over their bad behaviour during the year that had just passed. At least they could wipe their nose on a nice, clean white hanky!

Lars pulled himself together and pricked up his ears. He could now hear the sound of the Arctic Warbler, guiding them to a safe landing place in a copse of fir trees just behind the village.

'We need to land over there,' he said, pointing about ninety metres to the left. 'That way, we can get our briefing from my feathered friend. I must make sure I know what the Lapps want to hear from Lars Llangfjord!'

The broom glided down silently into the snow, parking itself very calmly for once beside the trunk of a fir tree.

'All of this extra weight seems to be making my broom rather sleepy,' said Bef, with a hint of concern in her voice. 'I shall stay here and check all is well with it, while you go about your business.'

Lars wasn't even listening. His Arctic Warbler friend was now perched on his arm and trilling merrily. Lars' face showed deep concentration as he listened to every word.

'It appears the reindeer are not eating well,' he explained. 'There is something wrong with the vegetation, maybe due to acid rain. The Lapps need to understand that the reindeer need additional vitamins. This is very good news for us … once I listen to the full reindeer story and then tell the Lapps what is going on, I am sure they will help me.'

The bird flew away a few metres, before turning back and chirping to Lars, clearly asking him to follow. The pair of them went off and disappeared on the snowy horizon.

Bef slumped to the ground, resting her feet on her broom and her back against a tree. A cone came crashing down and conked her on the head, but she didn't even seem to notice. She was worried about her broom. It wasn't like it to be so lifeless, or so tired.

'My dear broom,' she said tenderly. 'What is the matter with you today? You are really not yourself. Tell me what is wrong.'

The broom lifted itself ten centimetres and then dropped down again.

'Is your belly too full?' asked Bef. The broom shook from side to side, as if to indicate 'no'.

'Then have you not taken to Lars?' asked Bef, still probing in a gentle tone. Again the broom indicated that this really was not the issue. Bef laid her head against it. 'Speak to me,' she said quietly.

The broom began to murmur from within, at first slowly and then, as if it had verbal diarrhoea, spit out absolutely everything it wanted to get off its wooden chest. Bef sat up, looking very pensive indeed. A worried look passed over her face.

'But I have to right the wrong,' she said to her broom. 'Santa has made a terrible fool of me and, even worse than that, has tried to steal the hearts of children. You must see, my friend, that I cannot just sit back and let that happen. My children and you mean everything to me and without you I am lost, without a purpose, just a shrivelled up old woman with a head full of memories and many regrets.

'I have to go through with this now, whatever you think, but I will reflect on your advice. It is just so hard when you know that your town no longer wants you, that your festival is being cut back, that your postbox is sealed up and that children mock your clothing, all because Santa is wearing designer gear and offering tempting commercialised presents. If I do not make a stand, the children of Italy will be lost little souls.'

A tear fell down her cheeks as she sat there in the snow. Much of her fighting spirit seemed to have left her body and here, with just her broom for company, everything seemed different ... much less black and white and now a little grey around the edges. Deep in her heart, she now realised she wasn't doing anything out of revenge for being rejected by her fiancé, but acting because the children of Italy meant so very much to her. The traditions were important: they were everything she lived and breathed for, they bonded families and brought smiles where sometimes there could be despair and strife. What was a poor old witch supposed to do except fight for what she believed in most?

With these thoughts filling her head, her broom now seemed to have taken a vow of silence. The surroundings were so very still and she dozed off under the tree and stayed in that state for quite some time.

What awoke her was the sound of reindeer horns, being blown extremely loudly, as if in celebration. She rubbed her eyes and stared ahead of her. The Lapps were all dancing around in a circle and tossing Lars up and down in the air, as if he were some hero or winner of one of those very loud races that she had seen at Monza – Formula Uno or 1 or Grand Prix – or something like that anyway. Lars had obviously spoken to the reindeer and explained to the Lapps what was wrong with their herd. The important thing was that she could see he was already dressed in a Lapp costume. Part one of the plan had gone well.

She knew it was a waiting game now. Lars would have to spend time getting into the reindeer park and meeting up with Santa's reindeer. He would then have to work his way into the Post Office and seek out the Head Elf. Until the time came to apply for a position in the Post Office, she would have to find somewhere to stay.

That was now bothering her, as she had never been one for den building and getting poked by twigs. The memories of sleeping under the palm tree were still far too fresh and the weather had been a whole lot warmer there. Here, she would freeze to death within a few hours. There was only one course of action to be taken. She closed her eyes and clicked her fingers three times. A pile of gold coins came shooting out of the broom and landed in a heap by her feet. It was time to check herself into a hotel and bide her time. She shoved the gold into her rucksack and coaxed her dear friend into action.

'Come on broom. It's time for us to live the high

life for a few days – and I don't just mean circling around in the sky!'

She tapped her broom slightly and it responded by warming itself up for flight. On she hopped and it obediently began to fly her down towards Santa's village, crossing the Arctic Circle and celebrating that fact with a bounce and a sky-skip.

They circled over the twinkling lights of Santa's village, which shone magically in the gloomy skies, looking out for signs of a hotel. A big neon sign suddenly leapt out of the darkness, lighting up the roof of a hotel that almost appeared to have a chimney. This was also lit up brightly, but was unfortunately only a decorative block. Bef sighed heavily. Chimneys were simply her favourite entry method, but in short supply on this adventure. The broom put her down in the snow, sensing her frustration, and instantly became invisible. Bef hopped off, patted it and took herself through the big glass door of the hotel.

She was delighted to spot a sign boasting menus translated into nine different languages, particularly as one of these was Italian. She was more than a little peckish right now and could not wait to get a good plate of food in front of her – perhaps some nice tasty fish like salmon, followed by some home made berry ice cream. She was rather partial to a drop of crowberry wine too, as Santa had once sent her a bottle through the Elf Post and she had tippled it merrily back in Italy, enjoying every last drop.

By now, the thought of all this food was making her stomach rumble, so she strode over to the reception desk with great vigour and slammed her hand down on a little golden bell. A rather vacant-looking girl, with long blonde plaits down to her waist, appeared and looked Bef up and down.

'Yes, madam. How can vee help you?' she asked.

'A room, per favore, but it must be spick and span, with not a speck of dust or dirt or grime, or I shall sneeze all night and all of tomorrow too,' said Bef.

'I can assure you that all of our rooms are spotless,' replied the girl, in a rather defensive manner.

'Good,' said Bef. With that, she slammed a pile of gold coins down on the counter, much to the amazement of the employee. 'Take what is necessary,' instructed Bef.

'How long are you staying?' asked the girl, eyeing up the pile of gold and thinking this could well be a year-long stay.

'Just until I get a job in Santa's Post Office,' answered Bef.

The girl smirked far too visibly for Bef's liking. 'You won't get a job in there,' she said smugly. 'Only elves work in Santa's Post Office.'

'We'll see,' answered Bef. 'Now book me in for three nights and let me have a key. My feet are killing me with these makeshift, awful shoes on my feet.' She felt behind her, just to reassure herself that her big floppy shoes were still in her rucksack.

The girl frowned, not wishing to argue with a guest, but peeved that this woman thought she knew better than someone who lived and worked in this town. She put a key on the counter. 'Room 257,' she said curtly. 'Second floor. Breakfast is at 7am. Food is being served shortly.'

Bef took the key and walked towards the stairs. She took one look at the marble steps and knew her feet would be in agony if she tried to climb them. She looked over her shoulder and realised that the girl was busily gossiping to a colleague. They both burst out laughing, clearly amused by Bef's suggestion that she would become a postal worker. While their eyes were off her, Bef clicked her fingers and began to hover in the air. With another click, she shot up the flight of stairs without touching the ground once, using the elevation spell that worked a treat when there were fewer than thirty stairs to climb. The receptionist caught sight of something flashing past out of the corner of her eye, but Bef had already vanished.

'Where did that woman go?' she asked her friend. She received a shrug of the shoulders in response.

Bef found her room, pushed open the door and immediately began pulling the bed out. She then looked under all the chairs, to see how dirty it might be on the floor. She was disappointed to find not one speck of dust. She rushed into the bathroom and inspected the sink and bath. Again, they were spotlessly clean.

'Che peccato,' she said, as she thought what a shame it was that she couldn't get stuck into some grime removal – she was suffering such withdrawal symptoms.

She spotted a TV and then the remote control. She didn't quite know what to do, but started to push buttons, eventually deciding that an international news channel was a better choice than the latest toilet racing tournament in Lithuania, which she'd seen a thousand times or more over the centuries. Within seconds though, as she slumped back on the bed, she was bored and tired. The pictures kept rolling on and on and she only understood half of what was being said. Her eyelids began to close and her body gave in to its need for sleep.

Just as she dropped off, a nattily dressed presenter announced that a special appeal had been put out by the global pop group known as 'The Three Kings'. The images on screen switched away from Lapland's snowy wastes and to a very bright and sunny Dubai. There, sitting under the palm trees, in a relaxed setting, were Mel, Thaz and Gaspar. Mel introduced them all, while Thaz started to explain that they needed to get in contact with a woman called 'Bef' – a fan who had recently been in Dubai, but who was now travelling the world. Up flashed an image of Bef, which Mel had taken just before she'd left Dubai.

The report switched back to 'The Three Kings'. Gaspar was looking down the camera lens with his biggest puppy dog eyes.

'Please Bef, get in contact with us very quickly. We have something we have to tell you and we want you to talk to you before you do anything rash and we mean ANYTHING! We have spoken to someone from your village. It is vital you get in touch!'

The TV shot switched back to the news presenter in the studio; a man who looked more than a little bemused by this strange appeal. He was American and pronounced in his drawl, 'Gee, that fan must have made quite an impact on those guys. Whoever this Bef is, she must be quite some woman … let's take a look at her again!' Up flashed her picture once more.

At that moment, Bef rolled over on the bed and right over the remote control, sending the whole TV screen blank. She had heard and seen nothing of the broadcast.

Down in reception, the girl with the blonde hair was still chatting to her workmate. She too had missed the story of the need to find Bef. If she had not done so, she would have realised only too well that it was the rather abrupt woman, who had just paid in gold and was deluded enough to believe she would be working with Santa's elves soon.

For a good few hours, the girl kept repeating to her friend, 'That woman really was away with the fairies.'

Bef would have absolutely hated that, had she known, having had a feud with the head of the Florence branch of the fairies back in 1412 and never trusted a fairy since, let alone having had any thoughts of going away with them!

CHAPTER TWENTY-ONE

L ars was in his element. The Lapp village had taken him to their hearts and his belly was now full of warm reindeer milk and wonderful Lapp food cooked over a roaring campfire, which crackled with dried twigs, carefully selected to make the meal taste delicious.

He had also been given his own rather impressive blue and red Sami costume. All it had taken was a bit of whispering in the ears of the reindeer, to explain that their owners now understood their predicament and would be making sure their diet was much richer in future. The reindeer had responded by telling Lars he was enshrined in reindeer legend as the man who truly understood their needs. They added that, among those with antlers, he was regarded as a true king.

He was now riding in a sledge drawn by huskies and heading down towards Santa's village at breakneck speed, feeling rather giddy as they whizzed along. The Lapps had kindly offered to take him to the edge of the compound and this gave him the opportunity to catch forty winks. He snuggled up tight and cosy beneath the warm furs his hosts had provided within the rustic, wooden sledge. Only his nose and eyes were visible and these felt the bitter cold and withdrew beneath the warm blankets. Losing sight of the route ahead, he immediately felt even giddier.

There were butterflies in his stomach. He couldn't wait to meet the reindeer and get to work on the plan he and Bef had drawn up. He had been running it over in his mind and he knew exactly how it should pan out, in an ideal world. The experience in the Lapp village had given him the best possible way to win over the reindeer. He just needed to make sure Santa did not spot him and recognise him as the man he had once sacked.

The journey passed with the encouraging sounds of the husky drivers filling one ear and the incessant yapping of the dogs the other. He spent several hours in this state, wondering where Bef was right at this moment, but feeling too drowsy to really think about that too much. She was a resourceful witch and he knew she would be just fine.

He was jolted out of his slumbers by a sudden braking of the huskies. The sledge slid to a halt. Poking his head out of the covers, he saw a fence lit by the occasional lantern. The Lapps gestured to him to get out of the sledge. He trudged through the deep snow to reach the wooden fence and then looked to the night skies and studied the stars. Having done this, he walked down the fence for around one hundred metres, hopped over it and bent down, running his fingers across the wood.

'Bring me a lantern, please,' he urged and one of the Lapps obliged. Lars' face lit up, as he swung the lantern to and fro. 'Yes, yes, I knew it!' he shouted gleefully. 'This is the spot where I carved my initials into the wood more than two centuries ago. This is the lasting tribute to Lars Llangfjord, the best reindeer whisperer the world has ever seen!'

The Lapps slapped his back heartily. Lars waved them off, keeping a lantern in hand to guide him through the next stage of his mission. First, he had to find the reindeer. The park was large in size, many kilometres square and the herd could be anywhere within it. He called out for the Arctic Warbler, but heard no flutter of wings in the still night air. He raised his nose upwards, allowing his nostrils to sniff deeply. The scent of reindeer was very faint. The herd was some distance away.

He cupped his hands together and made strange noises, which then seemed to echo around, as if bouncing off moonbeams. At first, nothing else could be heard, but he tried again and then a third time. Suddenly, there came a response – a sort of grunting noise that was seemingly getting nearer. Lars held up his lantern and there, emerging from the darkness, he saw what appeared to be the head of the herd, a trailblazer sent to greet this stranger, who seemed to know how to communicate in Reindeer.

He began to murmur words no human could comprehend, but the stag came closer until it nuzzled Lars' hand and prodded his arm with its nose. Lars soon learned that the reindeer had been told of Lars Llangfjord in tales around the campfire, but had never dreamed of having the honour of meeting this maestro of the murmur themselves. They were delighted to have him among them and he was soon surrounded by the whole herd. Each reindeer approached him and, one by one, rubbed their nose on his hand and retired, to allow another of their number to take their turn.

'Why are you all looking so sad?' asked Lars, once all the reindeer had greeted him. 'This should be a joyous day for us all. I have waited a long time to return to you most noble of creatures.'

In his heart, he wondered if the acid rain was affecting these reindeer too, but there was something more than just a dietary problem here. His third finger on his left hand was twitching and, when it did that, there was always a real cause for concern.

The head of the herd began to explain and with every grunt Lars began to shake his head more and more.

'So worrying,' he said. 'It's just not right,' he

added. 'I won't stand for it,' he declared, jumping up and down in a fit of pique.

Lars was incensed. The reindeer had explained that they were being terribly overworked these days and now flying in the skies hundreds of times a year and not just at Christmas. This was all thanks to Mrs Santa Claus. She was described as a woman with an incredible urge to shop, not just to get retail therapy, but to satisfy what was almost an addiction to buy clothes and shoes and shoes and clothes, from the best designers around the world. Every time her desire to spend came on, the reindeer were hitched up to the sleigh and forced to fly her to her chosen shopping destination of the day: New York one day; Paris another … they were, quite simply, exhausted.

Their tale continued, as they explained that Mrs Santa Claus had now forced Santa to start wearing designer clothes and that it was she who had demanded he take over the present bringing duties in Italy. This was purely so she could visit all the fashion houses in Milan, on a very regular basis, to get even bigger discounts. These were given to her, because the shop owners were all parents who wanted their children to have the very best presents and they knew that, if they pleased Santa Claus, she would most certainly put in a good word for their children with her husband.

'This must stop. It must stop right now!' shouted Lars. 'While Lars Llangfjord still has breath in his body, there will be no over-flying of my reindeer friends. Similarly, there will be no taking over the duties of my dear friend Bef! This vain, over-fashion-conscious wife of Santa must be shown that reindeer are precious creatures that must be treated with the utmost respect. Lars Llangfjord is truly angry and it does not pay to make Lars Llangfjord mad!'

The reindeer bowed their heads in respect, knowing that, finally, they had someone who would go into battle for them. They formed a circle, as they huddled together on the ground, with just enough space in the middle of their circle for Lars to curl up between them.

'You are right,' he said. 'We need to rest and think of a strategy. We need to work with Bef, as we all want the same result here. I will rest for a few hours and then head into the village and see how the land lies.'

Lars snuggled up close to the reindeer, who kept him warm as he stretched out his old bones and lay his head on the back of one of the herd, using it as his pillow. This peaceful scene was only observed by the Arctic Warbler, which was sitting on the fence, close to where Lars had carved his name.

A few hours passed by and Lars awoke to find the herd getting to their feet. They seemed agitated and alarmed. A loud hooter was being sounded and they were having to respond to it.

'What on earth is that terrible noise?' asked

Lars. The head of the herd looked miserable as he explained that this was the summons always issued when Mrs Santa Claus wished to go shopping. They had no choice but to follow the sound of the hooter and report for duty.

'Go, if you must, this time,' said Lars, 'but I promise you that this will be your last shopping trip for that woman.'

The herd mooched away, with not a sign of happiness in their movement. Lars nimbly hopped over the fence and reached inside his Sami costume, pulling out a compass attached to a long, gold chain. He knew that, by following this and his finely tuned nose, he would reach the village in around thirty minutes – maybe less, if he picked his feet up, rather than shuffling through the snow.

Off he trudged, a lonely figure with a head full of worry and concern for his beloved reindeer. He almost failed to notice the first of the bright lights that shone out from Santa's village, but could soon see that the brightest of these was coming from a hotel. Something told him that this was where he needed to head.

As he continued to plod along, he was suddenly stopped in his tracks, as his feet bumped into something very solid. He toppled forward, landing with his chin in the snow and sprawled over the object that had stood in his way.

'Goodness me broom,' he declared in slight

annoyance. 'You could have told me that you were there. How's a reindeer whisperer supposed to know that you are blocking his path?'

The broom shook at this, a little peeved that this man should seek to scold. As he prepared to apologise and dusted snow out of his beard, he looked up to see Bef staring through a pane of glass. She beckoned to him to come inside, so with no further to-do, he did as he was told and joined her in the much warmer hotel.

'What in heaven's name is that terrible noise?' she asked.

Lars pricked up his ears, but had not really taken much notice of this before. He could now detect exactly what Bef could hear – a sort of screeching, wailing commotion that was getting louder and louder. The employees on the reception desk were covering their ears with their hands and turning up the volume of the music playing in the public areas. Outside, people were also sticking their fingers into their eardrums and huddling together, as if in fear.

Everyone was pointing down the street. Lars and Bef hurried outside to see what was going on. Spinning madly, as it moved down the thoroughfare towards them, was what looked like an out-of-control spinning-top of red and white. It whizzed and whirled and continued to emit the terrible noises that nobody within three miles could possibly have tolerated. As the spinning-top arrived at the hotel steps, it abruptly stopped whirring.

Suddenly, as it slowed down, it transformed itself into a woman with blonde hair, a red cape trimmed with white fur and an all-in-one red hot pants outfit, which contrasted perfectly with black fur boots.

'What are you two looking at?' she snapped. 'Out of my way,' she ordered. 'I need some bilberry juice NOW!'

'Whatever is the matter, my dear lady?' asked Lars diplomatically, secretly seething inside, realising instantly that this was the shopaholic Capriccia Claus.

'Nosy parker, squashed tomato, don't forget to eat it,' replied Mrs Santa Claus childishly, as she pushed him out of the way, almost barging into Bef in the process. She was now whooshing down towards the bar, knocking over anyone who crossed her path.

'Excuse me, please. Excuse me please,' asked a shrill little voice, which proved to be attached to an elf, but not any common old elf, but the Head Elf, according to his name-badge.

'I must apologise to all of you,' he insisted, 'but I am sure you all know how it is when Santa puts his foot down and stops his wife's spending. He has just put his chequebook into the fourth ice machine in the village vaults and frozen his assets. She does not take kindly to that. She had, after all, already summoned

the reindeer and now they are all uppity and goodness knows how we can deal with that right now!'

'No need,' said Lars, stepping up to the Head
Elf and holding out his hand in greeting. 'I have just
taken a degree in Reindeer Language and Literature
and, although not the best reindeer handler by any
means, I am the best for kilometres around. I would
urge you to let me attend to the reindeers' mood,
while you calm down that lady who, if I am not mistaken, has just poured her fourth glass of bilberry
juice and is now on the verge of asking for something stronger.'

The Head Elf looked the stranger up and down
quizzically. 'If you can do this, my man, I will
instantly give you a job. I am sure that, how shall we
put it … a more mature student like you will thank
their lucky Polar stars that they've found a job so
soon after graduating.'

'It's a deal,' said Lars, feeling rather triumphant.
Soothing the reindeer would be as easy as pie and
then he would have the ear of the Head Elf and be
able to get him to do whatever he wished. All he had
to do was work out how to control him in the Lynx
language that Bef was so convinced would work on
his inner consciousness and so control his brain.

Bef was looking highly impressed by Lars' quick
thinking and, as the Head Elf chased after Mrs Santa
Claus, began to clap slowly.

'My, my and fiddle my broomstick,' she declared.

'You have already worked more magic in a few minutes than I have done in the last six hours. That man will soon by putty in your hands, or as I like to say, mozzarella balls in your fingers. We just need to get me into the Post Office, so that I can assess the situation. Then we need to get a quick master plan together, to teach that dreadful woman a lesson!'

Lars headed out of the door and soon saw where the commotion was now centred. A posse of reindeer were all harnessed up to a sleigh, tossing their heads around in a most alarming fashion – alarming that is to all but the best reindeer whisperer the world had ever seen. Lars approached the sleigh and began to whisper in Reindeer. All of the creatures' noble heads turned to look at him as he whispered.

'Now, now my friends, there is no need for alarm. Our plan is coming together beautifully and I shall soon free you of all these wretched flights altogether. For now, I want you to put up a little bit of resistance, but then allow me to calmly free you and take you back to the paddock with, of course, a good supply of food for your trouble today. I promise you that things will change very soon, now that Lars Llangfjord is back in town.'

The reindeer understood perfectly and began to toss their heads around and grunt a bit more. This allowed Lars to play to the crowd and continue to utter strange sounds to them that no human could understand. Gradually, the reindeer pretended to calm down, each of them now brimming with hope that the demands on their time and strength would soon be eased, with a little help from the man about whom many generations of reindeer had spoken only good. Lars began to stroke each of them, before loosening their reins and freeing them from the sleigh.

'Is that wise?' asked one person in the crowd.

'Won't they stampede?' asked another.

'Not at all,' replied Lars. 'I have explained that it was just an unfortunate misunderstanding and that I shall take them back to their grazing land with a good supply of food, which I trust will not be a problem. Then we can all just calm down and allow things to return back to normal.'

At this, an elf dashed forward with a cart full of rich grasses and lichen for the reindeer.

'Excellent,' said Lars. 'Just the ticket!'

With that, he took hold of the cart and began to pull it along, following the reindeer, which were all calmly walking back home. A round of applause broke out in the crowd, with this almost drowning the words of the Head Elf, who had now appeared and observed the departure of the reindeer with Lars.

'I must reward that man with whatever he wants when he returns here,' he vowed. 'That man has more than spared my blushes today and one good turn deserves another.'

Walking away, with his back to the crowd, Lars picked up these words on the breeze and smiled to himself in a most satisfied way. Not only was he back with his beloved reindeer, but he was also about to be able to assist Bef with her plans.

Standing two steps behind the Head Elf was a woman dressed in the finest outfit that Jeremiah Needlebaum could produce. She was also grinning contentedly to herself. Her plan was more than coming together and she knew she would soon be installed as the latest employee in Santa's Post Office. It was now just a matter of time.

Chapter Twenty-Two

The Head elf woke up in a most grumpy frame of mind. He was NOT happy. His head was pounding with a most terrible headache and, to cap it all, he had slept for most of the night with his feet hanging out of bed without knowing it. That always left him in a foul mood.

Added to this, he could recall a most awful dream. All the presents that had been so carefully wrapped for children were unravelling around him, all around the Parcel Storage Facility and Parcel Carousel, which took presents from the Wrapping Room to the Sleigh Loading Bay. The dream had made him wake up with a jolt at 3am on the dot and he had hardly managed to get a wink of sleep after that.

He was not the only one to have had a dream. Lars' head had hit the pillow and he had, almost immediately, begun to experience the most beautiful visions in his sleep – a life in which he was back in charge of his beloved reindeer every hour of the day.

In Dubai, someone else was struggling to sleep, thanks to a dream that had slipped into his mind. Gaspar's dream involved trying to stop Bef from making a terrible mistake and going through with her plans. He had jumped on a camel that he had found tied up near a hotel on the edge of the desert and had urged Mel and Thaz to join him. Together, they had followed a star, which they had hoped would guide them to Bef. At that point, he had woken up, so was now frustrated, not knowing whether he had succeeded in his mission or not.

On this night of dreams, there was one person who missed out. Bef had slept very soundly indeed, snoring heavily and enjoying the comfort of a real bed and mattress for once. She had no need of dreams to guide her. She knew exactly what she wanted to do.

The Head Elf positively stomped into Santa's Post Office that morning. All the other elves dived for cover under the tables, as he sent various objects flying with the force of his boots on the wooden floor. As items shook and tumbled, the under-the-table elves tried to catch them.

'How many elves does it take to get out all the parcels for the children of the world?' shouted the Head Elf.

In unison, all the other elves replied, '91 Sir.'

'Wrong!' shouted the Head Elf. 'It takes 92 and

the 92nd is the most important of them all, as it is me!'

'Yes, Sir,' agreed all the other elves in perfect unison once again.

The Head Elf had almost failed to notice the new addition to the ranks standing behind a pillar. Lars had been waiting for the Head Elf's arrival and had been practising his Lynx for several hours, since tucking into a bowl of porridge served up by a local resident, who had befriended him following the reindeer incident.

'No, that is not the number you need,' whispered Lars from behind the pillar, as he stood almost directly behind the Head Elf.

These words came out of Lars' mouth, moved around a little in the air and then shot directly into the eardrum of the Head Elf, having negotiated the rather pointed tip of his long earlobes.

The Head Elf began to wobble from side to side. He appeared totally disconcerted and alarmed. He spun around and came face to face with Lars.

'So how many do I need?' he asked, in somewhat of a panic, as he looked into the eyes of the man that he trusted most in the world at this point: the man who had saved his blushes less than 24 hours before.

'You actually need 93,' answered Lars. 'For years, you have got the manpower projections wrong and it has always required the assistance of one more elf.'

Again, these words were whispered in Lynx, so

even the keenest-eared elf, Albert, who had popped his head up from below a table, did not hear what passed between the two.

'What does the 93rd elf do?' demanded the Head Elf, looking as though he were being tormented out of his mind by this thought.

'They should hold a position of great responsibility,' whispered Lars in his best Lynx. To the observer, it did not even seem as if his lips were moving, as he delivered these gems of wisdom, but as sure as eggs were eggs, they were entering the consciousness of the Head Elf.

'What sort of responsibility?' asked the Head Elf, in a state of confusion now, as all the other elves could plainly see. Not one, however, could offer an explanation as to why.

'They should be your second in command,' answered Lars. 'They should hold keys to every part of the Post Office, parcel areas and Sleigh Loading Bay and they should be responsible for seeing every single item of post that leaves the building for final checking. Attention to detail is everything.'

The Head Elf stopped spinning. He jumped ten centimetres off the floor and then tapped his head 93 times. 'I need a 93rd elf,' he shouted. 'Find me a 93rd elf!' he implored as he looked into Lars' eyes. 'Attention to detail is everything,' he roared.

The other elves looked bemused as they

gradually got back up on their feet and stared at their boss in his seemingly insane state of mind.

'What is everything?' bellowed the Head Elf.

'Attention to detail, Sir,' replied all the other elves in perfect unison again.

At that moment, Bef opened the door to the Post Office and stepped inside.

'This is the perfect 93rd elf,' whispered Lars.

'This is the perfect 93rd elf,' repeated the Head Elf.

'This is the perfect 93rd elf,' chimed all the other elves.

'I appear to be the perfect 93rd elf,' said Bef, with a true air of satisfaction and a smirk across her face. 'When do I start?'

The Head Elf looked her up and down. 'Something is missing,' he declared.

'She is missing an elf costume befitting of her status,' whispered Lars.

'You need to go for an elf costume fitting,' announced the Head Elf. He clapped his hands three times and the 62nd elf appeared by his side. 'Take the 93rd elf to the Elf Tailor,' he said.

The 62nd elf held out his hand and Bef took it in hers. With that, he led her out of a small wooden door that led to the inner sanctum of the Post Office, in which the craftspeople elves worked, fixing things, making items and creating grand designs for new features in Santa's village.

'The costume will be sorted within half-an hour,' declared the Head Elf. 'We shall then crack on with our work and make sure that, above all, we pay great attention to detail.'

'Quite right,' whispered Lars.

'Lovely to see you, my dear man,' said the Head Elf, as if snapping out of a trance. 'To what do I owe the pleasure?'

'I would like to play a more prominent role in the training of the reindeer,' said Lars quite bluntly. 'They seem to need a guiding hand and a proper keeper and it would appear as if your current reindeer elf is not up to the job.'

He looked the Head Elf in the eye and then, without moving his lips, whispered in Lynx, 'The man is not up to the job.'

'Excellent,' replied the Head Elf. 'To be honest, the reindeer keeper is not up to the job. You should step in straight away.'

'Fabulous news,' said Lars. He then took a step to the left and whispered, 'But let's keep this under wraps.'

'Quite so, quite so,' the Head Elf replied, tapping his nose, as if keeping a secret, while all the other elves wondered why he was talking to himself in such an erratic manner.

'Very well,' said Lars. 'I shall head to the reindeer compound and start having a chat to the herd.'

'Remind them that they need to fly in just a few

days,' urged the Head Elf. 'Christmas Eve is fast approaching and we have to make sure they are in the right frame of mind for it.'

'Indeed,' said Lars, as he shook the Head Elf's hand and then headed to the door.

Twenty minutes later, Bef re-emerged in the centre of the Post Office, wearing a smart yellow elf outfit with turquoise tights and sleeves. On her head, she was sporting a red elf cap, with a bobble on the end. Her shoes were yellow and pointed. On her back, she still wore the little rucksack that contained her precious 'scarpe' – the huge, floppy shoes from which she could not bear to be parted.

'The 93rd elf needs her medication, so has to carry this rucksack,' explained the 62nd elf, who had brought her back from the Elf Tailor. 'The Elf Tailor' isn't happy about it, as he says it ruins the look, but the 93rd elf insists,' continued the 62nd elf, showing a fair degree of angst over this breaking of the tailoring rules all elves had to follow.

He then proceeded to explain the full tailoring rule in exactly one minute – proving why he was and always would be the 62nd elf, as every statement of fact that he made, when quoting rules and regulations, could be timed at exactly 60 seconds.

'Thank you, thank you. That's quite enough rules and regulations quoting for one day,' insisted the Head Elf, still feeling decidedly grumpy about his night's sleep. Try as he might, he just could not escape the sight of all those parcels unravelling.

He clapped his hands three times and the 37th elf appeared at his side.

'Yes, Sir,' said the elf obediently.

'Take the 93rd elf on a grand tour of our marvellous facility,' said the Head Elf. With that, something stirred in his brain and he dived towards a locked safe. He tapped in a few numbers and the door shot open. Reaching inside, he retrieved an enormous bunch of keys. He waved them in front of the nose of the 37th elf.

'She will be the only other key holder in the Post Office,' declared the Head Elf. 'You must show her every door, every shed, store, exit door and safe. Show her which key fits which lock and make sure she grasps it all immediately.'

Bef smiled contentedly.

'Thank you, Sir,' she said. 'I am sure this induction will be most informative. I am very good with keys and am sure I can memorise every one.'

The Head Elf beamed. 'Excellent news,' he declared. 'Now, I need a cup of bilberry juice right away, or my toes will start to curl up.'

No sooner had he uttered this statement than the 11th elf, known as the Juice Elf, appeared with a cup of red liquid, which the Head Elf downed in one.

'Now I am ready for a full day's work,' announced the Head Elf. 'And I do not want to see anyone taking it easy, or putting their feet up! Get those elf sleeves rolled up and fasten them up with rubber bands, if necessary. We have a lot to get through in the next few days.'

'Yes, Sir,' replied all the elves in unison.

Walking towards an exit door, which was padlocked several times, Bef was muttering something under her breath. Only she knew that what she was pronouncing was the 'Canzone di Memoria e Chiavi' – a little ditty that helped a witch memorise any number of keys and locks and know immediately which could open which. She had to cast this spell once a year, around this time, so that she could always deliver presents … even in those cases where a chimney was blocked and doors were locked and preventing entry to a house. By flexing her fingers four times and then tapping each knuckle, she could make keys to doors fly into her hands, once the spell had taken hold. This skill had never failed her and it would not fail her this time either.

Meanwhile, back in Dubai, three members of a boy band called 'The Three Kings' were causing a stir at the airport. They had all arrived for a flight that would connect with another flight and then another that would fly them to the Arctic Circle. Having found no camels tied up anywhere, they had opted for the easiest option to go in search of Bef. Going by plane was much more comfortable anyway!

Chapter Twenty-Three

Bef was feeling mighty pleased with herself. The 'Canzone di Memoria e Chiavi' had worked a treat and she now knew every single lock and key in her charge. She could now, at will, open any door around Santa's vast empire and what an empire it was proving to be.

When she had learned about the Parcel Passageway, her eyes had opened as wide as those of the cats whose tails touched one of the electric fences around fields close to her home. Her fingers had tingled upon hearing of the Sleigh Loading Bay Area, the Reindeer Runway and the Sleigh Service zone. She had developed a slight twitch of the left eye when being shown the Wrapping Room, but there were other rooms about which she was truly intrigued.

These rooms had not been shown off, but merely mentioned in a whisper that was accompanied by the sort of knowing look that only an elf could make. The rooms in question were the Presents of Mind

Study, the Wishing Wall and the Room of Really Special Rewards. Each was causing pinging candy ball feelings in her stomach, as she longed to discover the secrets behind the names.

But what made her red in the face with ire, and a little bit green with jealousy too, were two other areas for which she now held keys. The first was Santa's Spa, which made her angry just thinking about him lounging around relaxing, while she was fighting a battle to retain the love of the children of Italy.

The second was an area whose name she almost spat out each time she muttered it under her breath, which she kept doing, just because it annoyed her so much and brought out the green-eyed monster within her. The zone in question was Capriccia Claus's Casa of Contentments.

Bef would have been mad about the woman now married to Santa having a house of contentments anyway, but the fact she had called it a 'casa' rather than a house, using an Italian name for house and not the English or American name, made it all the more painful. She had also not known Mrs Claus's Christian name until now. The fact this woman had now come to life with a real name made it all the more irritating. She could not, however, deny that the diva she had seen barging through the hotel was truly deserving of the name Capriccia. She was no doubt a silly, vain and dramatic creature, who always had to make herself the centre of attention.

Where Santa Claus's common sense had gone, she could not begin to guess.

With every key now memorised in her head, she was ready for action. The Post Office was manic. Sackload after sackload of letters kept arriving, each bulging, heavy and requiring a team of six elves to drag them into the Post Office for sorting by country. Letters from children in America were sorted out from those from children in England, Spain, Canada, Australia and, though it pained her to see it, even Italy. The Linguist Elves then took over, translating the letters and working out how to pen a reply to each child. Once letters were signed by Santa, all that remained was to put Santa's personal postmark on the letters – a stamp carrying a special image of Santa on the outside of the envelope.

Seeing Santa's image applied to each envelope was like a big red rag to a bull for Bef. Seeing stamp after stamp of this man in his bright red outfit stuck to the clean, white envelopes was more than she could bear. She sat there in her brand new elf outfit racking her brains as to what she could do about it, but it was so long since she had cast most of the spells in her 'Grandissimo Libro di Scongiuri' – the humongous book of spells and charms she had inherited from her mother. Recalling what was in that book, sitting on a shelf back in her little house in Italy, was almost impossible.

She sat and she sat and she sat, knocking her

head periodically, as she tried desperately to remember a spell that could come to her aid. Suddenly, one elf working behind her, who was very displeased with one of his colleagues, shouted out, 'For goodness sake use your imagination!'

At that, Bef sat bolt upright on her toadstool shaped and coloured seat.

'Mamma mia! Of course! The 'Immagini-frustrazione' charm,' she declared.

Now this charm was a very special one that came to a witch's assistance whenever a particular image or picture was causing her distress. Undoubtedly, this was the case right now, so she tapped her head again, in an attempt to remember the details. At that moment, the 27th elf appeared in front of her waving a special camera.

'You need a security picture,' said the 27th elf. 'Smile please and smile as if you were the one delivering all the parcels to the children of the world. That's how Santa likes his elves' security pictures to look.'

Something clicked in Bef's brain and she smiled the most beautiful smile anyone had ever seen. A warm glow came over her face as she tilted her head slightly to one side and looked straight into the camera lens. The elf clicked.

'Beautiful,' he said.

'Can I have a copy, please?' asked Bef sweetly.

The 27th elf looked deep into her eyes and found

it hard to refuse such a polite request. 'It's against company policy,' he said, 'but as it's you, I will send you one as a special favour by elf-mail.'

'When will I get it?' asked Bef.

'In a day or so,' replied the 27th elf.

'But I would love to send a copy to my sister today. She would be so proud of me becoming the 93rd elf … and SECOND IN COMMAND.'

The 27th elf suddenly remembered Bef's position of high authority and caved in. 'I will send it straight away,' he said, stuttering slightly.

'Perfect,' replied Bef.

When it arrived ten minutes later, it looked wonderful. Bef had a beautiful glow about her face and a serene smile. The picture was just what was needed to replace Santa's stamp with one carrying her own image. Now she had remembered the finer details of the 'Immagini-frustrazione' charm, this was child's play. All she had to do was find some pepper.

'Do we have any pepper in the elf canteen?' she asked the nearest elf to her.

'Yes, 93rd elf, I believe we do,' replied the slightly nervous elf, who was one of the youngest of all elves. Desperate to please, he went scurrying off to the kitchen and returned with a bright green pepper pot.

'Perfect. I like to smell it, so that I can cure my migraines,' lied Bef.

With that, she poured a little pepper into the

palm of her hands. At that moment, someone grabbed hold of her wrist. She froze.

'What are you doing?' asked a voice. Luckily, it belonged to Lars.

'I'm about to cast the 'Immagini-frustrazione' spell,' she replied. 'I want to get rid of all the stamps that carry Santa's image and have my stamp stuck on instead.'

'The elves will notice,' warned Lars. 'You must not attract attention to yourself in this way. When will the image change?'

'As soon as I shove pepper up my nostrils, sneeze and utter the word, 'scambiare', she advised.

'OK,' said Lars. 'At that point, I will step in.'

Bef took a pinch of pepper out of her hand and shoved it up the other nostril. She quickly grabbed another and pushed it up the other side of her nose. Within two seconds, she gave the loudest of loud sneezes imaginable and scattered pepper dust halfway across the Post Office, while shouting out, 'scambiare'!

'What does that mean?' said one elf to another.

'She must be saying 'bless you' to herself,' replied his workmate.

In actual fact, in that instant when the word came out of her mouth, all the Santa stamps on letters leaving the Post Office instantly became Bef stamps, just as she had planned. Her beaming smile and turquoise and yellow outfit had completely replaced the image of a jovial man in a red suit.

Elves sticking the stamps on letters were chatting away as Lars cast his eyes around the Post Office. But one, a bit of a loner, sitting some way apart from the others, suddenly leapt off his toadstool and cried at the top of his voice, 'What is going on?'

Bef looked alarmed, as the whole Post Office fell silent. All eyes were looking at her with deep distrust. The 93rd elf was ready to run, until a message that she could not understand was communicated on the tannoy. Lars had leapt into action and was whispering in Lynx to the elves, entering their deepest sub-consciousness.

'There is nothing amiss here,' he whispered. 'This is just another picture of Santa when he was younger. It is natural that he should wish to change his picture from time to time.'

'There is nothing wrong here,' shouted out the elf who had jumped off his toadstool. 'It is perfectly natural that Santa should wish to change his picture from time to time.'

'It is perfectly natural,' chimed all the other elves in unison. The stamp fixers carried on sticking on the Bef stamps.

'Lovely new picture of Santa,' said one.

'I quite agree,' said another.

'What next?' asked Lars, hopping around Bef's desk. He was very proud of his Lynx skills.

'I need to find out more about the operation here,' said Bef, mumbling so no elves would hear. 'I need to find the best way of taking over all Santa's deliveries, but I need to enter each area and discover what happens there. We then need to control the reindeer, so Santa cannot fly and then I must take to my broom and take over the whole present drop.'

'How are you going to find out about the operation?' asked Lars.

'By dead of night, when all the elves are asleep in their dormitories. I have been given my own bunk – luckily a bottom bunk, but in a dormitory of three top elves. The other two are in bunks above mine, so I should be able to sneak out with my keys and explore. Once I know how to close down the whole operation here, we will be in business.'

'It is too dangerous for you to do this alone,' said Lars. 'But I have to stay with the reindeer and make sure I have their complete trust. I am worried to think of you creeping around by night, sneaking into rooms and trying to leave undetected.'

'Are you mad, man?' asked Bef. 'Pazzo, perhaps? Sneaking around by dead of night, creeping into rooms and leaving undetected is what I do best! I've been doing it for centuries!'

'Fair point,' said Lars. 'But I will only let you do this alone, if you are sure that you will be safe.'

'100 per cento,' asserted Bef.

Lars bowed his head and began to back away. 'So if you are sure that all the reindeer are fully licensed to fly, I will bid you farewell,' he said loudly, ensuring all elves believed his visit had related to some sort of document needed for his reindeer.

'Certain,' said Bef, tempted to wink at him, but restraining herself, to avoid suspicion.

Both Lars and Bef thought they had pulled all this off beautifully, but in a corner of the Post Office sat an elf a little less convinced by the whole scene. This was the 81st elf, otherwise known as the 'Safety-first Elf', as he controlled all elf and safety matters in every part of Santa's empire, including the reindeer park. He tapped his fingers in annoyance on his desk. Nobody had come to him to ask about reindeer licences. How could this upstart of a 93rd elf tell the reindeer man he had no worries about his licensing? He knew full well that this was not the case.

Something was wrong with this whole set-up and there was something decidedly fishy about the arrival of these two strangers and the weird behaviour of the Head Elf. The more he thought about it, the more he knew he was right and, the more he knew he was right, the more he knew it had nothing to do with not being able to speak or understand a word of Lynx. The more he thought about it, the more he knew he would fret while trying to get to sleep in a three-person dormitory, in which one of the strangers would be in the bottom bunk!

Bef was not aware of any of this. She had her mind on other things … on finding out what went on in all the different rooms and zones she had not yet seen, on discovering what on earth the Casa of Contentments could be and, above all, unearthing her former fiancé, Santa Claus.

Since she had been here in his homeland, she had not spotted him, heard a peep out of him, or felt the tingle down her spine that told her he was nearby. People kept talking about him, stating what he would and would not like or agree with, quoting him and referring to his instructions, but there had not been one single sighting, even during the incident in which his wife had so upset the reindeer and the Head Elf.

Bef was mystified as to where he could be. She was puzzled as to why he was not managing his operation in a more hands-on way. She was absolutely desperate to know if he was spending all his time in 'Santa's Spa'. Surely he had not become as vain a creature as his wife, but then, she had to recall how she too had succumbed to vanity and changed her own appearance. That saddened her and was playing on her mind more and more. What was the point of winning back the hearts of her Italian children if they did not recognise her? As this thought struck home, a tear began to trickle down her cheek – a tear that nobody seemed to notice thank goodness – apart, that is, from the 81st, ever-so-aggrieved elf, who had not taken his eyes off her since Lars had left the Post Office. He could always scent an opponent and there was a very strong whiff of opponent wafting up his nose right now.

Chapter Twenty-Four

Bef turned in for the night as a woman on a mission. She would have the perfect opportunity to slip out and investigate all parts of Santa's empire, once all the elves were asleep. She needed to see inside the rooms she hadn't been shown and have a better look at those she had only had a few seconds to glance at, before the 37th elf had locked them up again.

She was determined not to fall asleep. She would wait until the two elves in her dormitory had dropped off soundly. She would then creep out of the room, as quiet as a mouse, so as to have a very good nose around, with her big bunch of keys in hand. She settled down in the bottom bunk bed and waited.

The two elves in her room were complete opposites of each other. The 55th elf was a talkative chap, who had made her feel very welcome and had made sure she got her full rations at dinner. She could already hear him snoring in the top bunk and knew he was deep in slumber. The other, the 81st elf, was very frosty indeed, snapping at her when she asked a question and looking at her only out of the corner of his eye. He was in the middle bunk and, for absolutely ages, she had no idea whether he was sleeping or not.

Bef lay still, waiting for some sign that he had dropped off and, shortly after the clock turned midnight, she heard him snore. That was her cue to slip out of her bunk and tiptoe to the curtain dividing the dormitory from a long corridor, which connected all dormitories to the Post Office.

She left barefooted, but with her rucksack on her back. A few yards down the corridor, she emptied it and put her huge floppy shoes on her feet. They would not make a clicketty-clack noise on the stone and they made her feel very safe. She continued to walk down the corridor, totally unaware that someone was spying on her from behind a curtain. The 81st elf was far from asleep and feeling exceedingly pleased with himself. His imitation of a snoring elf had been spot on.

Bef studied the keys and decided to first revisit the Sleigh Service Area, just behind the Post Office, in tin-roofed buildings that smelled of oils and polish. She knew that this was where the team of Melfchanics lovingly tended to Santa's sleigh, checking out the undercarriage before each flight, greasing the runners so the sleigh could easily slide on to any roof, cleaning the brass on the reindeer harnesses, polishing the bells, waxing the floorboards and maintaining the upholstery. One room was also set aside for any paintwork repairs – usually caused by Santa scraping the sleigh on a chimney.

Bef looked around the room, trying to work out what could be done in here to prevent the sleigh taking off, but she was no mechanic.

'Fiddlesticks,' she muttered. 'Only Leonardo da Vinci could work out what could ground a sleigh!'

After a few seconds of deliberation, she headed to the Wrapping Room, which had filled her with awe when its door had first been swung open by the 37th elf. The Wrapping Room was actually an enormous hall, with a spectacularly carved wooden roof and shelf after wooden shelf fixed to the walls. These were all filled with rolls of wrapping paper, ribbons, lace, net, cardboard, bows, gift cards and decorated bags.

Over one million different types of wrapping paper, of all colours, patterns and designs, dazzled her. The team of Wrapping Room elves used twelve very tall ladders to reach the highest shelves and pull out the roll that they wanted for a particular present. This would then be handed down to an elf a few rungs below them, who would pass it down to another elf, who would make sure the elf at the bottom of the ladder could rush it off to the wrapping tables.

These tables, of which there were three, were each

precisely as long as eight reindeer stood nose to tail in a line. Exactly one hundred pairs of scissors hung from them and, as a roll of paper reached the table, it was unrolled to the length required for a particular present and then cut by the nearest elf to that point, using the closest pair of scissors at hand. The roll was then rushed back to the ladder, passed back up and returned to its rightful position by the elf at the top. Speed was of the essence!

No unauthorised person could ever enter this room, but Bef just waved her pass across a special detector and walked through the security beams. She then turned the key in the lock.

The room seemed much larger now there were no elves at work in it. Bef gazed around and felt queasy. 'How could I ever compete with this?' she asked herself. 'This room alone is probably bigger than my entire house back in Italy.'

This thought depressed her slightly and, as she looked around the Wrapping Room, she could not think of any mischief in there that would ground Santa's sleigh on Christmas Eve.

A keen pair of eyes drilled into her as she left the Wrapping Room from a back exit. Bef had somehow sensed, to the 81st elf's amazement, that there was a metal panel in a fireplace that was never lit. This, if tapped five times, lifted and revealed an entrance to a tunnel. This was not any common or garden tunnel, but the famous Parcel Passageway.

The Parcel Passageway ran underground from Santa's Post Office to the Sleigh Loading Bay. The presence of this dark and secret tunnel was only revealed to elves that had been with Santa for more than ten years. At that point, they could become trusted Despatch Elves and drag carts of presents along the tunnel and towards the Sleigh Loading Bay. Bef chortled in amusement at this. She had only been here five minutes, but she already knew about it!

The Parcel Passageway was not a place to enter at this time of night. It was slightly spooky, lit by only lanterns hanging on the rock walls, which were re-lit daily by the Lantern Lighter Elf, should their lights go out during the day.

Carved into the rock walls were different numbers, which showed how many parcels had been delivered by Santa each year. The Stonemason Elf theatrically performed the carving on December 26th, after Santa had returned from delivering all the presents. The numbers could only be carved using a special chisel called the 'Chisel of Consignments'. This chisel was handed down from Stonemason Elf to Stonemason Elf, so the first numbers carved into the rock had been there donkey's years.

As Bef shuffled along the tunnel, she felt some of the numbers carved into the rock and marvelled at just how many presents Santa delivered each year. She had never been expected to deliver that much coal, fruit and candy. Inside, she wondered whether she could actually take on such a big responsibility. Why on earth did Santa wish to take over Italy and add to his workload?

All the time she walked along the twisty, winding tunnel, she was unaware that, as she went round each corner, beady eyes were watching her. The 81st elf was creeping along behind, desperate to know who this woman was and why she was so keen to explore Santa's empire, in the middle of the night and wearing ridiculously large shoes!

She never looked back as she made her way along and so never saw him staring angrily at her, shaking his head at her actions and trying to blend into the rock as much as possible, so that if she did turn around, she might not see him in the shadows. After all, the light of the lanterns only stretched so far and there were lots of dark, secret hidey-holes for a nasty elf to use to his advantage.

The Parcel Passageway was very long and, as Christmas approached, could be packed with carts of parcels, all queued up and awaiting handling. Once they reached the Sleigh Loading Bay, they were loaded up into a metal casing, exactly the same size as the back of the sleigh. This moved when an elf wound a cranking wheel with all of his or her might. The casing then pushed the presents, ever so carefully, into the sleigh. Once full, this was wheeled out on to the Reindeer Runway and hitched up to a team of reindeer.

When Bef reached the Sleigh Loading Bay, she started to contemplate Plan B, in case her Plan A did not work. Plan A was to ensure the reindeer refused to fly, but what if one team of reindeer decided they would carry on helping Santa? Plan B would be to mess with part of the system, such as the cranking wheel, or maybe to block off the Parcel Passageway, so parcels could not be loaded. As for Plan C, that would involve stopping Santa himself from flying. She hadn't yet figured out how to do that.

She touched the cranking wheel and then moved back and looked at the Parcel Passageway again. For one fleeting moment, she thought she saw something move down the tunnel. She rubbed her eyes. She must have been seeing things. There was nothing there. She looked up at the ceiling of the tunnel. It wouldn't take that much to cause a rock fall to occur and block the entrance to the Sleigh Loading Bay, but her 'Incantesimo della Roccia' had failed her miserably back in 1449, when she'd been trying to escape from a mad dog, which she'd disturbed in a castle, by accidentally landing on its tail. The spell hadn't worked and so, instead of keeping the dog back behind a pile of rocks, she had been forced to take off with it still clinging to her dress by its teeth. It had only let go as they had soared above the castle ramparts, but had taken with it a huge chunk of her precious dress. She had given the castle a miss for several years after that!

'What is she up to?' whispered a sly little voice, as the elf watched her from the shadows of the tunnel. He was mightily relieved she hadn't spotted him, as he'd only just managed to squeeze into a crevice in the rock in the nick of time, after she had spun around unexpectedly. 'This woman is up to no good,' he told himself, over and over again.

Bef was muttering to herself. 'Shall I, or shan't I?' she kept saying. 'Do I wish to know how he and his wife live in luxury, while I still dwell in my little medieval house? Will I cry when I discover what life is like here, or become so angry that I can't be rational and carry out my mission?' She paced up and down and down and up and the answers seemed no clearer after twenty-two times of doing this.

'Oh goodness,' she eventually declared, 'I must learn to make decisions a lot quicker than this. I am just a silly old woman who needs to be loved. What Santa does in his spare time is not important. I must win back the hearts of my children, no matter what it takes.'

With that, she paced back up the Parcel Passageway, causing a certain elf a great deal of alarm, as he was now ahead of her. He scampered as fast as he could, but she was positively marching up the tunnel at a very fast pace. The floppy and huge shoes that should have been a hindrance to her seemed to actually help her move faster.

With Bef nearly upon him, the elf suddenly

managed to scamper up the rock wall and lay on a stone ledge on the tunnel roof. He prayed she wouldn't look up as she marched underneath. Luckily for the 81st elf, she didn't and, once again, he found himself behind her, following her every move.

Halfway down the tunnel, she stopped and started to feel the walls with her hands. 'Reveal the door!' she declared loudly and a whole section of rock suddenly moved to the left. Now she found herself facing a very thick, pine door with ancient keyhole and lock. She shuffled the keys around in her hand and instantly found the right one. She pushed this into the lock and slowly turned it, so as to not create too much noise. She opened it up and immediately faced a sign that read,

'PRIVATE: Access For Santa and Trusted Elves Only'.

Bef walked very slowly now. She had not seen any of this part of Santa's empire, yet this was what intrigued her the most. A series of corridors lay ahead, so she needed to choose one. She decided to follow the corridor with a sign pointing towards The Presents of Mind Study. She reached a big blue door and tried the brass handle, to see if it would open. It wouldn't, so she began to search through the keys, identifying the correct key for this door. As the keys jangled, she didn't hear the door from the Parcel Passageway open, or detect the shuffling sound that accompanied the 81st elf passing through the door and past the warning sign. She also failed to see him peering round a corner as she entered the Presents of Mind Study.

The cream coloured room had a shiny wooden floor and a heavy, carved oak table. It was very much like a library, with hundreds of books sitting in bookcases suspended on the walls. All of these related to gifts, with books detailing toys, games, dolls, toy cars, cuddly bears, clothing, computer games and much more that children might wish to receive for Christmas. It had been explained to Bef that Santa and the Head Elf would enter this room with the letters from all children who had asked Santa to bring 'some surprises'. Together, Santa and the Head Elf would stage a snow shower thought session, to determine what the best surprise could be for each child.

The snow shower involved putting a picture of the child inside a revolving, see-through sphere that generated a snowstorm of snowflakes around the child. After a 66-second snowstorm, the snowflakes would merge and spread, to create an image of what the ideal present would be for that particular child. Santa and the Head Elf would then consider all possibilities, using the many books on the bookshelves.

Bef could not deny that she was impressed by the snow shower system. 'Fiddlesticks and flabbergastedness,' she exclaimed to herself. ' All of this is far too clever. How can I compete? How can I thrill children as much as this?'

These words appeared to be uttered to the open air, but walls had ears – very pointed, very sharp ears in this case … the ones belonging to the 81st elf.

'Very interesting,' he said to himself. 'Very interesting indeed. Who is this woman and what is her purpose here?'

Bef was still mumbling in a mixture of Italian and English as she headed towards the Wishing Wall. This had two entrances: one from the private area from which she was emerging and one from the Post Office. Having not been told much about this part of the empire, she was extremely grateful for the 'Elf Information' poster, which explained it all to her. It read:

The Wishing Wall is a place at which each elf may make a wish for a child, who may not otherwise receive many presents. In making a wish, that elf must forego a present of their own, but the goodness in their heart increases each time they do this unselfish thing, making them happier elves. If you wish to make a wish for a child, repeat the name of the gift you wish to give them three times and watch the silver orb at the top of the wall open and accept the wish. You gift will then be sent out to a child, who might otherwise receive nothing, or very little.'

'Che bello,' said Bef. 'How very nice indeed. What a lovely idea.'

With this area now ticked off her list, she only had a few more to explore. The first of these was the Room of Really Special Rewards. Bef was truly dreading entering this room. She imagined it would be full of over-priced toys and dolls that really spoilt children clamoured for and mentioned at least ten times in their letter to Santa. She felt it would be full of bright pink and gaudy blue items for girls and boys, which were totally unlike her plain and simple offerings of coal and candy. She feared opening the door, as she was sure she would be violently sick on the spot and puke all over her lovely, big, floppy shoes. But she had to know and the only way to do that was to put the key in the lock and turn it.

As she did this, a snide little voice was muttering to itself, 'How dare she enter this room. She is not worthy to even discover what goes on in here. She is a spy. She is an infiltrator. She is a demon and a devil in disguise. She is a nobody trying to be a somebody. I must stop her!'

The 81st elf closed his eyes as she entered the room. Bef found herself inside an enchanting area, light and airy with crystal chandeliers cascading light downwards on to a marble floor, but with clouds suspended above the chandeliers, giving the impression of sky and sunlight. Calming music automatically played the moment the door was opened and, ahead of her, she saw ten enormous bottles of what appeared to be perfume, each with a tap and each surrounded by tiny little tube and glass stoppers to put into the top of them.

Each of these enormous bottles was labelled, with the labels reading: Kindness, Generosity, Politeness, Consideration, Helpfulness, Selflessness, Happiness, Health, Humour and Wisdom.

'How does this work?' Bef asked herself, as she found herself mesmerised by the beautiful décor of the room, right down to gold skirting boards and beautiful, gold embroidered wall hangings.

She looked around, but found no Elf information poster, much to her disappointment. The only clue to what might occur here seemed to potentially lie in a huge, gold covered book, which lay open on a small table. She scurried over to it and turned the pages. As if by magic, words leapt out of the book and started to be spelt out in the air in front of her.

'In this room, we provide the means to reward very special children, who do not demand toys and money, sports clothes and new dresses, but who ask very little and so deserve an awful lot. These are the children who do not push themselves to the front, talk loudly, interrupt others and upset people with their behaviour. These are the children, who are not angels, but who are rays of sunshine for those around them. These children do not put themselves forward for a gift from The Room of Really Special Rewards, but are nominated for such a magnificent gift by their family, their friends, their teachers and their acquaintances.

'When Santa becomes aware of such children, he makes sure a very special reward is included in their sack or stocking … a very small tube of essence, which is secretly hidden in the sack and undetected. This will give the child one of the best rewards they could receive in life – Kindness, Generosity, Politeness, Consideration, Helpfulness, Selflessness, Happiness, Health, Humour or Wisdom. A child may receive up to ten of Santa's Special Rewards during their lifetime and the more they bring joy to others, the more they will receive. Rich will be the child that receives them all.'

A tear trickled down Bef's cheek, as she marvelled at the sheer beauty of this very special room and thought of all the children who would receive a drop of essence and be made wiser, kinder, more helpful or full of laughter, not to mention the other six possibilities. This was one of the most touching things she had ever experienced and was so tempted to fill a few tubes herself and take them to some of the precious Italian children that she knew. However, she did not wish to destroy any of the beauty of this room and so left it quietly, closing the door gently and turning the key with the utmost respect.

Darting eyes watched her closely from behind a very large vase that filled an entire corner of the passageway leading to the door. One thought was running through the head of the peeved and alarmed 81st elf, 'So what are you going to do next, you less than dear lady.' Bef was also asking herself that question.

CHAPTER TWENTY-FIVE

Bef shuffled along the corridor in a state of total confusion. She was still so angry about Santa taking over her VIPB patch in Italy, but was equally filled with joy by the things she was discovering in his empire. None of this had existed when she was due to marry the man. The more confused she became, the more she shuffled her shoes, causing the 81st elf to snigger from the safety of his latest hiding place.

Bef resolved to do something she was sure would leave her in no doubt that there were parts of Santa's empire that had to be removed from the VIPB world. She decided that her next port of call had to be Santa's Spa, which she was sure would be full of ridiculous luxuries and totally unnecessary pampering.

She marched forcefully and arrived at the door to the spa, easily identifying the right key. She had picked up on a bit of gossip about the spa, whilst working in the Post Office. A few elves had been laughing the day after the Capriccia incident, saying that Santa had been driven into the spa to try to recover from all the stress that his wife had caused him that day. Others had mentioned that he was spending a lot of time in the spa, to get into peak condition for his Christmas deliveries. They also said he would be back in there immediately after Christmas, recovering from the strain, whilst all the elves, who had been working at least twelve-hour days, would be expected to get back to work as usual. Bef had rolled her eyes at this, thinking such behaviour typical of the man she had once adored, but who was no longer at the top of her gift list.

Now she was inside the spa, she was determined to discover what fascination it held for him. The first thing she came across was a big tub of bubbling water, called 'The Packuzzi'. She could see water jets and holes making the water froth and so could not resist taking off one of her floppy shoes and putting her foot inside the tub. How it tickled! She couldn't help laughing and chortling and enjoyed it so much that she whipped off the other shoe, sat on the edge and dangled both feet in. She was having so much fun that she failed to notice the 81st elf enter the spa and hide behind a wardrobe containing Santa's bathrobes.

Once she had been tickled on the soles of her feet to the extent that she could not take any more, she pulled her feet out, picked up her shoes and poddled off to something called the 'Riderotherapy Pool'. A sign on the wall reminded Santa that he should only spend twenty minutes in the pool at most times of the year, but that he could spend up to an hour in here after a strenuous sleigh ride.

Bef found this a load of nonsense. 'Poppycock, if ever I saw it,' she said.

The next discoveries were the 'Sledmill' – a walking machine that it was said would get Santa into the best possible condition before his Christmas deliveries – and the 'Towing Machine,' on which she had a little play. Bef didn't find this very entertaining at all, even when two massive hand-shaped devices emerged and clamped on to her legs, to try to condition her and allow her to tow a greater weight. It made her muscles ache far too much and also made her bottom a little uncomfortable and numb. She hoped the 'Sledmill' would be much more enjoyable.

She put her floppy shoes back on her feet and stood on the machine, facing all the buttons and controls. The base of the machine began to move and she started to walk with it, but had whacked the speed up exceptionally high, reckoning it could entail no more effort than broom flying. Unfortunately, she just couldn't keep up with it and also kept stepping on her floppy shoes, leaving herself unable to pick up her feet and getting them in a terrible tangle. The more she messed up, the more she laughed, finding the whole thing a real hoot.

'Favoloso! Ridicoloso! Umoroso!' shouted Bef out loud, as she got into yet another muddle and landed flat on her bottom. She couldn't get enough of this machine and decided to turn up the speed even more. This resulted in her being thrown off it, with the machine catapulting her about 1.5 metres in the air and jettisoning her on to the top of the 'Rodeo Reindeer'. This plastic, bucking reindeer automatically started up and threw Bef up in the air and off the side at all angles, so that she was left hanging on by all possible means – reins, a firm foot grip around the reindeer's neck and a tight knee hold.

'Even better!' she exclaimed, as she fell off the reindeer for about the tenth time and just collapsed in a fit of giggles.

The 81st elf was watching this entire scene and shaking his head in horror. How dare this strange woman find Santa's exercise equipment so hilarious! How dare she move from piece to piece and not care how much she tarnished it by simply sitting on it, or dangling her feet in it. He was sure her feet would be smelly. She looked like the sort of woman who would have cheesy feet! She was also obviously insane and who knew how much damage an insane person could cause. And why did she keep coming out with words in a funny language? He had seen more than enough.

He was just about to march forward and confront her, by throwing a medicine ball at her in the first instance, when he heard a truly recognisable sound outside. He would have known the sound of Santa's footsteps anywhere. What he didn't realise was that Bef also recognised them. She had first heard them at that VIPB Conference so long ago and had fallen in love with the sound of those feet. Now she felt nothing but anger mixed with fear. These were the footsteps that were taking her Italian children's love away from her. These were the footsteps that could foil all of her carefully made plans. She did what any woman would do under these circumstances and hid behind the Rodeo Reindeer.

Santa entered the spa and looked around. He could smell something in the room. Someone was here; he knew that without a doubt and nobody but NOBODY was allowed in here without his permission. The only elves with any permission to enter were the pool cleaning elves and the towel refreshing elves. None of these should be here in the middle of the night and he was only here himself because Capriccia was in the middle of another hissy fit.

He stuck his nose in the air and started to follow the trail of the elf scent he had detected. Something was confusing him. There was another scent in the room too – a scent that took him back a long way. He just couldn't remember to where that was. Could it be the smell of the sequoia trees in California, or the smell of salt wafting around Sydney Harbour? He couldn't quite place it, but it was definitely here.

Then the scent of elf became much, much stronger and the other scent had faded away, to become almost non-existent. His nostrils were tingling now, as the elf giving off the scent was very close by. Santa opened a cupboard door and found a trembling, pale-faced creature hiding between the bathrobes. The 81st elf had been discovered!

'What are you doing in Santa's spa and why, may I ask, are you hiding in my bathrobe cupboard?' bellowed Santa. 'Come out at once!'

The 81st elf took a step outside of the cupboard in a very timid way, his head bowed and his sly eyes looking at the floor for once.

'I am awaiting an answer,' roared Santa, tapping his foot up and down impatiently. 'Elves need very special papers and permissions to enter this room. I believe you have none of these!'

The 81st elf considered pretending this was all down to some health and safety matter, which was, after all, what his job was all about, but decided on a much better plan. He would tell Santa that it was all the fault of the new 93rd elf. He would explain that he had been trying to collect enough evidence to take to Santa, to prove that the woman was a danger.

This was exactly what the 81st elf did best, if the truth be told – telling tales, getting other elves into trouble and making himself seem very clever indeed. There seemed to be no reason to change his habits now.

'I am not the only other person in your spa, Sir,' he said, trying to be humble, which didn't suit him at all. 'I was following the new 93rd elf, who is really up to no good. She is the reason I am in your spa and you will find her right over there.' He pointed a wizened finger in the direction of the Rodeo Reindeer, but then realised that, by hiding in the cupboard, he hadn't seen where the 93rd elf had hidden. His eyes scanned the room, but he could not see her anywhere.

Santa looked at him as if he did not believe a word he said. He had heard that the 81st elf was a troublesome creature and one who caused a lot of ill feeling in the Post Office. He had also heard that the 81st elf did not speak Lynx, which was always a very bad situation indeed. Right now, he didn't even know who the 93rd elf was, or where she could possibly be. It all seemed to be a lie dreamed up on the spot.

'So pray tell,' said Santa, 'where is this 93rd elf?' He looked into the 81st elf's eyes. The 81st elf trembled at the knees, as Santa was just like a headmaster at times.

'She was over there, so she must be hiding somewhere around that area,' replied the 81st elf, bouncing over towards the Rodeo Reindeer. 'She was messing about on your fitness equipment and laughing out loud. She has been visiting all parts of the village with her bunch of keys and going into forbidden rooms. She talks in a funny way and speaks a strange language. She seems to make notes in her head and she wears ridiculous shoes too.'

Santa wasn't remotely interested in any of this garbled tale until the mention of the shoes. 'Ridiculous shoes?' he queried. 'What do you mean by ridiculous shoes?'

'Well, they are big' and floppy and she slops around in them as she walks,' explained the 81st elf, somehow thinking that he was getting himself off the hook now. Who would have thought that a mention of the woman's shoes could do that?

Something had stirred in Santa's brain … an image of really ridiculous, over-sized shoes. He then recalled the scent that he had picked up when entering the room.

'Where is this elf?' he demanded, still not sure whether to trust this tale.

'In this room,' replied the elf, in absolute confidence.

Santa shook his head. 'Only you and I are in this room and there is only one door. The elf that you mention does not appear to be here, or here, or here,' he said firmly, pointing as he talked. There were no more cupboards in which to hide and there was no sign of another elf anywhere.

The 81st elf looked truly puzzled and anxious, but had another plan. 'I do not know where she is right now,' he said, 'but I do know that she will not be asleep in the dormitory where she should be. Let's go there right now and I will prove it to you.'

Normally, Santa would not have co-operated with an elf in such a way, but the mention of the shoes bothered him.

'Very well,' he replied. 'We shall head there right now through a secret passage. I must blindfold you first, but it is the quickest way, by far, to reach the dormitories.'

With no further delay, he pulled a woollen scarf from his pocket, which was especially used for blindfolding elves that did not need to know certain things. He tied the blindfold around the 81st elf's eyes and led him by the hand to the side of the Packuzzi. There, he lifted a tile in the floor and revealed a passageway beneath the floor. Both he and the 81st elf descended.

The tunnel was not as well lit as the Parcel Passageway, but Santa picked up a lantern and held it high as they made their way to the dormitories. It only seemed to take about a minute and then they were heading up some steps and emerging through another trap door positioned somewhere along the corridor that led to the room in which the 81st elf occupied the middle bunk.

Santa removed the blindfold. The 81st elf felt very smug now. He triumphantly flung open the door to the dormitory. 'See,' he said, 'the bottom bunk is empty!' He waved his hand towards the bed, but hadn't actually looked at it before speaking. When he did, he found, to his horror, that the strange 93rd elf was fast asleep in the bottom bunk. What was more worrying still was that there were no huge shoes to be seen. It seemed as though she had been asleep and tucked up in bed all night.

Santa stared at the 81st elf in a most annoyed fashion. He then looked at the sleeping 93rd elf. For one moment, he had wondered if his former fiancée had entered his village, but this was an attractive woman, free from warts and wrinkles and, above all, ridiculous shoes. He had no doubt the 81st elf was leading him a merry dance and, if there was one thing Santa did not appreciate, it was just that … especially just a few days before Christmas Eve.

Santa glared and his face wrinkled. Not only had this elf lied to him, but he had also prevented him relaxing in his spa for a few hours. He now felt tense and even more stressed than he had when heading to the spa for a nice relaxing time in the Packuzzi. Even more annoying was the fact that this elf had awoken memories of a former fiancée about whom Santa felt terribly guilty. He knew he had not treated Bef very well and did not like to be reminded of it.

'I am demoting you from your position as 81st elf, to that of 66th elf,' said Santa. 'You will swap jobs with the 66th elf with immediate effect and you will forego your gifts this Christmas. I will also expect you to work as a cleaning elf for a whole month, as a punishment for your lies and silly story. As for the trespassing in my spa, you will forego a week's wages. Let this be an end to your nonsense and let us hope that you learn your lesson.'

The 81st elf scowled nastily, but knew he had to accept this punishment.

'Now gather your things and head to a general dormitory. I will have the Head Elf re-bunk you,' said Santa haughtily. 'We cannot have you staying in this room, after all that you have said about one of your colleagues.'

With that, he pushed the 81st elf back through the door and buzzed a device in his pocket, which summoned the Head Elf. He and the 81st elf made their way along the corridor.

Back in the dormitory room, Bef opened one eye. She had longed to open both eyes and take her first glimpse of Santa, but had managed to restrain herself and put herself into a dozing mode by uttering a very quick sleep spell. What had really saved her though was landing right on top of the secret passage door when flung off the Rodeo Reindeer. What a stroke of luck that had been. Even better was the fact that the spying elf was being moved away from her. The night had been truly successful.

Santa was also feeling better: exercising authority was something he greatly enjoyed and he had never liked what he had heard about the 81st elf.

But one person was not feeling good, or

charitable, or even a little bit sorry for his actions. The 81st elf was absolutely fuming inside and was not going to accept his punishment without a fight. How dare Santa demote him and not even question the weird woman who had become the 93rd elf so very quickly? How dare he make him swap roles with the 66th elf? How dare he take away a week's pay and his gifts? He would make Santa eat his words.

As the Head Elf took him to a general dormitory, many of the other elves woke up, thanks to the commotion, and were delighted to see the horrible 81st elf taken down a peg or two.

But the 81st elf himself had a plan up his sleeve. If Santa and the Head Elf would not believe him, he would take his tale to someone he admired greatly, someone he was actually a teeny bit in love with and someone who would definitely quiz the 93rd elf. That someone was Capriccia Claus and he knew that the place to which he had to head to find her was Capriccia Claus's Casa of Contentments, the one area of Santa's empire that the underhand 93rd elf had not yet visited. The 81st elf resolved to have a shock in store for her when she did and he had little doubt in his mind that she would be paying her visit very, very soon indeed. He knew a nosy individual when he saw one!

CHAPTER TWENTY-SIX

Capriccia Claus's Casa of Contentments towered above Santa's village as a five-storey high
emporium of girl power and pleasure that reflected
how much Capriccia loved to spend money and
pamper herself. It was painted bright pink, with
fuchsia-coloured window frames and stuck out like
a sore thumb – an eyesore set against the gloomy
skies of the Arctic Circle. Its best point was that it
truly communicated the extent of Capriccia Claus's
shallow, petty nature.

Floor one of the Casa of Contentments was
dedicated to perfume, with every shape and size of
smelly fragrance imaginable lined up on the longest
dressing table in the world, which stretched right
around the edge of the room and then worked its
way into the middle via a series of twists and turns.
Capriccia had not only tried to buy every type of
perfume on the planet, but often had nine or ten
bottles of each, just in case she ran out. Actually, to
say she tried to buy these perfumes is not strictly

true. She had, instead, followed the tactic she always used when shopping – announcing that she was the wife of Santa Claus and stressing that it would be very wise if the shop gave her the items she desired most for zilch, zero, a bit fat nothing – totally free of charge. Many shops foolishly did this, just to stay on the right side of her. After all, she was *quite* famous.

Floor two of her Casa was full of hair and beauty products that were oh so Capriccia. It had her own brand of 'hair pretensions', which she had developed with the help of some of the elves, and 'Flake Facials', formed from local snowflakes, mixed with a very special cream.

There were 'Northern Highlights', which changed colour throughout the day, both as the light changed and according to Capriccia's mood. Then, there were 'Skylashes', which Santa had discovered for her on his travels, along with a very special 'Elf-Tanning' product that turned her skin a most unusual shade of olive-brown and which had to be applied with special mitts made by the sewing elves.

Floor three was a paradise for any lover of clothes. Capriccia had collected dresses, suits, trousers, evening wear, coats, hats, blouses and skirts from all the top fashion houses in Milan, Paris and New York and had rack after rack of clothes in her walk-in wardrobe, which covered the whole of floor three of the Casa of Contentments. Most items had been worn once at most, but were there for show and just in case she needed them. The truth of the matter was that it was really far too chilly in Santa's village to wear any of them, but that didn't stop Capriccia from satisfying her whims. As she told people, 'at least I can wear them in my Casa.' The reason for this was that she kept the temperature throughout the Casa at a whopping 30 degrees Celsius, partly because she wanted to wear these outfits and mostly because she knew it was far too hot for Santa and he wouldn't always be there checking on her spending.

Moving up one floor took you to the jewellery floor, full of glittering gems on necklaces, bracelets, earrings of all sizes, bangles, ankle chains and tiaras. The diamond, sapphire, ruby and emerald headband collection was particularly notable. Some of the elves had to wear sunglasses, when entering this room to help dress Capriccia, such was the glare and shine from all the gold and silver. If a shaft of sunlight happened to come cascading through the window and fall upon a diamond, it sent prisms of colour all around the room and meant that the elves had to lie down in a dark room for thirty minutes, as they were not used to such light.

But the top floor was Capriccia's real passion, as this was the floor dedicated to her shoes. She had every kind of shoe ever designed – stilettos, sandals, platforms, Cuban heels, diamond-encrusted beach shoes (though she hardly ever went near a beach), gold slippers and exquisite ballet pumps. Each pair was under CCTV surveillance, as Capriccia prized her shoes more than anything in the world and could not bear the thought of mangy moths eating them. Protecting them from the effects of any elf dust descending on them was also her top priority.

Such was her love of her shoes that she had insisted that she have a bedroom created inside all the rows and rows of footwear. She slept here when-ever she wanted to escape from Santa, or sulk after their latest row.

While 99 per cent of the elves loathed Capriccia and her diva ways, the 81st elf adored her. She was his perfect woman and he had developed an enor-mous crush on her. Her long, blonde hair, which tum-bled to her waist, (at times when she was going natu-ral and not using her hair pretensions), mesmerised him with the way it swayed and moved. Her bright blue eyes hypnotised him, even though she was over 1.8 metres tall – nearly a metre taller than him. Her slender, thin body never looked skinny to him, while most of the elves found her positively scrawny. Her mood swings never seemed to affect the 81st elf, while most of his workmates would take cover the moment she started to scream, which was a very reg-ular occurrence indeed. Whenever she stamped her feet, in whatever footwear she had chosen for that particular hour, it was the 81st elf that came running.

Santa had met Capriccia thanks to a little cun-ning on her part. She was working in a patisserie in Pavlovagrad at the time – a little village 1000 elf-miles south of Paris and 2000 elf-miles west-south-west of Moscow. A child had written to Santa and asked him to bring her a particular cake made only in her patisserie, as part of his Christmas gift list. Elves were sent to collect the cake, but Capriccia had seized her opportunity and insisted that she hand-deliver the cake to Santa. The rather intimidated elves had caved in to her request.

When she arrived with the cake, she asked Santa to sample some, but had cleverly put a love potion in that slice. Within a month, they were married and she had thrown out a drawing, which he had kept for many years, of some old witch from Italy to whom he had said he was engaged. Her name was 'Bef' something, but Capriccia couldn't remember the rest. The woman was so ugly, she could never be a serious love rival.

The only thing that had made Capriccia take much notice of this woman was the fact that she was the VIPB in Italy and that was not Santa's patch. Capriccia had instantly said, 'That's something that's got to change very fast indeed,' realising that, if Santa controlled Italy, she would have lots of excuses to go on shopping trips to her favourite city of all – Milan. There, she would be in shoe heaven. No old witch was going to stop her from seeing this plan through.

Gradually, her plan began to work. Every time she went shopping in Milan, she would make some very loud comment such as, 'Do you really still want that old, ugly witch to bring you presents, when you could have a handsome man like my husband look after your children's wishes?' People started debating the point, which was exactly what Capriccia had wanted.

Next, she started leaving pictures and posters of Santa wherever she visited in Italy, asking people to pass them around. Finally, she revamped her husband's wardrobe, dressing him in Armani and Versace clothes and making him a true Italian fashion icon. Faced with this competition, she was sure the ugly, old witch would have no chance of surviving.

Capriccia had been delighted when she had heard that the old witch's festival was finally being downsized and her postbox boarded up. She was over the moon when Santa was asked to give a radio interview in Italy. She was completely ecstatic when she forced him to start delivering in Italy, even though he had resisted for a full year and two days and said that it wasn't right, not right at all in fact, to take over the Befana's patch. Having accused him of still being in love with the old witch every day for three months and four days, Capriccia finally won. Santa could simply take no more of her jealous outbursts and so finally agreed to accept letters from Italian children and take on the Italian gift deliveries.

While Capriccia had felt triumphant, the reindeer and elves were not at all happy. The Befana's deliveries had to be made on January 5, just after their own Christmas rush and exhausting sleigh runs around the world. This was a time when they were used to putting their feet and hooves up and having a good old rest, so there was a lot of mumbling and moaning in the ranks. Capriccia paid no attention to this. She had got her own way – AGAIN!

The 81st elf just loved how strong, forceful and downright evil Capriccia could be. He saw a lot of himself in her – an outsider in Santa's village, a non-Lynx speaker and an individual who like to do their own thing. That's why he considered her his perfect woman.

Having been demoted by Santa, following the spa incident, the 81st elf could not wait to see Capriccia. He was not only angry with Santa and absolutely determined to destroy the 93rd elf, but also highly upset. His role as the health and safety expert meant that he was the one who could grant reindeer licences, every time Capriccia wished to fly off on a shopping trip. That meant lots of lovely contact with her. Those days were currently over, all because of that infernal and untrustworthy 93rd elf. He had to get Santa's decision reversed and only Capriccia could do that.

Capriccia had no real affection for the 81st elf. He was just useful to her, as he never said 'no' to her requests to fly and her shoes and clothes collection had swelled enormously since he had arrived in

Santa's Post Office. She liked to make him think that he was special, but she was only using him for her own purposes. The 81st elf, however, could not see this.

So, when the 81st-elf-who-was, but who was now demoted to a role as the 66th elf, came calling at the Casa of Contentments, it was as much as she could do to answer the intercom buzzer to him.

'I must speak to you, Madam,' he said politely, 'about a most grave danger within the Post Office.'

He said this extremely seriously, but Capriccia just yawned. She found most things concerning the Post Office completely beneath her and wasn't remotely interested.

'Really,' she said, in a bored tone, while continuing to file her very long nails.

'Yes, a danger most grave,' continued the 81st elf, failing to notice the yawn, or the fact that Capriccia was now inspecting her nails for signs of cracks in her polish. 'It concerns the new 93rd elf,' he explained, not being remotely put off by Capriccia's failure to listen to him. 'She is up to no good, no good at all. She has been spying and touring Santa's empire by dead of night,' he spluttered, in sheer annoyance at the 93rd elf's actions.

'Perhaps she is bored,' said Capriccia. 'Or maybe she is sleep walking.'

The 81st elf realised he was not getting the reaction he had wanted. 'She is really quite pretty,' he said slyly, knowing just how jealous a woman Capriccia was.

Capriccia looked up. 'Pretty?' she said. 'How pretty?'

'Well,' said the 81st elf, having to think quickly, so as to not upset Capriccia too much, 'obviously not as beautiful as you, but pretty in a certain light.'

Capriccia had lost interest again. 'How pretty can an elf be?' she was thinking and this made her realise that this elf was probably no love rival at all. The 81st elf detected this waning of interest. He had to think of something else.

'She has even replaced Santa's picture with her own, on the stamps that are leaving the Post Office on the children's letters,' he said, very decisively and tactically.

Capriccia sat bolt upright and arched her back. 'WHAT?' she yelled, causing some of her perfume bottles right down on the first floor to shake. 'I have been asking to have my picture on stamps for years now and not once has Santa allowed me to do it!' Her face had turned a funny shade of purple and the 81st elf was delighted. Now he was getting a reaction.

Capriccia leapt to her feet. 'How has this happened?' she yelled. 'Who employed this 93rd elf? I thought the Post Office only needed 91 plus the Head Elf!'

The 81st elf had a glint in his eye. 'The Head Elf employed her and Santa has not seen fit to remove her.' He was now struggling for some other piece of information to feed to Capriccia that would really set the fireworks off. He looked around him at the rows and rows of shoes and it came to him. 'And she wears the most grotesque, huge, floppy shoes that I have ever seen. She should be sacked on that point alone,' he asserted.

The 81st elf thought he had been very clever here, tapping into Capriccia's love of fine shoes, but he had actually been cleverer than even he knew. Capriccia somehow remembered the drawing she had thrown out on marrying Santa ... that old drawing of the ugly witch to whom he had been engaged. She would never forget looking at it and thinking how ridiculous and huge the woman's shoes were – an abomination, in fact! Her mind was now whirring. Surely this ugly old witch wasn't here, in Capriccia's own village, trying to steal Santa back?

Capriccia's face was now navy blue with anger and her Northern Highlights had turned green – a sure sign that her jealousy level was sky-high. 'How old is this woman? Does she have warts? Is she as ugly as ugly can be? Does she have a tatty old dress full of patches and darning? Does she have a broomstick?' All of these questions were fired at the elf in front of her, like a barrage from non-stop water cannons.

'About 30 or 35. No visible warts. Quite pretty. Arrived in a very stylish outfit. No broomstick has been seen,' he replied, hoping he had answered her questions in order. He desperately tried to think of something else that would grab her attention. 'Oh, and she has a very strange habit of always wearing a rucksack on her back, which she won't take off, no matter what,' he added.

He gave a half-smile, which he instantly wished he hadn't done, as it always tended to make him look rather creepy. He stared at his feet, hoping that the glazed look in Capriccia's eyes meant that she hadn't noticed.

Capriccia was thinking hard. Could the old witch have a daughter, or great-great-great-great, oh she couldn't be bothered to work out how great, grand-daughter? Could they be out for revenge? Who else in the world would have inherited floppy, grotesque shoes? She had to see this 93rd elf for herself and get to the bottom of this. What was in the rucksack? That was a mystery she ought to solve too.

'Bring me one of the letters with the stamp on, so that I can see this woman for myself,' she ordered. 'And do it quickly!'

The 81st elf bowed until his cap touched the ground. 'Of course, Madam. I will do it right away, Madam. Will Madam then request that Santa restore me to my former position, with my former responsi-bilities?' He looked at her hopefully, but it was point-less. She was pacing up and down the room and not listening to a word he said.

Capriccia continued to pace the floor for a full five minutes, before stopping dead in her tracks, staring him out, clapping her hands together and yelling, 'Go, go, go. What are you waiting for? Time is of the essence. If letters are going out with this woman's picture on them, the mail must be stopped. Get on with it and bring me the evidence!'

The 81st elf scowled slightly. He hated it when she shouted at him, but then she flashed her turquoise eyes at him and gave him a false smile.

'Please. Pretty please,' she said.

That made the elf's day and he scurried to complete his mission about as happy as a now-demoted-former-81st-elf could be.

Chapter Twenty-Seven

The 81st elf rifled a letter out of one of the postal sacks. He could not wait to take it to Capriccia. He also knew she wouldn't be able to wait too long for him to deliver it to her. Patience was not her greatest virtue. When she wanted something, she wanted it NOW!

He had carefully sneaked up to a bag of outbound mail and tucked a letter inside his tunic, while nobody was looking. He was sure he knew what his beloved Capriccia's reaction would be when she saw it. Sure enough, she screamed just as loudly as he had imagined and started to send bottles of perfume flying around the room, as she spun in a terrible rage. She wanted to storm off to Santa and show her husband the upstart's stamp, but she restrained herself. What she really wanted to now was the identity of the 93rd elf.

So it was, that Capriccia took herself, in a reasonably calm state, (by her standards anyway), to the Post Office, where she knew the Head Elf would attend to her needs. The moment she walked through the door, all elves downed tools and sat like statues, as if petrified by what this unpredictable woman might do. But Capriccia had a very carefully planned request to make and was not her usual self. She was strangely rational and reasonable, which confused a lot of little elf heads.

Straightening her spine at the counter and drawing to her full height, she said she needed an elf to clean her shoe collection, but this request came with some rules attached. Firstly, the elf selected for this mission had to be female. Secondly, as the shoe collection was so precious to Capriccia and, of course, so valuable, it had to be the very top ranked female elf employed in the Post Office.

The Head Elf instantly knew this meant sending the 93rd elf and also knew it was more than his life was worth to refuse Capriccia's request. He approached his 93rd elf slightly nervously and told her what she was expected to do. He was surprised when she seemed positively pleased to be sent over to the Casa of Contentments. In fact, she seemed to beam at the very mention of the word 'cleaning' and be smiling about the task ahead.

Bef certainly was smiling. She was desperate to know what sort of woman had stolen Santa Claus away from her. She was positively itching to know what went on in the Casa of Contentments. She was determined to put the final pieces of her plan together and take over Santa's gift deliveries.

From the moment Bef stepped foot in the five-storey Casa, she hated everything about it. The perfumes made her nose tingle, which resulted in a sneezing fit. On the second floor, she was creeped out by all the false things around her – nails, hair, Skylashes and more. On floor three, she was disgusted by just how many designer clothes this one woman had, particularly because, until recently, she had boasted just one tatty dress to her name. On floor four, she covered her eyes on seeing all the flashy, gaudy jewellery. As for floor five, she felt physically sick and pukey looking at the sheer number of shoes that Capriccia possessed, none of which were remotely practical. For Bef, this just summed up the shallow, fickle, petty personality of the woman Santa had married. What on earth had possessed him?

When she arrived on the fifth floor, she could see no sign of Capriccia. She began to wander between the shoes, picking up pairs she felt particularly ridiculous and shaking her head from side to side while looking at them. Capriccia was crouched behind one of the long tables of shoes and was spying on this upstart of an elf for several minutes. When Bef mocked a pair of white stilettos with real bilberries growing on them, she felt particularly precious about her shoes. She sprang out from behind the table and stood just sixteen centimetres from Bef's face.

'So, my shoes are not to your liking then?' she asked angrily, staring straight into Bef's eyes.

'No, they are not,' replied Bef, perhaps a little too bluntly.

'Well, after all, you are only an elf,' said Capriccia, in a most condescending manner. 'Look at your own feet, for instance. Look at those crazy elf shoes you are wearing. I mean … what on earth would someone like you know about shoes?'

Bef arched her back. Bef stuck out her chin defiantly. Bef then remembered she needed to keep schtum. 'I did not choose these shoes,' she said tetchily. 'They were given to me as part of my uniform.'

She was quickly realising that every word that came from this vain, self-obsessed woman's lips was making her dislike her even more than she had thought possible. This reflected in her face, as she looked Capriccia in the eye and could not do anything but grimace while looking at her.

'Oh, I see,' said Capriccia, ready to lay the first part of her trap for this know-it-all 93rd elf. 'Then tell me what your real taste in shoes might be. Maybe delicate and petite? No, I can't see that. My bet is that you like your shoes very large and very floppy, with little fashion sense behind them and just a ridiculous effect when plonked on the end of your feet.'

Bef arched her back again, but counted to ten under her breath, 'uno, due, tre, quattro, cinque, sei, sette, otto, nove, dieci.' She opened her mouth and spoke. 'Perhaps you are right. Maybe I do like my shoes rather larger and more comfortable.' She almost added, 'than these horrors', while staring at a pair of pink, orange and blue platform shoes decorated with dried reindeer droppings. She thought better of it.

'But, each to their own,' she continued. 'Where would you like me to start cleaning?'

Capriccia looked less than pleased. She had wanted to discover more about this woman and possible links to the Befana, but saying she liked slightly larger and more comfortable shoes was not enough to go on. She couldn't accuse the 93rd elf of being someone else, unless she had definite proof. She stared at the rucksack on Bef's back. How strange that this elf chose to carry this around with her. How strange that she would not remove it to do the very manual work Capriccia was giving her. What was inside that was so precious to the 93rd elf that she would not take the rucksack off her back?

'I think it would be far easier for you, if you removed your rucksack,' said Capriccia, simpering and fluttering her false Skylashes to try to catch the elf off guard.

'No, that won't be necessary,' replied Bef. 'It helps keep my posture correct and that is everything when you are a model.'

'A model?' sneered Capriccia cruelly. 'A model what?' She smirked at the very thought of this woman being on one of the catwalks she would often visit, when at a fashion show in Paris or Milan.

'A model citizen, of course,' replied Bef, having no idea what other sort of model there could be.

Capriccia thought she was being deliberately rude and smart and was not best pleased. 'Oh, how droll. How very amusing,' she said. 'Well, don't blame me if you get chronic backache! That might be a just reward for the lip you've just given me.'

Bef frowned. 'I haven't given you either of my lips,' she replied, in a very matter-of-fact way. 'In fact, I like my lips and have no intention of giving you one. Get your own lips!' She almost forgot she was supposed to be a dutiful elf and not a tetchy old witch from Italy!

Capriccia seethed. She needed a plan B, but she wasn't the brightest button in the box and was struggling to think of one. The more she thought about what could be in the 93rd elf's rucksack, the more it annoyed her. The more she looked at Bef, the more unsettled she became.

This thought filled her head all the time the 93rd elf was cleaning her shoes, a job that she annoyingly seemed to relish. The truth was that Bef was truly loving it, as her mania for cleaning completely took over, as if she were at home sweeping, or cleaning up after other people. She made each pair of shoes completely spotless and even went back to inspect each pair a second time, to ensure that they were perfectly polished or wiped.

This high standard performance by the 93rd elf irritated Capriccia to an extent she hadn't thought possible. This elf was too good at things by far and also quite pretty, in the right light, as the 81st elf had suggested. Capriccia paced up and down her bedroom, trying to think of a plan to stop this elf in her tracks.

'She is stealing my limelight. Stealing my limelight,' Capriccia wailed to herself, like some sort of lone wolf out in the woods howling to the moon. 'Stealing it with every passing second. Stealing it from under my very nose. Probably stealing my husband. Stealing everything.' She sank back on her bed and then sat bolt upright, as if a wave of electricity had passed through her body. 'Elfreka, I've got it!' she exclaimed. 'Why didn't I think of this sooner? She's stealing it alright!'

She went back to find Bef, now on the third clean of some shoes. Capriccia put on her most sickly smile.

'Many thanks. Now, it's time I let you get back to your work at the Post Office,' she said, in a truly false tone, which anyone with a pea for a brain would have known was not sincere. 'I shall be in trouble for keeping you here any longer. You can get back to stamping letters, or whatever it is you do. Some may even be sent to your own country … where was that again?'

Bef opened her mouth and was about to say 'Italia', when she realised this was a trap and Capriccia was on to her. Instead, she summoned up a number of letters in her head and jumbled them up. 'Lesser Natalia,' she replied, leaving Capriccia with a puzzled look on her face. 'It's very close to South Africa and not too far from Mauritania,' she added, knowing Capriccia was not the sort of woman to own either a map or a globe.

'I shall bid you farewell, Madam,' she continued, leaving Capriccia with the same gormless expression that she wore for eighty percent of her day.

With that, Bef headed to the elfelator and travelled down to the bottom floor of the Casa of Contentments, hurrying to get back to the Post Office as fast as possible. She had hardly parked her bottom on her special toadstool, when a whirlwind of blonde and green hair came hurtling through the door. The whirring stopped and the figure of Capriccia arrived at the front desk. She banged her fist on the counter three times, which summoned the Head Elf.

Bef didn't know what came over her, but she suddenly had the urge to shout out, 'Scarper,' causing one-third of the elves to take cover.

'One of my most precious pairs of shoes is missing,' shrieked Capriccia, causing all elves to place their hands over their ears, whether they were under the tables or still on their stools. 'I want every elf that has been on duty at my Casa today to empty their pockets, their bags and their elf lockers immediately. We must search for the stolen goods. I am going on a shopping trip to Italy tomorrow and I MUST take the stolen shoes with me.'

She banged her fist on the counter again, just to make the point even louder and clearer.

The Head Elf had turned white with fear. Capriccia was almost breathing fire and this mode always spelt trouble.

'All elves that have been at the Casa today are to empty their pockets and bags right now,' he said. 'Line up in front of me here and we shall have an elf inspection.'

Twenty-two elves in total formed a line, with Bef at one end of it. Her face was strained with nervousness and she felt thoroughly depressed. Her shoes were about to be discovered in her rucksack and that would instantly give her identity away. Santa would be called and she would be sent away before carrying out her devious plan. She wanted to cry.

One by one, the elves down the line emptied their pockets and bags in front of both the Head Elf and Capriccia. The 81st elf was looking on from the edge of a shelf on which he was perched and was positively laughing to himself, as he saw how awkward the 93rd elf looked. As they went down the queue, Capriccia poked a few of the elves she didn't like anyway, just to make a proper show of what she was doing. Her only intention, however, was to have the contents of the 93rd elf's rucksack revealed.

The elf two places before Bef was so nervous that he developed a coughing fit as Capriccia reached him. Another elf had to rush off and bring him some water. The elf standing next to Bef fainted as Capriccia reached him and had to be stretchered off to A2E (Accidents to Elves). Bef thought of running away before she was forced to unzip her rucksack, but there was no escape and her broom was still at the hotel. She would have to reveal her big, floppy, laughable shoes.

'Well, well, we have but one left,' said Capriccia gleefully. 'And it happens to be the one who was actually on the shoe floor for several hours,' she added with great satisfaction. 'Get that rucksack off your back, unzip it and show us all what is inside.'

Bef slowly took the rucksack off her back, letting its straps fall off her shoulders. She swung it to the floor and bent down to unzip it. She thought the massive shoes would instantly spring out, but nothing happened.

'Come, come. What's the matter?' demanded Capriccia. 'Tip that bag up and empty out its contents.'

With a very heavy heart and shaking hands, Bef picked up the bag, turned it upside down and shook it. She heard the contents fall out and hit the floor, but had by now closed her eyes and was awaiting the fiery blast from Capriccia.

'What is this? What on earth is this?' asked Capriccia angrily. Bef opened one eye and saw that Capriccia was holding up one remarkably smelly and holey sock, so full of moth bites that Capriccia had not been able to avoid sticking her fingers through the holes. It now looked like she had a sock puppet on her hand.

Bef's eyes grew wide as she looked at the floor and found that the heap of things that had fallen out of the bag also included some check-patterned knickers, an apple, a woolly hat and a pair of bright fuchsia pink stockings. She had never seen any of these items in her life!

Capriccia was seething. There wasn't a sign of the big floppy shoes she had been expecting to find. Bef was breathing a huge sigh of relief. There wasn't a sign of the big floppy shoes she had been expecting to find in there either! Where had they gone?

Suddenly, she remembered that her broom had the power to transport her shoes into its safe-keeping, if it felt there was any danger to Bef, but to do so meant that she had to have shouted out the word, 'scarpe' or 'shoes' in English. She knew she hadn't done this, so was racking her brains as to what had happened, as Capriccia glared angrily into her eyes.

'What did you call out when I entered the Post Office,' demanded Capriccia.

Bef had to think hard, but then smiled to herself, causing Capriccia huge distress.

'Scarper,' said Bef, half chortling, while trying to look serious. She realised that her broom's hearing hadn't been quite right for some time, but she was truly pleased that it had been a little wonky on this occasion. It had set the 'Retrieval of Shoes' procedure into motion, purely thanks to mishearing the word she'd shouted out. The broom had quickly whipped up whatever it could from washing lines and kitchens and replaced the shoes with this collection of strange items.

Capriccia glared at the 93rd elf. 'Well, it would appear that my shoes are not here,' she said, 'meaning that I will have to make my shopping trip to Italy tomorrow without my favourite stilettos. This is a BIG issue … I have to make at least six TV appearances, while in Milan, to promote Santa taking over as the official VIPB for Italy this year.'

Bef scowled. Capriccia thought she had exposed some link to the ugly Italian witch. There was a bitter look in the elf's eyes and Capriccia had her fingers crossed behind her back, hoping for an emotional outburst that would confirm her association with the witch. She was, therefore, crestfallen when the 93rd elf merely said, 'Does this mean that Madam requires the reindeer tomorrow?'

'Of course I do,' said Capriccia, now truly annoyed, as her plan had failed. 'Only a dumb person would ask that question. I shall be delighted to get away from this infernal place for a while and hit the shops looking for my new Christmas wardrobe. The WIFE of Santa has to always look her best.'

She over-stressed the word 'wife' by at least sixty per cent and smirked slightly as she did so. This woman might have her heart set on Santa, but she would get him only over Capriccia's dead body. Capriccia still held the upper hand. She just didn't hold the key to this woman's identity.

Bef was more worried about the reindeer than Capriccia's nastiness and was crying silently inside at the thought of Santa delivering to her Italian children. She was sure Lars knew nothing about their last-minute shopping trip to Italy, coming as it did at a time when the reindeer needed all the rest they could get before their Christmas gift deliveries. Capriccia clearly had no feelings for these precious creatures. Life was just one big shopping expedition to her.

Bef sighed heavily, causing Capriccia to glare at her once again.

'Very well, Madam … I will inform the reindeer master,' she said. Then, as she looked up to see a snide little elf sitting on a shelf, scowling nastily at her, she added, 'And ask the new 81st elf, who was the 66th elf before the demotion of the former 81st elf, to prepare the licences.'

Both Capriccia and the former 81st elf had faces lined with anger, as one left the Post Office, slamming the door behind her and the other fell off his shelf as she did so!

CHAPTER TWENTY-EIGHT

L ars steamed when he heard about Capriccia's demand to fly to Milan. He was red in the face, even before Bef had chance to tell him. The Arctic Warbler had been perched on a branch close to the Post Office and had heard all the commotion as it unravelled.

Bef was blue in the face, due to excessive amounts of huffing and puffing and worrying about Capriccia's appearance on all the Italian TV shows she'd mentioned.

When Lars briefed the reindeer, he asked them to refuse to fly, which they did, each and every one of the herd digging in their hooves and claiming to have gone lame, or suffered a little tummy upset thanks to acid rain, or gone down with Arctic reindeer flu.

Capriccia was wild with anger when told that there were no reindeer to fly her to Milan. She was not taking this lying down, however, and first went storming off to Santa, who told her it was best to keep the reindeer fresh for his flight. Having got no support there, she turned to the former 81st elf, knowing he was more cunning than she was.

He told her to tell a new mother and father deer that, if they and their friends did not fly her to Milan, they would never see their cute little baby reindeer again. The reindeer herd, Lars and even the Arctic Warbler, put their heads together. All had to agree that not seeing the darling baby was a price too high to pay. The 81st elf's blackmail tactic had worked.

It was with a heavy heart that Lars watched the reindeer take off for Milan on the Reindeer Runway. All he could do was plot what to do next with Bef.

Now Bef knew that she simply had to take over Santa's Christmas deliveries and that would mean removing him from the scene. To do that, she had to get into close contact with him. She tapped her head many times, for almost twelve hours, but was still no clearer about how to remove him from his own village.

Her opportunity to share his company came faster than expected. No sooner had Capriccia taken off on her shopping trip, than Santa suddenly informed the Head Elf that he wanted both him and the 93rd elf to attend a snow shower, to decide how best to approach the children of Italy. On the one hand, Bef was livid about this and hopped up and down on one foot for a good five minutes, letting off the steam that would otherwise see her explode like a pressure cooker. On the other hand, she saw this as a massive chance to gain more information about Santa's present run. When told about the snow shower, Lars was ecstatic.

'This is marvellous news,' he exclaimed, with a degree of excitement Bef hadn't seen for at least two days. 'I can work on the mind of the Head Elf and make sure that he persuades Santa that certain parts of his mission are foolish, at best, and absolutely ridiculous, at worst. Leave it to me.'

Lars was true to his word. Within a couple of hours, he had called into the Post Office to chat to the Head Elf. He started talking about his concerns about the reindeer and then continued by telling the Head Elf how worried he was about Santa's plans for Italy.

'The reindeer are so exhausted already, they really cannot take on extra deliveries,' said Lars. 'It is highly likely they could suddenly nosedive into the Trevi Fountain in Rome, or splash down unexpectedly in a canal in Venice. As for flying over the volcano of Etna, I believe even the legendary Befana had trouble with that, being blown off course by volcanic forces.'

The Head Elf had leaned over the desk very close to Lars' ear. 'The reindeer could nosedive into the Trevi Fountain,' he said.

'Quite,' said Lars.

'They could also unexpectedly splash down in Venice,' he added.

'Indeed,' replied Lars.

'And then they would have virtually no chance of getting Santa around Etna, if the legendary Befana could not manage it,' said the Head Elf.

'So true,' said Lars.

'What a terrible, terrible calamity waiting to happen,' added the Head Elf.

'How wise you are,' said Lars.

By the time he arrived at the snow shower with Bef and Santa, the Head Elf was very hot under the collar indeed. He could not wait to tell Santa that taking over Italy was a bad idea, but had to wait a fair time before being able to make his point. Bef had her own opinions on the matter.

Santa called both of them into the room and looked extremely serious as he drew their attention to the matter in hand – his present deliveries in Italy. Bef had never seen him look that serious, other than the day when he had sacked Lars from his role as 'Reindeer Whisperer'. The 'Presents of Mind Study' created an atmosphere that seemed to make things even more intense, so all had very studious faces as they tackled the issue.

'The first question, of course,' said Santa. 'Is what we should give to the children of Italy as a present?'

'Coal and candy,' said Bef, almost forgetting she was supposedly undercover and not the Befana,

316

but the 93rd elf. She rubbed the bottom of her nose in a way that reminded Santa of someone, but he couldn't quite place it.

'My sleigh would get far too dirty,' said Santa, scoffing at the idea. 'And anyway, that's what the former Very Important Present Bringer gave them. No wonder they want a change!'

'Well, if you think so,' said Bef, tapping her foot angrily. This also made Santa remember something vague, from many years before. He looked under the table at the 93rd elf's footwear. He then looked at her face. No, it couldn't possible be …

Bef flushed red in the face with embarrassment and concern. Her old habits had almost given the game away. Luckily, the Head Elf came to her rescue before Santa noticed.

'Coal and candy is the best idea,' he said. 'The Befana knew her stuff.'

Bef beamed. Santa again looked at her very oddly.

'Well, Capriccia suggested a designer bag, belt, scarf or hat from Milan,' said Santa, slightly annoyed at being contradicted by two people.

Bef had her mouth open, ready to answer, but the Head Elf leapt in.

'Impossible,' he said. 'The reindeer are already exhausted. There is no time to source such presents.'

'Well, what do you suggest then, Head Elf?' asked Santa, more than a little peeved.

'Nothing at all,' said the Head Elf. 'Taking over Italy is a huge mistake. The reindeer are already so exhausted, thanks to your wife's shopping trips, that they could crash into the Trevi Fountain, or splash down in a canal in Venice. As for navigating around Etna … well … they have no hope,' he said, laughing ever so slightly. 'If the legendary Befana found that difficult, you and the reindeer have no chance!'

Bef was positively beaming with happiness. 'I have to agree,' she added.

Santa was not happy. He rose to his feet. 'This snowstorm is concluded,' he said haughtily. 'I shall take over Italy, on the advice of Capriccia and I shall take the children exactly the sort of present that I would give to other children outside of Italy. I shall make every effort NOT to crash into a fountain, a canal or even infernal Mount Etna.'

He stomped off in such a cross manner that the ground shook.

Bef looked at the Head Elf.

'Well, 93rd elf,' he said, 'I think that went very well indeed!'

Bef was not quite as pleased. Santa was clearly determined to deliver to her Italian children. That she could not have. His deliveries would be on Christmas Eve and hers only on January 5, so he would have stolen her thunder by then. She had to find Lars.

In the meantime, however, someone else was

looking for Santa … well, to be precise, two people were looking for Santa. One was Lars, who was determined to stop the reindeer flying to Italy, as well as round the rest of the world, given what Capriccia had just done. The other person looking for Santa was Capriccia, who had arrived back from Milan and been informed that her husband was not around and in an important snow shower with the 93rd elf!

Capriccia was in the middle of a tantrum. How dare her husband invite the 93rd elf to a snow shower and spend special time with her when his wife was away! She was angry beyond all levels of anger on the angry scale and went all around the village looking for her husband, to show him the letter with the 93rd elf's stamp. But find him she could not.

That was because Lars was even angrier with Santa. His anger went back years, to the day Santa had sacked him as the Reindeer Whisperer. This anger was made even deeper by the treatment of the reindeer. Little wonder then, that he had lured Santa to a cabin deep in the woods, claiming that Capriccia had bought special presents for the Italian children and these were awaiting his approval.

Santa had arrived at the cabin looking forward to finally getting an answer to his snow shower question. He was surprised to find neither presents nor Capriccia. All he could see was a roaring fire, ideal for toasting his frosty toes, so he sat down in an armchair and enjoyed warming up. The moment his boots were off and he was at his ease, Lars leapt out with a very long rope, which he wrapped round and round Santa's body and slightly large tum and tied in a massive knot at the back.

'It's you,' said Santa, recognising Lars as his former Reindeer Whisperer.

'Indeed it is,' replied Lars.

'What makes you come back for your revenge after so many years have passed?' asked Santa, baffled as to Lars' sudden appearance and motives.

'I am here to assist a lady that you wronged,' said Lars. 'I am also here to protect my reindeer. I know full well that you are treating them with no respect, by allowing your petty wife to fly them off every time she fancies a new pair of shoes or a bottle of perfume. It is not right and it MUST stop.'

'Who is this lady that you mention?' asked Santa. 'Could it be the Befana, by any chance?'

'What makes you ask that?' said Lars.

'Well, I have just met someone called the 93rd elf, who reminded me greatly of her. Is the 93rd elf her great-great-great-great … oh, I can't be bothered working it out …granddaughter, out to get revenge on me for falling for Capriccia?'

Lars laughed out loud. 'You foolish man! That was the Befana and she is about to pay you back for your arrogance, thinking that you could steal the hearts of children from her. You will soon discover it is she who will be delivering presents to your children and not the other way round. Sit there Santa and reflect on your mistakes. You may then realise the trouble you have caused to man, woman and reindeer alike!'

Lars ran out into the snow, leaving Santa struggling with his ropes. In the meantime, Capriccia had entered her whirlwind phase of rage, spinning through the village in her typical frenetic manner. All the elves knew this, so when Bef returned to the Post Office, she was immediately told that Capriccia had come looking for her and assumed she was somewhere with her missing husband. Bef had not lingered, sensing that the place to which she needed to head was the Wrapping Room.

Sure enough, she found Capriccia spinning through it, causing roll after roll of wrapping paper to tumble from the shelves, ribbon to unwind and sticky tape to spin out of control across the floor. It was just like the dream the Head Elf had experienced and parcels that had already been wrapped were starting to unravel, the more that Capriccia spun around, causing everything to become dislodged and unstable.

Bef stood in the centre of the room and waited for Capriccia to stop spinning around and around her – it was making her positively sick. The wrapping elves had all taken cover, but the chute that took wrapped parcels out to the loading bay area was still running. Some elves had even jumped on it to hitch a ride and then jumped off, before they were dumped into a skip intended for some far-flung country or other.

Bef stood her ground and gradually the speed of spinning lessened … and lessened … and slowed right down until Capriccia came to an abrupt standstill, looking straight into the eyes of the 93rd elf.

'You,' she said, her voice trembling with anger. 'You, you know-it-all elf! You infiltrator. You husband stealer. What have you done with Santa?'

'Nothing at all,' said Bef. 'You, on the other hand Capriccia, plotted to meet him, drugged him and then made him marry you. When you did that, you knew he had a fiancée in Italy and you thought nothing of stealing him away from her. Now you must face your punishment and pay for your actions, not to make me feel any better, but to stop you from working those poor, poor reindeer to death.'

With that, Bef suddenly produced her broom and pointed the end of it at Capriccia. She closed her eyes, tapped one foot and shouted the word, 'Confezionamento'. In an instant, a roll of clear bubble-wrap leapt from a shelf and started to circle Capriccia, packaging her up, while still allowing her angry and aghast face to be seen during the wrapping process. A roll of brown paper followed suit, adding other layers, which then hid most of her completely, except for her feet. Next, some brown parcel tape spun around and around her, tightening the packaging and making it secure. The broom then blasted a huge gust of wind at this Capriccia package and sent it down the parcel chute, just as the labelling mechanism posted a label for Hamburg, Germany on to the package. Unable to jump off the chute, Capriccia tumbled into a parcel load destined for collection by Santa's sleigh in Germany. Very soon, she would be whisked far away from Santa's village and up into the night sky, way out of harm's way and far, far from Bef's eyes.

A clap of delight rang out. Bef turned around to find Lars applauding.

'Excellent work, comrade,' he said. 'Now we must block the parcel tunnel, so when Santa escapes from his ropes, he will still be unable to force the reindeer to fly, as there will be no parcels to deliver.'

'Easily done,' said Bef, hoping desperately that she could block the tunnel with the 'Incantesimo della Roccia' spell that had failed her so miserably previously. She closed her eyes and tried so hard to get it right, as she muttered under her breath. In the distance, a rumbling noise could be heard, as the roof of the Parcel Passageway tumbled down, blocking off the Sleigh Loading Bay.

Bef held her breath for a few minutes, before hearing a fluttering above her. Through a slit in the roof flew the Arctic Warbler. It landed on Lars' arm.

'You have managed to block the Parcel

Passageway,' said Lars, 'but we have not yet completely won the day. There is one load of presents ready for take-off on the Reindeer Runway and one team of reindeer harnessed up and ready to fly. I cannot allow Santa to exhaust my precious friends. I must fly the sleigh myself!'

'But you have no experience of flying,' replied Bef, with a fair degree of concern in her voice. 'It is far too dangerous for a non-Very Important Present Bringer to try to become one without training. You would be risking your life, as well as that of your reindeer. I cannot allow you to attempt it!'

'Then you will teach me,' said Lars. 'Take off for England now and I will follow your broom path, directing the reindeer to chart the exact same course that you take. When we arrive in England, I will deliver the presents as normal. I believe the flight to Britain is relatively easy from here. With your guidance, we will avoid harm and injury.'

Bef considered the suggestion. 'Very well,' she said. 'Time is of the essence. Let us fly now!' She mounted the broom, stroked it and started to talk to it kindly. 'All of our supplies are still on board and ready for delivery, at last!' she declared triumphantly. 'Jump on and let's get out to the Reindeer Runway now!'

With that, Lars leapt into the passenger berth and the pair of them soared upwards towards the glass ceiling of the Wrapping Room. A pane of glass shifted as they approached, allowing the broom and its passengers to have safe passage. Off they flew and, within seconds, landed by the sleigh and reindeer waiting on the Reindeer Runway.

'Follow my lead,' cried Bef, as Lars leapt off her broom and jumped into the sleigh. 'We shall set off for Big Ben in London!'

Lars jumped into the sleigh and started to coax the reindeer, as Bef hovered on her broom ahead of him. The reindeer began to hoof the ground and then started to gallop along the Runway, getting up to a great reindeer speed. At that moment, their hooves left the ground and they began to follow the path set by the broom. The broom and sleigh together soared up into the sky.

Bef looked backwards and urged Lars and the reindeer on, giving them huge encouragement, as they flew together for the first time. Looking backwards instead of ahead of her, she failed to realise that looming directly in their flight path was the five-storey pink monstrosity of a building that was Capriccia Claus's Casa of Contentments. Similarly, she did not notice that, standing on the very top of this building and waving his hands furiously, to try to distract the reindeer, was the very aggrieved 81st elf, who had come in search of his beloved Capriccia and discovered she was nowhere to be found.

The broom did its usual thing and cleared the Casa of Contentments at the very last minute, but

Lars did not have time to think that quickly. He was heading directly for the top floor of it or, to be more precise, for the 81st elf. He noticed, with seconds to spare and shouted something in reindeer that to you and I translates as, 'Lift yourselves, as fast as you can, right now!'

To a reindeer, the whole team did just that, lifting their hooves as high as reindeer can, just managing to avoid the building. However, the last two reindeer in the team were not completely free of danger. Although they had escaped hitting the Casa, they had not avoided the 81st elf. He was now clinging on to their legs for dear life, as they soared high into the night sky.

Lars looked downwards and saw the 81st elf trying to clamber up into the sleigh. 'Faster, faster,' he urged, 'and then turn back round and brake with all your might.'

The reindeer shot forward, almost overtaking Bef on her broom, and then doubled back, jamming on the hoof brakes at the same time. The sleigh jolted very hard – an impact that the 81st elf could not overcome. Down he tumbled, losing his grip and falling down on to a huge goose-feather mattress that Capriccia liked to sleep on in summer, when she would take to her Casa's roof, light heaters all around her bed and drift off under the stars.

'To London,' shouted Lars.

'To Big Ben,' replied Bef. 'We must cover Britain

before all the children wake at around 5am! Are you ready for the challenge of being a Very Important Present Bringer?' she yelled.

'I've waited centuries,' replied Lars.

Off the pair headed, to deliver their presents to all the children of Britain, with Bef charting the course and Lars and the reindeer delivering presents down chimneys, through windows, in sheds, in bedrooms and in sacks left in all manner of peculiar places. Even Bef was amazed by some of this, but Lars coped admirably and once they had granted the wishes of the children of Britain, the two of them were again circling Big Ben, causing a strange ring of light around the monument, which made passers-by at ground level stare up in amazement at the weird phenomenon in the sky.

'Goodbye Lars,' said Bef. 'I am sure the reindeer will guide you back to the village. It is now time for my broom and I to fly to America and then to other parts of the globe, delivering my wonderful coal and candy. Washington here we come!'

With that, she was gone, flying off into the distance and fading out of Lars' view very quickly indeed.

'God speed, Bef,' he cried. 'Best of luck!'

CHAPTER TWENTY-NINE

When the three strangers from Dubai finally arrived at Santa's village, after many delays, broken planes and weather issues, the elves were in a state of total confusion. The blocking of the Parcel Passageway had sent some of them into bewilderment – a state that usually meant a three-day recovery period for an elf – while others were convinced they had seen Santa flying off with the reindeer. Only the Head Elf seemed unperturbed. 'The reindeer will not be exhausted any more,' he kept repeating.

Standing close to a parcel depot, Thaz was sure he saw a parcel of brown packaging and tape, with two kicking feet poking out of it, being sent off along a sleigh carousel destined for Hamburg. Meanwhile, Mel swore he could see a little person bouncing up and down on top of the tallest building in the village, shouting something that sounded like, 'Get me off of this mattress. I can't stop bouncing and it's a health and safety hazard!'

The hottest boy band in the world, 'The Three Kings', were determined to find Bef and pass on the news they had received from their visitor from Italy, having had no luck in getting a response from her following their TV appeal. They thought someone here, in Santa's village, was bound to have seen her, but every time they asked someone, all they got was a shoulder shrug or a blank expression.

The only glimmer of hope came from a girl on the reception desk at the hotel, who had said that a very strange woman had stayed there recently, but had left when she became an elf.

'Well, the words, 'very strange', certainly sound like Bef,' said Thaz. His two band members had to agree.

There was a fair bit of head scratching, tapping of brows and doodling on paper, as the three of them debated their next move. Apparently, Santa was missing, according to some elves at least, as was Mrs Claus. That did sound to them as if something had happened involving Bef. They were determined to find out more.

As they took a stroll outside, walking through snow that Gaspar had really missed since his exploits with Bef, Gaspar saw the outline of a body that looked strangely familiar. The body was no more than a metre tall, but had hair sticking up another 45 centimetres, a little like candyfloss. In the gloom, Gaspar could also just about make out that it was wearing red and white, striped pyjamas.

'It's the 'Terrible Torta', ' yelled Gaspar.

'Who?' asked Thaz and Mel together.

'Bernhardt Bürstenfrisür,' shouted Gaspar. 'Quick, follow him! He must know something.'

The three of them tracked the little fellow through the snow, as he ran and ran and ran to a log cabin, some distance from the main part of the village. They listened as clanking and clanging noises came from inside the cabin and then watched in amazement as Bernhardt emerged with Santa. Both were running, as far as their legs would carry them, towards some pine trees.

'I bet he has a broom there,' shouted Gaspar. 'Run as fast as you can. We have to stop them and explain all.'

'All the hours the boy band spent in the gym really did them proud as they ran through the snow, chasing a man whose leg span was only about twenty centimetres and a rather overweight Santa, who had eaten one too many mince pies. They caught them up, just as they reached the pine trees and at the point where Bernhardt was about to start up his broom, with Santa as a passenger.

'Stop right there,' shouted Gaspar, surprising himself with his own forcefulness.

Bernhardt spun around and looked him in the

eye. 'I thought I had seen ze last of you,' he cried angrily.

'Me too,' said Gaspar, 'But I am delighted to meet you Santa. There are things we have to explain to you about Bef who, if I am not mistaken, you are about to chase somewhere in the world. She thinks her Italian children and her town don't love her any more, but she does not know the truth. We do. Once we tell her the real situation, we are sure that she will listen and we can bring an end to all of this misunderstanding and ill feeling. Chasing her with the man known as the 'Terrible Torta' can only end in more heartache. I beg you not to fly with him.'

Santa studied him. 'You are a kind boy,' he said. 'I can see that. But surely Italy wants me to take over the present bringing. My wife said so.'

'Your wife was very much mistaken, Sir,' replied Thaz, stepping forward in the snow, keeping one eye on Bernhardt for any sign of sudden movement that might require defensive action. 'We have spoken to the representative from her town. Things have gone terribly wrong there since she left. Everyone is miserable. Things are falling apart. She needs to return and see how much she is loved, then this whole drama will end.'

Santa listened and looked at Mel. 'I suppose you wish to tell me the same?'

'Yes, Sir,' said Mel. 'Our forefathers told us we

should always protect Bef and that's what we're doing, at any cost.'

Bernhardt shrieked loudly. 'Poppycock! Lies and propaganda! Don't listen to these losers … let us chase her in America and put an end to zis in ze best possible way!'

Santa looked at the little man in his pyjamas and then at 'The Three Kings'. 'Do you have anything that I could use?' he asked.

He did not have to say any more. Gaspar reached inside his coat and produced some of his now very effective potion.

'Sorry, Bernhardt,' said Santa. 'I have to believe these boys.' He threw the potion towards Bernhardt, as 'The Three Kings' and he turned away. Within seconds, Bernhardt had slumped to the ground.

'Do you know how to fly a broom, boy?' asked Santa, looking at Gaspar.

'I've been a passenger,' said Gaspar. 'Unfortunately, though, I have no idea how to chart a course.'

'Leave that to me,' said Santa.

Within seconds, they were flying high above the village, with Gaspar trying to coax and steer the broom, as he had seen Bef do, while Santa offered directions. They flew for many hours, until they saw the bright lights of New York and the Empire State Building. Scattered on the roof were some odd black lumps.

'That's coal,' shouted Gaspar. 'We collected lots of it. She's already passed this way, so I have no idea where she will be now.'

Santa stroked his beard, while trying to hold on to the broom and not fall off. 'There is a very tricky delivery just after this,' he explained. 'Knowing the Befana, she will have seen delivery to the White House as a real challenge, one she will not have been able to resist. Getting in there is quite difficult, you know ... let's head there and I'm sure she will be there, trying to figure it out.'

The pair charted a course for Washington and soon saw the unmistakable outline of the White House. There, sitting on the roof was a woman on a broom – one looking extremely puzzled and frustrated and muttering to herself so much that she didn't spot the other broom descending from the sky. It landed right next to her, causing her to jump!

'Mamma mia,' she exclaimed. 'What are you doing here, Gaspar and why are you with Santa? Please tell me that this man has not brainwashed you.'

'No, quite the opposite,' explained Gaspar. 'I have explained to him why you have done what you have done, but also explained to him that you have acted without having the benefit of all of the facts. Luckily, Mel, Thaz and I have those at our disposal, as we had a visit from a representative from

Italy, from your town, where things are dreadful since you left and everyone is terribly unhappy.'

Bef sat bolt upright, her ears pricked and her eyes glistening. 'Terrible?' she quizzed. 'Unhappy? Please tell me more.'

'Your village is full of dust. All brooms have flown off. There is a weird singing and a noise like a wind. The dust makes the children wheeze. It gets on to cappuccinos. It even slides into pillow-cases and the village has lost its 'icon' … yes, that's how you were described. It has no fabric to hold it together. People miss you like crazy and want you to go home. They have even written this letter.'

With that, Gaspar dived into his pocket and produced the letter that Signor Passarella had given them.

Bef started to read it and tears rolled down her face. She wiped her nose on the sleeve of her red dress, into which she had changed, when dumping her elf's outfit on the roof of 10 Downing Street.

'There's even a weird sound of your shoes shuffling down the street,' said Gaspar, ready to convince her once and for all to return home.

She blinked away the tears. 'What have I done?' she said, looking at Santa.

'It's my fault for listening to my petty wife and believing that I could take over in Italy,' said Santa. 'I should have known the love for you was too strong there, but Capriccia went on and on about it, as it suited her shopping trip schedules and gave her reasons to go to Milan. I was taken in by her tales.'

'But I have delivered some coal and candy instead of your presents and blocked the Parcel Passageway too,' explained Bef honestly.

'Can you reverse the spell and do you know to where you have delivered?' asked Santa hopefully.

'Possibly,' she replied. 'If I can remember.'

'Well, in that case, I could fly back and still get my deliveries out on time, if I have a long chat with a certain Reindeer Whisperer, the best in the world in fact, and give him his old job back,' said Santa. 'This broom appears to be very speedy and I have a good captain aboard with me here. Gaspar and I could return to find Lars and you could proceed to Italy, to prepare for your special day, while ridding your village of all those woes. First though, I could let you into a secret as to how to deliver these presents to the White House. What do you say?'

'I'd say that was very fair and that I have been a silly woman to feel aggrieved that you left me. I should have been happy to have known you at all.'

Santa shook his head. 'No, it was I who was wrong and I should have realised that you were far too good a person for me to marry. I am so sorry.'

Bef wiped away her tears. 'Enough of this emotional nonsense,' she said. 'Show me the White

House secret. It might come in useful for some building or other in Italy.'

The pair of them huddled together and Santa told her the secret, causing her to chortle loudly. In an instant, the pair of them disappeared, leaving Gaspar on the White House roof. They then reappeared equally as quickly. Presents had been successfully delivered and Gaspar did not have a clue how!

With that, Santa jumped back on the broom and Bef took to hers.

'See you at my festival, Gaspar,' she shouted, 'And bring the boys!'

CHAPTER THIRTY

Dust lay everywhere. Nobody recognised Bef as she walked up the street, with her shoes carefully hidden at first, as she did not want people to know she was back until she saw the truth for herself. Windowsills were piled high with dust. Children were coughing. The men in the piazza were covering their coffee cups, to try to prevent more dust falling in. As she walked along the street, the weird wailing, which had been barely detected from a distance, got louder and louder until all inhabitants of the village covered their ears.

'What is to become of us? It is louder than ever!' shouted one man. 'If only the Befana would come home!'

'Don't raise your hopes,' said another. 'The letter doesn't seem to have done much good. We should never have sent Passarella to do the job.'

Bef walked further and noticed that her postbox had been re-opened and that posters advertising her festival had reappeared with a 'We hope to be able to lay on our festival' note added to the top. There was no sign of anything to do with Santa.

She reached into the rucksack and whipped out her floppy shoes. She placed her trusty friends on her feet. With that, she shuffled down the street, causing no interest at first, as the weird shuffling sound had filled eardrums for quite some time now. It took a little child to look down at the shoes on the stranger's feet and cry out, 'It's the Befana's shoes!'

A murmur went round the village and hundreds of faces appeared at windows, doors and out of cars, cafes and even the church. Bef spotted Marianna as the murmur of one phrase got louder and louder, that phrase being, 'It's the Befana's shoes.'

Suddenly, Marianna stood on the church steps and yelled out, at the top of her voice, 'What joy! It's the Befana herself.'

All eyes began to scrutinise this woman in the fashionable red dress. All then agreed. 'It's the Befana herself!'

Cheers went up around the village and a wave of noise moved up the mountainside and out into the surrounding countryside and villages. Joy was everywhere.

'Yes, yes, it is I,' said Bef, 'but you cannot call me the Befana. Now, what a sorry state of affairs we have here. I have come home to sort this mess out, so let's start with the dust.' She clicked her fingers and at least a hundred brooms flew back into the village and into the hands of their owners.

'Now let's sort out the wailing,' she said, tapping her ears five times. The wailing stopped and the church bells started to ring, as if a wedding were taking place.

'And, finally, let's get my festival organised,' she declared triumphantly. 'There is no time to waste, as I have three extremely important visitors coming to see it. We must put on a display better than all the others and show that our traditions cannot be beaten!'

The villagers scurried around and plans began to be made for everything from people dressed like her descending on wires from different buildings, to a competition to create the best design for her shoes. Things had never been so lively!

She shuffled up to her house, leaving everyone to get on with different tasks. She pushed open the heavy door and found a package behind it, which made it really difficult to gain entrance. This made her more than a little tetchy. When she reached down, she discovered it was wrapped in exquisite paper that she had seen in Santa's Wrapping Room. It also had a gift card signed 'S'.

She opened it carefully, to find it was a phial from the Wisdom bottle in the Room of Really Special Rewards. With it lay a little note that read:

'You wisely chose to rejuvenate yourself with the

help of Old Father Time, but this potion will give you the wisdom to decide whether to stay as 'Bef', or return to your former self. Whichever you choose to do, your choice will be a wise one, for all the right reasons.

Bef opened the phial and breathed in the potion. Her broom, which had already settled back into life at home, having shot down the chimney and rested by the fireplace, lifted itself off the ground a couple of centimetres in expectation.

'I've decided broom,' its mistress said with great authority. Broom held its breath until she declared very proudly, 'Bef is here to stay!'

Broom was secretly pleased and wriggled a little. It instantly knew that many more exciting adventures lay ahead!

The End